# The
# Unforgiving
# SEA

Karen V. Robichaud

**THE UNFORGIVING SEA**
Copyright © 2014 by Karen V. Robichaud

Scripture taken from the HOLY BIBLE, NEW INTERNATIONAL VERSION®. NIV®. Copyright © 1973, 1978, 1984 by International Bible Society. Used by permission of Zondervan. All rights reserved worldwide. Scripture quotations marked HCSB are taken from the Holman Christian Standard Bible®, Copyright © 1999, 2000, 2002, 2003, 2009 by Holman Bible Publishers. Used by permission. Holman Christian Standard Bible®, Holman CSB®, and HCSB® are federally registered trademarks of Holman Bible Publishers.

Printed in Canada

ISBN: 978-1-4866-0719-8

Word Alive Press
131 Cordite Road, Winnipeg, MB R3W 1S1
www.wordalivepress.ca

**WORD ALIVE**
—P R E S S—

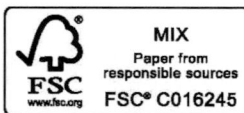

MIX
Paper from
responsible sources
FSC® C016245

Cataloguing in Publication information may be obtained through Library and Archives Canada

In memory of Baby Boy Eardley
September 22, 2012


And for my precious granddaughter, Cierra Laine Eardley.

*After every storm there is a rainbow of hope…*
*here I am!*

— Anonymous

*"Having faith and a good conscience.
Some have rejected these and have suffered the shipwreck of their faith."*
(1 Timothy 1:19, HCSB)

# Acknowledgements

I would like to thank my friends, Lorna and Matthew Colwell of Ottawa (formerly of White Head Island, New Brunswick), for patiently answering my questions about lobster boats and lobster fishing.

A special thank you to my daughter, Candice Eardley, who read and proofed early manuscripts. Without her by my side, this book would not have come to be.

Finally, to Evan Braun of Word Alive Press, thank you so much. Your copy editing has made me a better writer.

## Chapter 1

# LOGAN

I wake to the scream of a fighter jet flying low overhead. Seconds later, another jet shrieks over the roof of our house. The walls shake. The windows rattle. I flip over onto my side, look out the window. A blaze of red-orange flame lights up the dark sky as the CF-18's afterburners kick in. I catch a brief flash of metallic silver reflecting off the full moon as the jet banks sharply to the right and then vanishes.

I lie back down and pull the covers up to my chin. My father, Captain Luc Blanchard, is a CF-18 fighter jet pilot in the Canadian Armed Forces. He's in a cockpit of one of the CF-18's that just flew overhead. It's my dad's last night on the graveyard shift. Tomorrow, he and I are playing tennis at the indoor courts on base against my friend, Jared, and his father, who is my dad's co-pilot and friend. I feel my hands turn into fists as I close my eyes and pray silently for my dad, something I do often because I secretly worry about him crashing. For the next minute, it's just me and God. I feel my hands unclench, my entire body relax. Once done, I turn over and fall back to sleep.

An hour later, my alarm wakes me. Outside, the winter sun is rising in the east, the sky a subdued pinkish grey. I hear the crunch of tires on snow as a car drives past in the street. Yawning, I push back the blankets, preparing for another ordinary day in my ordinary life. Funny how that is, how you can get out of bed, shower, eat, and get ready for school, the whole time having no clue it's going to be the worst day of your life.

The sound of my mom humming drifts up the stairway and into my bedroom. Mom's a hopeless hummer. Happy, she'll hum one of her favourite hymns. Sad or stressed, she'll hum tunelessly, continually, something that drives me nuts. When my dad was deployed to Libya, she was super stressed and hummed constantly, crazily. To me it sounded like a swarm of bees were in the house.

I listen for a moment, smile. I recognize the hymn, 'Be Thou My Vision.' That's because my dad's shift ended fifteen minutes ago. He'll be home any time now. That never fails to set her off on a happy humathon. Over her humming, I hear the clatter of dishes and silverware. The aroma of bacon and eggs wafts in under the gap in my door. My stomach gives a loud grumble. These days, no matter how much I eat, I'm always hungry.

I shower fast, then check my face in the mirror. I rub the fine blond fuzz, groan in despair. My mom, who blames it on peri-menopause, has more hair on her chin than I do. I dress in blue jeans, a black hoodie over a red long-sleeved T-shirt, and white socks. I take the stairs two at a time, jumping the last four to the floor. The thump echoes through the house.

"Logan," Mom scolds from the kitchen. "Don't do that. You're going to fall and kill yourself one of these days."

"Never happen, Mom," I say as I enter the room. I grab a banana from the glass bowl on the counter, peel it, and take a huge bite.

Mom's dressed in salmon-coloured pants and top, a uniform she wears for her dayshift as a physiotherapist at the town hospital.

"How'd you sleep?"

"Fine." I shrug.

She frowns. "You look tired."

The sun shines in through the window next to the stove, highlighting the natural auburn in her dark brown hair. Mom and I share the same hair colour, deep blue eyes, and slender build.

"Mom, I slept fine." I sigh. "Is breakfast ready? I'm starving."

"Almost," she says, turning bacon over in the frying pan. "What time are you and your dad playing tennis today?"

I swallow the last of the banana and toss the peel in the garbage bin. I slip up beside her and reach into the frying pan to snatch a slice of bacon.

"Logan, don't. You're going to get burned by hot grease," she says, but her eyes hold a smile.

Grinning, I blow on the strip of bacon and pop it into my mouth.

Mom scoops scrambled eggs from the pan, adds bacon and hash browns and hands the plate to me. "Here, go sit down and eat."

I stare at the plate, aghast. "That's it? Two slices of bacon and that little bit of eggs and hash browns?"

"Three slices of bacon. You just ate one, remember?"

I hold my plate out and make the sound of a puppy whining.

She laughs softly, shakes her head. She adds a bit more eggs, hash browns, and a slice of bacon. "That's it. Save some for your dad."

I carry my plate over to the table, popping a slice of bacon in my mouth before I even sit down.

"You didn't answer my question," she says.

"What question?"

"What time are you guys playing tennis?"

"Oh, right. Four o'clock." I pick up my glass of orange juice and gulp half of it down.

Mom joins me at the table. She spreads pomegranate jelly on a slice of toast while eyeing me. "So you'll be home around five-thirty?"

"Six," I mumble around a mouthful of eggs.

Although I favour my mom for looks, I share my dad's quiet nature. My one-word replies or silent nods usually exasperate my mom. But today, she only says tenderly, "I have an Easter play rehearsal at the church after work, so I'll be late. There's a chicken casserole in the fridge. When you get home, would you throw it in the oven at 350 degrees for forty-five minutes?"

"Literally throw it in?"

"Ha-ha, aren't you the funny one." She glances at the watch on her wrist. "Mmm, your dad's late. Wonder what's holding him up." She starts humming like a madwoman.

I shrug, wish she'd relax. He probably just stopped to talk to someone.

A few minutes later, Mom drains her coffee, pushes back her chair, and rises. She moves behind me, wraps her arms around my shoulders, and pulls me back against her. She stops humming only long enough to kiss the top of my head and say, "I have to run upstairs and finish getting ready or I'm going to be late."

I nod and clean the last of my breakfast. I stand, pick up my dishes, and carry them over to put in the dishwasher.

Ten minutes later, I zip up my jacket and slide my backpack on. I grab my Calgary Flames wool hat from the top shelf in the closet, yank it on my head.

"See you, Mom," I shout.

"Have a good day, sweetie. I love you," she calls out from her bedroom upstairs.

"Love you too," I call out and then open the door. A blast of frigid air instantly cuts through my clothing to my skin. I shiver hard, pause at the open doorway. The sun is higher now, the sky a cloudless, crystal blue. But on this cold prairie morning, with the temps in the single digits, the sun's rays are weak. They do nothing to warm the air or melt the light dusting of snow that fell overnight. It's the twenty-first day of March. Spring supposedly. I snort, wish spring really would arrive.

A movement to my right catches my eye. I turn my head and see a shiny black sedan advancing up the street. I draw in a quick, sharp breath. I step back inside, shut the door fast. I stand frozen in the foyer, pulse thudding in my throat. The black sedan is called the "death car" by the kids on the air base. It's the car used by the notification team when they come to inform a family that their loved one is dead.

Whenever us kids on base saw the death car approaching, we would do one of three things. The first group would turn white and take off running for home. The second group would stand defiantly and fix their eyes on the car in an unblinking stare, as if by doing that they could will it away. The third group would stop what they were doing, close their eyes, and pray. I belong to the third group. I'm a Christian and believe strongly in prayer.

I take a breath and slip over to the narrow vertical window at the side of the door. I peer outside, looking right. The car keeps coming, passing the homes that line both sides of the street. As it nears my house, I hear the low drone of its engine, the grinding crunch of its tires on the snow-covered road.

From her bedroom on the second floor, Mom hums away, mercifully unaware.

Standing rigid, I close my eyes, bow my head, and pray fervently.

When I open them again, I see the black car reach our driveway. My heartbeat booms in my ears, drowning out all other sounds. I whisper a prayer: "Please Lord, make it keep going."

Finally, thankfully, the car moves past our house and proceeds on down the street.

I release a long shaky breath. At the same time, I'm appalled that I feel so relieved when I know another family is about to receive the most devastating news possible.

The sedan brakes to a stop two houses down from ours. My stomach plummets. Keltie MacClellan, my girlfriend, lives there with her parents and older brother, Lachlan. Her father is a CF-18 fighter jet pilot who serves in the same squadron as my dad.

I fell hard for dark-haired Keltie back in September—specifically, September 7. That was the day she stepped into my homeroom. She paused at the doorway, surveyed the room. And our eyes met. Her warm green eyes held mine for a long time while I tried to breathe normally. Then she walked gracefully down the aisle and took the empty seat in front of me.

She turned around, said hi, and smiled. Her smile reached down deep inside me. I felt my heart turn to liquid in my chest. I smiled back and somehow managed a hello. But it came out too loud, a shout really, and everyone in the room turned and looked at us. My face burned.

Keltie didn't seem to mind. She just smiled at me again. And that was it. She owned my heart.

I spent the rest of that class staring at the back of her neck, breathing in the scent of her glossy dark hair. It smelled like cinnamon-and-apple shampoo. She was so pretty, yet so unpretentious. I liked that about her.

When first-period math ended, she rose and left the room. I followed her. She strode briskly down the hall. I picked up my pace, pursued her. Then she turned a corner and vanished. I mournfully walked to my next class. I searched for her at noon in the cafeteria and again at three-thirty when school let out, but I didn't see her again.

That night I couldn't sleep, my mind whirling with thoughts of her. But then, with much dismay, it hit me that she'd left class awful fast. She'd nearly run the four-minute mile down the halls. And she hadn't been looking for me all day. I told myself that her smile hadn't been special for me. After all, I had to admit that when I'd smiled back at her, she'd seemed to remember how to breathe just fine. I prepared myself for the inevitable heartbreak. She wasn't interested in me, would never be. I comforted myself with the thought that it would have to be enough just to see her in math class each morning.

Still, I showered the next morning, soaping and shampooing myself until the water ran cold. I arrived at class early, clean as a whistle, dressed to impress—and found Keltie, already sitting in her seat, a smile on her face, waiting for me. Since then, we were a couple.

"Oh, Keltie," I say sadly, eyeing the black sedan sitting ominously in front of her house.

Suddenly, the white reverse lights come on and the sedan slowly backs up. It halts, pulls up into our driveway and glides to a stop. It sits there, engine idling, its exhaust blackening the snow-covered asphalt beneath the tailpipe. Two men in uniforms sit in the front seat, peering out the windshield to our house. The passenger is wearing a white chaplain's collar. It's Pastor Reimer, from our church.

The horror hits me like a hammer blow to the chest. I gasp, stagger back. Outside, the engine shuts off. The doors click open, shut again. The men start toward our door. Their footfalls on the walkway sound like thunderclaps, shattering the early morning quiet. Seconds later, there's a knock on the door.

My heart stops cold for a second. Then it continues, but beats erratically, like I have a severe arrhythmia.

Mom stops humming. "Logan, are you down there? Will you get that, please?"

The low murmur of the men's voices come from the other side of the door. There's a second knock, harder.

My heart pumps chaotically in my chest. My legs start shaking. I think I'm going to be sick.

"Logan, will you the answer the door!"

I stare at the door, helpless, unable to speak or move.

There's a third, more forceful knock.

My entire body's trembling now. My hands are clammy. My breathing is harsh, ragged.

Mom pounds down the stairs. "Logan, didn't you hear me?" she asks, annoyed.

I look at her, numb.

She sweeps past me with a frown. "What's wrong with you? Why didn't you get the door?"

She reaches for the doorknob and pulls open the door, looking into the sorrowful faces of the two uniformed men standing on the doorstep. Her eyes flick to the black sedan in the driveway, then back to the men. Her eyes lock on Pastor Reimer's face, her expression one of pure horror. And then she pitches forward.

For as long as I live, I'll never forget that day. Never forget Mom blacking out like she did. It was a terrifying thing to see. She didn't gasp, lose colour, and crumple to the floor. She didn't moan, go weak at the knees, and slowly slide down. She just pitched forward like a great felled tree. If Pastor Reimer and I hadn't caught her, she would have hit the floor face-first.

We carry Mom into the living room and lay her on the couch. Pastor Reimer uses smelling salts to bring her back around. The harsh odour is nauseating, and I know it will linger in the room for hours. After a few minutes, she sits up, but looks dazed.

Pastor Reimer sits down next to Mom. I sit on her other side, watching her closely. I'm scared she's going to faint again and fall face-first on top of the glass coffee table.

Later, Mom asks Pastor Reimer something about moving off-base. With his kind brown eyes, he reaches over and takes her hand. In a gentle, hushed voice, he tells her not to give that one thought. She'll have all the support she needs, can take all the time she needs.

Mom nods, but looks so vacantly at him that I wonder if she really understands what he's just told her.

I, on the other hand, understand perfectly. At the words *off-base*, my stomach gives a violent wrench, like I'd just stumbled over the edge of a two-hundred foot cliff. Stunned, sick, I look out our living room window to the houses that line the street. I've lived the past four years on Canadian Forces Base Cold Lake, Alberta. All my friends live on the base. In fact, I've lived all of my thirteen years on air bases across Canada. Now I'll have to live in a city or town with civilians? It shocks me that I know almost nothing about civilian life. It's all so foreign. I feel an icy hard dark spot, like a cancerous tumour, settle in my chest.

When I'm sure Mom isn't going to pass out again, and neighbours start showing up with food, I slip down to the basement. I need to be alone. I need to be around my dad's things. I remove his red and black Wilson BLX racquet from its case, draw it back, and swing it in a forehand stroke, one Dad patiently taught me until I had it perfect.

I set the racquet down and move over to his golf bag. I run my fingers over the iron clubs and feel suddenly better. Somehow, being down here surrounded by Dad's things makes it all seem unreal, like I'll wake up any second and realize I've been having a horrible nightmare. My dad isn't dead. His CF-18 didn't develop catastrophic engine system failure. He wasn't really trapped in the cockpit of his fighter jet as it, still carrying thousands of pounds of volatile fuel, plummeted to the ground. Like Jared's dad, his co-pilot, he ejected safely before the F-18 crashed in a fireball. Hope blooms in my chest. I stand silent, listening for the front door to open, for the sound of my dad's voice.

But as Mom's soft sobs and the murmur of solemn voices filter down through the floorboards, my hope vanishes. With a bolt of shock I realize it's true— horrifyingly, unbearably true. I will never talk to my dad again. I will never play tennis or golf with my dad again. My dad is dead. Sure, I know and believe he's in Heaven and I will see him again there, but right now, I don't care about that. I want him alive and with me now.

Like the engine failure in my dad's fighter jet, my grief is also catastrophic. Unable to stand under the enormity of it, I slump against the foundation wall, slide down it to the cold concrete floor. I draw my legs up and wrap my arms around my shins. Leaning forward, I press my face in my knees to keep anyone upstairs from hearing my shuddering sobs.

## Chapter 2

# OLIVIA

I lie on my back in bed, staring up at the ceiling. I tell myself to just breathe in, breathe out. It's that simple. Yet it seems beyond me. The pain in my chest is excruciating. It feels like someone is stabbing me with a steel ice pick, jabbing in and out of my chest, shredding my heart to pieces. In agony, my breath grows more shallow and rapid.

I press a hand to my chest, certain that I will feel this pain, that I will grieve for Luc every minute of every day for the rest of my life. I don't know how I will bear it. I've read that when some people who have lost a partner first wake up, for a second or two they forget that their loved one is dead. Then they remember, and it hits them with an acute jolt of shock all over again. But for me, a believer, at least there's the trust that I will one day be with Luc in Heaven. That's the only thing bringing me relief from this pain.

"Luc, oh, Luc," I cry out. My words are too loud in the quiet hotel room.

I hear the sound of rustling sheets from Logan's bed. I quickly stuff a pillow in my mouth, smothering my next sob. I glance at the clock-radio on the night stand between beds. 1:07 a.m. No surprise. Since Luc's death, I jolt awake in the dead of night, every night, heart pounding, crying out for him. Not wanting to wake Logan, I try to muffle my sobs by putting the pillow over my head, or burying myself under blankets. Still, he always hears. Each and every night, he hears.

The first night after Luc's death, I awoke Logan with my sobs. He hurried into my bedroom. He sat on the edge of my bed, put his arms around me and rocked me, telling me that everything would be all right. That he'd take care of me. All that while tears poured down his pale young face, his thin body shaking uncontrollably.

I don't want that to happen tonight, yet I'm unable to stop another sob. It seems to echo through the small room. I turn so that my back is to Logan. But

I'm too late. I hear the rustle of sheets and the groan of the mattress. He's awake and is getting up. I hear him squat down next to the side of my bed.

He yawns. "Mom?"

I feel sorry that I woke him and want him to go back to bed. I keep my eyes closed and pretend to be asleep.

He gently touches my shoulder. "Mom, I know you're awake. I heard you crying."

I turn and face him. The drapes on the window are old and thin and let in the bright glow of the streetlights. I can see him clearly. He looks about ten years old, squatting in his pyjama pants and T-shirt rubbing his eyes.

"Oh, Logan, I'm sorry. I didn't mean to wake you."

"That's okay. Are you all right?"

I sniff and nod. "Yes, yes, don't worry. Go back to bed."

"Do you want a drink of water?" he asks gently.

Behind me, under the window, the room's air conditioning unit kicks on noisily. Like the drapes, it too is cheap. It either runs constantly, turning the room into a morgue, or it shuts off too soon and the room grows unbearably stuffy and hot.

"No, no, I'm fine," I say, fighting to keep my voice steady. "Go back to sleep."

He waits, watching me. "Are you sure, Mom? We can sit up and talk if you like."

A shaft of yellow light falls across his face, making his skin look jaundiced and his cheeks hollow. He lifts a finger to his mouth and chews at the corner of his nail. He bites a piece of skin off and turns his head, spitting it out.

"That's sweet of you, but there's no need. Besides, we have to be on the road early tomorrow morning. Please, Logan, go back to bed."

He doesn't move, stares at me, starts chewing at the corner of another fingernail. That causes another ice-pick-like jab to my heart. Luc used to do the same thing when he was worried. It's a Blanchard trait. I turn my head and take in a small breath.

Logan sits down on the edge of the bed. "There's a little coffee pot there with tea bags and powdered cream. I can make you a cup of tea."

"Thank you, sweetie, but no," I say, my voice quavering. "Go back to bed."

He shakes his head. "I'll sit here until you fall asleep again."

*Who's the parent and who's the child here?* I think, not for the first time since Luc's death.

I shake my head right back. "Go back to bed."

He doesn't move, yawns again.

"Logan, I'm fine," I say firmly. "Go back to bed *now*."

He blows out a breath, stands, but still he hesitates. "You'll wake me if you need me?"

I reach up and touch his hand, hanging loosely by his side. "Yes, I will."

Defeated, he nods, then walks to his bed and climbs back in.

"Good night, sweetie," I say tenderly.

"Night, Mom." He lays on his back, sniffs audibly. "What a stink. I thought this was a non-smoking room."

"It is now, but it's an old motel. There's forty years of cigarette smoke in the carpet, drapes, and furniture."

"No kidding." He yanks the blankets up over his mouth and nose.

A door slams in the room beside us, followed by a deep male voice and a shrill female voice. The TV goes on and laughter and voices from a sitcom carries through the wall.

"Nice," Logan says. "I think the walls are made of cardboard."

"I have earplugs in my suitcase if you want them."

"No, never mind," he grumbles.

I settle down in the bed. My pillow is soaked with tears. I flip it over and stare miserably up at the ceiling. I blink repeatedly to force myself to stay awake until Logan falls asleep again.

I pray that my decision to move back to my hometown of Shipwreck Cove, Nova Scotia, is the right one for Logan. He was so shocked when I told him. Gradually, his shock gave way to anger. Not only because we were moving to a province thousands of kilometres from all his friends, but because we were moving in with my mother, a nurse, who had recently begun operating a special care facility for the disabled from her house. Logan's anger, understandably, turned to horror when he realized he'd be the lone male in a house with six women, four of whom were complete strangers.

The first night, we stopped in Regina, Saskatchewan. The second night we spent in the tiny town of Paradis, Manitoba. Tonight we're in Wawa, Ontario. We ate supper in a little diner and then took a room in this old motel. It has rained every one of the days we've been on the road, a miserable, cold early-April rain that chills you right to the bone. But then, it's either rained or snowed every day since Luc died. It's like when he died, the sun decided to never shine again.

To add to Logan's misery, we're making the five-day journey in a lime-green station wagon. He complains that I poke along, barely reaching the posted speed limit, always sticking to the slow lane. He says that at the rate we're going, it'll take us a month to reach Nova Scotia, not that he cares if or when we get there, mind you. He's just humiliated when lines of cars pass us all day long.

We hadn't even made it out of Alberta on the first day when I saw him lift his eyes from his cell phone from which he constantly texted either Keltie or Jared to watch a line of cars pass. Then he looked at the speedometer, grimaced, and shut his eyes tight. I thought he was in pain, but when I asked him what was wrong he said, in such a dismayed tone that made me afraid he was serious, "Mom, an old lady on a bicycle could pass us right now. Speed up, please, or I'm going to jump out of the car right now and kill myself."

Abruptly, the air conditioner gives a noisy shudder and shuts off, yanking me back to the motel room. In the sudden silence, I hear Logan flip over on his side, turning his back to me. Minutes later, I hear his steady breathing. He's asleep.

I let out a long breath, close my eyes, and try to go back to sleep. Unbelievably, the air conditioner clicks on again and blasts cold air that reeks of mould and stale cigarette smoke right into my face. Outside, a semi drives past the motel on the main road into town, the sound of its Jake brakes shattering the night. I groan and pull the blankets over my head.

## Chapter 3

# LOGAN

At dawn, I stare out my bedroom window at the magenta and pink glow in the sky announcing a new day in Shipwreck Cove.

Gram's house sits on a triangular piece of rocky land off the Lighthouse Road, facing the sea. There's a short front lawn and long, grassy backyard. My bedroom on the second floor looks out to the Bay of Fundy, and the Atlantic beyond. The narrow inlet in front of Gram's house is called Rum Runner Cove. There's a thin, rocky piece of land that juts out into the sea on both sides, leaving only a slender entrance into the cove's calm waters.

Because the two-story, blue cedar-shingled house sits at the edge of the sea, it's almost always shrouded by fog. It shudders each time a blast of wind hits it. All the windows rattle and the wind slips in through the cracks around the sills, screeches down the chimney and into the living room, sounding like a ghoul. The musty odour that rises from the cellar is appalling. To me, it smells like a graveyard down there.

Two fat grey gulls suddenly streak past my window and I recoil, startled. I step up to the window again and look down, peering through the mist. A gust of wind sweeps in off the water, flattening the grass on the lawn, pummelling the branches of the tall old pines planted years ago by my grandfather as a windbreak around the house.

Straight ahead, a half-mile out from land, the tall, red-and-white-striped lighthouse at Skull Island takes shape. To the west, Deadman's Head becomes visible. To the east, I make out the rocky shoreline of Devil's Point. From the lighthouse comes the mournful wail of its foghorn. Far out in the bay, I hear the harsh clang of the bell buoys.

I look left, to the sharp bend in the road. The chill wind slides in through a tiny gap in the window, whistling icily in my ear. At the bend, the land juts out to sea. I watch the surf there explode against the rocks, hurling a wall of white spray so high that it crashes down on Lighthouse Road. The right-hand lane there is always wet, the large boulders of the seawall below the road heavily coated with slimy green moss.

I turn my head and peer to my right. Two kilometres up the coast is the town of Shipwreck Cove with its two wharves. There's the wharf used by the town fishermen, appropriately named Fisherman's Wharf with its weigh station and lobster pound. Past that is the public wharf, called Galen's Wharf, after some guy from town who was a WWI flying ace who died when his plane was shot down in France only a week before the war ended. Galen's Wharf is where, in the summer months, most of the town's recreational boaters berth their powerboats, sailboats, and other pleasure craft.

The businesses and homes of the town sit huddled together in the shape of a horseshoe, facing the harbour. Nearly all of the town's population of seven thousand live in that area, close to the downtown. Not us, though. It kills me that Gram's house is so far from town.

I stare bleakly at the ocean, letting out a heavy breath. I just can't understand Mom's way of thinking. I truly believe she's lost it, gone right off the deep end. What else can explain her moving us from beautiful Alberta to a coastal town in Nova Scotia? To a town that's shrouded constantly by thick fog and battered nonstop by incessant, stabbing winds that reek of dead fish and rotting seaweed? And moving us into Gram's place, an old damp house that smells of mould even on a blazing hot July day?

I understand that Mom's had a tough life, losing her father to the sea when she was a child, and now my dad. I decide that all that grief has broken her. Like one of Gram's fine china plates crashing to the floor, Mom has shattered into a thousand jagged pieces. Despite my love and compassion for her, she often drives me crazy. More often, it angers me.

Sure, we've visited Gram before, at Christmas and in the summer. But she worked then as a nurse at the town's hospital and lived alone. I was horror-struck when Mom told me Gram was operating a special care facility from her house, that we were moving in with her and four disabled women. I begged Mom to please not move us back east. When that didn't work, I pleaded with her to move us to Halifax. That way we'd be in a city, close to Gram, and could visit her often. I figured that was a fair compromise on my part. When that didn't work, I threatened to run away, told her she'd never see me again.

Mom only nodded understandingly. She tried to reassure me, told me I'd adjust. I scowled, tried to reason with her. She hugged me and said I'd be happy in time. I pulled out of her embrace, telling her I'd never forgive her. Sick of my sulking, she said she wasn't going to argue with me anymore. She said we both needed to be with family, and Gram needed our help caring for the four women. More importantly, she said she felt God was leading us home.

I lost it then. I yelled at her, my tone laced with bitterness, "God is leading us home? The same God who allowed Dad to die such a horrifying death?"

"Yes," she replied gently, "and the same God who asks us to trust Him, and teaches us that the best way to forget our own troubles is by caring for others." Then she turned back to the living room window of our house, gazing out as if she couldn't wait one more second to leave.

Right then, something struck me. In the weeks since Dad had died, she'd lost weight and walked with stooped, defeated shoulders. She'd taken to wrapping her arms around her chest and hugging herself tightly. But as she stood staring out the window, decision made to move back to Nova Scotia, I noticed that she stood straighter. Her arms were at her sides. When she looked at me, her eyes were slightly less shadowed by grief and there was a tinge of hope in them. And she smiled. A shaky smile, but still, her first since Dad died. So I lost the glare and bit back a sarcastic response.

Before dawn on a Tuesday in early April, while everyone slept, we locked the doors of our house, stowed our suitcases in the trunk, and silently climbed in the car. As Mom started the engine, I cast a last glance at our home of four years. It looked cold, dark, empty. Like Mom, Dad and I had never once lived happily in there.

Mom backed out of our driveway, her hands gripping the wheel so tightly her knuckles turned milk white. She didn't look back once. But when she glanced at me, I saw, in the glow of the dashboard lights, that her eyes brimmed with tears.

I looked back over my shoulder to Jared and Keltie's houses and watched them both until we turned the corner. Acute sorrow squeezed my chest. My breathing turned ragged. It took everything in me to hold back my tears. My heart felt torn in two. One half, full of love and compassion for my mom, fought with the other half, filled with anger and bitterness toward her. With each passing kilometre, the war worsened and my sullenness increased.

All these months later, I still can't understand Mom's way of thinking. How can she be happy waking up each morning in a town covered with a tarpaulin of wet, grey fog? A town with a grim name like Shipwreck Cove? A town surrounded by places with even grimmer names, like Deadman's Head and Skull Island?

A town where almost everyone either fishes for a living or works in the fish-processing plant located five miles outside town? A town where the tourists flock in the summer, inexplicably to me, and get robbed buying knickknacks from the shops on Harbour Street with stickers on the bottom that say "Made in China"?

I lean my forehead against the cold window pane. *Give me the smell of jet engine fuel over the smell of the ocean any day.* And because thoughts of airplanes naturally lead to thoughts of my dad, the profound sorrow of missing him once again immobilizes me. My chest hurts. My throat aches, a lump the size of a tennis ball stuck in it.

I straighten up and slide the window up to draw in some fresh air. Below my window, I hear Gram's wind chime, which she made from scallop shells she found on the beach, clanking in the strong wind. The wind chime hangs from a corner of the small roof over the front step. In the summer, the shells tinkle softly in the warm breeze coming off the water. Now, in the brisk November wind, the shells clack together harshly. I stick my head out and look down and see that two of the shells are broken. I make a mental note to bring it in today before all the shells are destroyed. I pull my head back inside. Dense, piercing fog rapidly follows me, filling the room with the stench of salt and seaweed. A chill dampness coats my face, my bed, the wood floor. I grimace and slam the window shut.

Muted voices, clanging pots, and the aroma of coffee and bacon drift up the stairway and into my room. I close my eyes, preparing myself for another day of torture as the lone male in a house with six females. Four of whom I think are not so much physically disabled as just plain crazy. And two others, Mom and Gram, I seriously wonder about.

## Chapter 4

# LOGAN

As I descend the stairway, I hear women's voices coming from the kitchen. When I step into the room, the conversation instantly dies. Mom and Gram have their backs to me, Mom bent over at the open fridge door, and Gram frying bacon at the stove. The four residents sitting around Gram's kitchen table all look over to the doorway, staring at me.

I stop dead in my tracks and stare back. They've done this since the day we moved in and I still can't get used to it. Four sets of wrinkly, watery old eyes staring at me like they've never seen a teenage boy before.

Gram smiles over her shoulder at me. "Good morning, sweetheart."

"Morning, Gram," I mumble.

"Hey good-looking, whatcha' got cooking?" says Shaye with a bold wink.

Gram turns and waggles the egg flipper she's holding at Shaye. "Now, Shaye."

Shaye, at fifty, is the youngest of the residents. When she was nineteen, and a university student in Halifax, she was struck down by a taxi one day while crossing a street. She was in a coma for two months. One leg is now shorter than the other, and she walks with a limp, dragging her good leg a little behind her. She also suffered an injury to the part of her brain that controls inner inhibitions and will now make what Gram calls *inappropriate* comments, but what I call just plain dirty. And she flirts with any male she sees. Being the sole man of this house, she's been torturing me since I got here.

"Top of the day to you, love," says Audrey Piper in a thick British accent.

I pretend I don't hear her. I think thin, grey-haired Audrey is the looniest of the bunch. For one thing, she isn't even British. Since the stormy February night in '02 when her husband and teenage son died when their car slid off the road and down an embankment into the icy water of the bay, she has believed she's the English actress Helen Mirren.

Mom shuts the fridge door, turns, and carries a carton of orange juice over to the table and sets it down in front of Audrey.

"Here you go, Audrey." Mom glances at me. "Morning, sweetie."

I glower at her, but she's already turned her back to me and doesn't notice.

"Go ahead, sit down, Logan," Gram says. "Your breakfast is almost ready."

I shift my eyes to Audrey and see the second reason I consider her the craziest of the bunch. She just put an imaginary cigarette to her lips and is touching the flame of an imaginary lighter to its tip.

*Unbelievable.*

Wanting to put as much space as possible between me and the four residents, I take the middle chair in a row of three. That leaves an empty chair on either side. I'll let Mom and Gram sit next to the crazies.

"Do you want ham or bacon with your eggs, Logan?" Gram asks.

"Bacon," I mumble.

"Bacon, *please*," says Mom. "And he can get it, Mom. You have enough to do around here already. You don't have to wait on him."

Gram's kind blue eyes wrinkle up as she gives me a loving smile. "That's all right. I want to."

"Bacon, please," I say quietly to Gram.

Mom lifts a brow. "Last time I checked, there was nothing wrong with your legs. Next time help your grandmother out and get your own breakfast."

Audrey is blowing invisible smoke at me. I groan inwardly. *Give me a break here, Mom.*

Gram walks around the table and sets my breakfast down in front of me. She puts a hand on my shoulder and gives it a warm squeeze. "Eat up while it's hot, sweetheart."

My irritation fades and my body relaxes a little. I love Gram to death and just a tender glance or touch from her instantly lightens my dark mood.

"How come he gets bacon and eggs and I don't?" blurts Maxine Michaud, who sits on my left at the end of the table, her eyes locked on my breakfast.

Maxine, wearing a large faded blue housedress, carries a hundred pounds too much on her five-foot frame. She's a diabetic and has high cholesterol and high blood pressure. Yet she shamelessly cheats on her diet. When no one's in the kitchen, she'll raid the fridge and cupboards for sweets, carrying them off to her bedroom to eat in secret.

"Because you're on a low-fat, sugar-free diet, Maxine," Gram answers her. "We've talked about this before. Besides, you did have bacon and eggs."

"Turkey bacon and egg whites you poured out of a carton. That's pretend bacon and eggs, if you ask me," Maxine says with disgust. "Not the same thing at all, not by a long shot."

Gram casually flips an egg in the frying pan, paying no attention to her.

Maxine flicks her eyes over my way and stares longingly at my breakfast.

I act like I don't notice, then pick up my fork and, because Mom and Gram aren't looking, dig in without praying first.

"Young man, would you be kind enough to give me a light?" Audrey asks.

I drop my head over my plate and eat faster.

"Logan," she says.

*Leave me alone*, I scream silently.

"*Loooogaaannn*," she warbles in her old lady voice, believing she's Helen Mirren on stage in some musical and can actually carry a note.

My shoulders tense, my mood darkening again. I jerk my head up. "What?" I snap.

She smiles sweetly, holding out the imaginary lighter. "My lighter seems to be out of fluid. Do you have a light, love?"

I scowl at her. "That's not a real lighter, and that isn't a real cigarette, either. Don't be so mental, okay, Audrey?"

Mom whips around from the counter and glares at me like I'd just burst out laughing at a funeral.

"That is rude, Logan," she says sharply. "It's Mrs. Piper to you."

"Actually, love, it's Ms. Mirren," Audrey corrects Mom.

Gram raises her eyebrow at me. "Yes, we don't speak to each other like that in this house," she says, but tenderly.

Face burning, I stare down at my plate, able to feel six pairs of eyes locked disapprovingly on me. I hear murmured tsking.

I want to dump my plate of food on the floor, jump up from my chair, and bolt out of the house. I think about hitchhiking to Alberta and never coming back. Instead, with a shaky hand, I pick up my glass and gulp down my orange juice. As I do, I see Audrey pretend to pick up a box of matches on the table. She opens the case, slides a match out, strikes it against the imaginary box, and lights her cigarette. She blows out the pretend match and drops it on her plate. Then she takes a deep drag on the cigarette, exhaling the invisible smoke out of the side of her mouth.

I look at Mom and Gram. I can't understand how they, both qualified medical professionals and allegedly sane women, think it's better to go along with Audrey's delusions. But they either don't see me or ignore me, for neither one will meet my gaze. I hear Audrey inhale deeply again, then I feel her breath on my face as she blows the imaginary smoke in my direction.

That's it. I can't take it. I start shovelling the food in my mouth, wanting to get out of the house as fast as possible.

"Slow down before you choke, Logan," says Mom.

I scowl at her, shove a half-piece of toast in my already full mouth. Then I put my hands to my throat and fake a gagging gesture.

Mom narrows her eyes, then looks at Gram for help. Gram only shakes her head slightly. Mom doesn't say anything further.

Audrey grinds out her pretend cigarette in a pretend ashtray and leans back in her chair. "Shaye, did I ever tell you I won an Academy Award for best actress for my performance in *The Queen* in 2007?"

"Oh, please, spare us," Maxine snorts.

"Pardon me, madam?" says Audrey, her fake English accent more pronounced.

"You never won an Academy Award, and you're not Helen Mirren. Your name is Audrey Jane Piper. You worked in the fish-processing plant."

Audrey lifts her chin. "I'm sorry, but you are dreadfully mistaken, my dear."

"Audrey, you worked on the canning line with me for twenty years," says Maxine.

"I assure you, madam, I did no such thing."

"Aw, you did too, you crazy old thing."

"Maxine!" Gram scolds her. "You just heard me tell Logan that we don't speak to each other like that in this house."

"Well, Winnie, she's lying and I can prove it," Maxine tells Gram triumphantly. "I have a picture of the two of us working on the line in 1980. It's in a box in my bedroom."

Audrey lifts a hand and waves Maxine's words away. "Balderdash," she huffs. "I had the lead role in *The Duchess of Malfi*, at the Royal Exchange Theatre in 1980."

"The Duchess of Malfi?" cries Maxine. "Come on, Audrey. Stop it, will you? You've lived your entire life in Shipwreck Cove. We lived next door to each other, went to school together for goodness' sake."

"Clearly, madam, you are mistaking me for one of your uncouth, illiterate friends from this horrid little town," Audrey counters, snobbishly looking down her nose at Maxine.

Gram frowns in disapproval. "Audrey, that's enough."

"It's Helen, dear heart, Helen Mirren. I keep telling you that," Audrey says with an audible sniff.

Grace, who nodded off at the table and missed all this, jerks awake, blinks twice, and then shouts at Gram, "Vinnie, could I have some of your nice strawberry jam, please?" A sausage rolls off her plate to the table.

Maxine, sitting on Grace's left, flicks a glance at Gram. Seeing that the coast is clear, she swiftly reaches out a hand out, grabs the sausage, and pops it into her mouth. She closes her eyes and chews, a look of pure ecstasy on her face.

Shaye, sitting on Grace's right, leans sideways and shouts into her ear. "It's Winnie, not Vinnie. I've told you that at least a thousand times. Turn your hearing aid on, woman."

Grace, a frail, white-haired woman of eighty, wears hearing aids in both ears, but refuses to turn them on because she says there's nothing wrong with her hearing. She also suffers from narcolepsy. She nods off about twenty times a day. Often she'll fall asleep right in the middle of a conversation. Then, seconds later, because she hallucinates during these sleep episodes, she'll let rip with a hair-raising scream. I still can't get used to it.

"Jam's on the table," Gram tells Grace.

"Pardon me, Vinnie?" says Grace.

Shaye gives a weary sigh, reaches across the table for the jam, and passes it to Grace.

Grace accepts the jam and smiles at Shaye. "Thank you, Fay, you're a dear," she hollers.

Gram puts a hand on a hip and takes a good look around the table. Satisfied that everyone has their breakfast, she picks up two plates of eggs and toast and carries them over to the table. She sets one plate down on the red placemat on my left, then moves around me and sits on the chair to my right. "Come and eat now, Olivia," she tells Mom, gesturing to her left.

Mom sets the coffee pot back on the burner and joins us at the table. I relax slightly now that Mom and Gram are on either side of me.

"I heard the Coast Guard has called off the search for Jeremy Tanner," Gram tells Mom.

"Oh no," Mom says, shaking her head. "His poor parents. It's terrible. That's the second young fisherman lost at sea since I've moved back home."

Gram nods slowly, sadly. "It's heartbreaking."

The four residents all murmur in agreement.

For the next few minutes, everyone is silent. The only sounds are the soft clatter of silverware and Grace's false teeth clicking as she chews.

"That was simply delish, my dear," Audrey says quietly to Gram while dabbing daintily at her lips with a napkin. She drops it on her plate and pushes the plate away. "I believe I have time for another cigarette before they call me to shoot my next scene." She places another fake cigarette between her lips, pretends to light it again. When she sees me watching her, she winks and blows imaginary smoke again. I smell coffee and eggs on her breath. Gross.

I freeze, my fork held in the air over my plate, body tense. Across the table, I see Grace's eyes close, her chin drops, and a soft snore escapes her mouth. To my left, Maxine stares hungrily at my plate.

Gram reaches out and tenderly squeezes my arm. "Pay no mind. Go on, finish your breakfast," she says in a low voice so only I hear.

Suddenly, Grace lifts her chin and screams so loud that I jump an inch off my chair and drop my fork on my plate with a clatter. Then Shaye finds my leg under the table and starts running her foot up and down my shin, the whole time smiling brazenly. I jerk my leg back, but she quickly slides her other foot up under the cuff of my jeans and runs her big toe along my calf.

"Hey, gorgeous," she mouths silently at me so Gram won't hear.

That's it! I can't sit here with these four certifiable nutcases a second longer. I jump to my feet and the legs of my chair scrape harshly across the wood floor. I stomp out of the room and down the hallway to the front door.

"You didn't finish your breakfast, Logan," Maxine shouts. "Can I have it?"

"No, Maxine!" Gram says at once.

"Gentle steps, please, Logan," Mom calls out to me.

"Yeah, you don't need to stomp around the house like a pack of wild horses, mister," Maxine yells, pouting because she can't have my breakfast.

What I want to yell back at Maxine is: *It's not your house!* I haul on my running shoes, grit my teeth, and say nothing instead.

"Maxine, mind your own business, please," Gram reprimands her.

*Thank you, Gram,* I say to myself.

"Logan, do you want a drive to school?" Mom asks. "I have to go to town in a few minutes to mail something."

"No!" I yell from the hallway, lacing up my shoes as fast as I can.

"All right, have a good day at school, sweetie." She's oblivious to my anger.

"Yes, have a good day, sweetheart," adds Gram, apparently also oblivious.

"Yes, have a good day, *sweetheart*," all four residents call out in unison and then crack up in laughter.

"Girls, honestly," says Gram.

Their laughter only increases.

I drop my head and close my eyes for a few seconds. I then yank open the door and step outside. I slam it so hard behind me that the glass rattles and the blinds covering the window swing wildly back and forth. See if that gets Mom and Gram's attention.

## Chapter 5

# LOGAN

Outside it is foggy and damp. I stomp over the dead leaves that cover the paved driveway. I feel them turn to a slippery mush under my shoes. I remember overhearing Mom tell Gram last night that she had missed the vivid Nova Scotia autumns when she was in Alberta. I roll my eyes at that. Maybe the colours are more vivid here, but in Alberta I could pick up a fallen birch or poplar leaf and it would be so dry it would turn to powder in my hand. Here, with the constant fog, the leaves lay in dark, sodden clumps on the ground or against curbs. It's just another thing about living in this seaside town that I find depressing.

I look at Gram's van as I tromp past. It's a battered, pale blue, ten-passenger Ford. The words *McPhee's Special Care Home* are painted in black letters on the sides. I hate the thing. If I see Gram, Mom, and the four residents tooling around town, on their way to prayer meeting or Sunday services, I duck in an alley fast. I'm terrified Gram will see me and toot the horn. I can just imagine those six prayer warriors all waving madly at me from the van windows as they drive past in full view of the townspeople. Or worse, stopping and trying to coax me to jump in and go to church with them, something I stopped doing since Dad died and refuse to do each and every Sunday morning when Mom and Gram practically beg me to attend with them.

I look at Mom's slime-green station wagon parked beside Gram's van and grimace. I despise the car; the colour alone nauseates me. I wish it would roll down the driveway, across the road, and straight into the sea.

Unbelievably, only a month after Dad died, Mom sold his sapphire blue four-wheel-drive pickup. She told me she didn't think she could bear to sit in it ever again. Right up until the day she sold it, I would sneak into the cab of the truck, breathing in the lingering scent of my dad's aftershave. The scent faded a little more each day, and I'd been terrified for the day it would be gone forever. It made no sense to me at all. Why hadn't Mom wanted to keep it and breathe in Dad's scent for as long as it lasted?

My dad's been dead for eight months and still I think of him at least fifty times a day. But his face is already blurring, its sharp angles less defined. I'm scared that I'll forget what he looks like, so I keep a picture of him in my wallet and look at it ten times a day, memorizing his features. I know there'll never be a time when I don't miss him anymore, but I never want there to be a time when I can't remember what he looked like.

I stop at the end of the driveway and shove my hands deeply into my jeans pockets against the early-morning chill. I look left and then right. The Lighthouse Road is deserted. I cross the road to a worn path through the rocks and boulders of the seawall that leads down to Rum Runner's Cove. A minute later, I emerge from the path onto the beach. I stop and look out to sea. I like it here down at the cove. It's not a good spot for swimming, because of the rocky beach, so I'm the only one who ever comes down here.

The fog's dissipating, but I still can't see farther than thirty feet out. The wind blowing in from the bay is so full of salt I can taste it on my lips. The tide's retreating, leaving long tendrils of dirty foam on the sand that look like whitish-yellow pythons. Seagulls shriek at each other, foraging through the crab and clam shells covering the sand.

I study the debris washed up on the beach by the tide, noticing a piece of driftwood bleached so smooth and white that it looks like a human femur. To my right, a white plastic jug with a frayed yellow rope tied around its neck. A foot away is a plastic water bottle with an inch of sand in the bottom. I step up to it and kick it over to the rocky seawall.

I spot a chard of sea glass on the sand right in front of me. I pick it up and study it. It's a vivid azure blue with slivers of turquoise running through it—a rare find. Most sea glass I find is white. I shove the piece in my coat pocket. I'll add it to the collection I keep hidden in an old shoe box on the floor at the back of my closet. I hide it there because I don't want Mom finding it and thinking there's even one thing about this place I like.

The fog soaks my hair, leaving water droplets on my eyelids and face. I lean forward and shake my head to remove the droplets, then wipe the moisture from my face with my coat sleeve. I look down the beach in the direction of town and then up to the Lighthouse Road. The road runs parallel to the water until a half-kilometre from town where it becomes Harbour Street. I debate whether to climb up and follow the road to town.

I decide to walk along the beach for as long as possible. The last time I walked to town along the shoulder of the highway, two cars stopped, the drivers offering me a lift. I declined both offers. Ever since my dad died, I rarely feel the urge to talk to anyone, and I avoid people as much as possible. I doubt if I've said more than ten words in school since arriving last April. Some of the kids have tried to befriend me. One girl, Sophie Thibideau, invited me to the Friday night youth group at her church. It's the same church Mom, Dad, Gram, and I attended when we visited Gram, the same church Gram, Mom, and the four loons all attend. I politely declined. She's cute and seems nice, but she's not Keltie, who I miss terribly. Eventually everyone got the message and now leaves me alone.

Thinking of Keltie, I pull out my cell phone, but then remember the time difference. It's not yet 5:00 a.m. in Alberta. I shove it back in my coat pocket.

A gust of raw wind kicks up. My hair lifts in the breeze, my scalp and neck freeze. I pull the hood of my hoodie up over my head and turn the collar of my jacket up against the wind. I get a whiff of mould and sniff at my coat collar. I groan aloud, disgusted, mortified. The jacket reeks of mould.

*Oh, I hate that old dump of a house,* I think, clenching my fists.

The musty odour rises up from the dank cellar and clings to everything—the walls, the furniture, and our clothing. That's it, I decide. I intended to go to school today, but not now. How can I, smelling like an old potato sack?

I hate it here. I hate my life. I want to scream until my lungs burst. Instead I pick up a flat stone and hurl it across the surface of the water. It skips once and sinks.

*Dirty looking water.* It has nothing on the crystal blue glacier water that fills Alberta's lakes and rivers. I pick up another rock, this one flatter, and throw it with more force. It skips across the water five times before sinking. I hurl three more, each one harder than the last, until I cool down.

Breathing in the damp, briny air, I walk along the firm sand in the direction of town.

## Chapter 6

# CADE

I'm standing at my office window gazing down on Harbour Street when I see Olivia Blanchard step out through the doors of the post office.

My heart dissolves in my chest. "Olivia, there you are."

I lean to get a better look at her and smack my forehead against the glass. I wince and then refocus, following her with my eyes as she walks up the sidewalk and stops in front of the library, directly across the street from my window.

I stand frozen, staring at her, half-stunned. Despite the two decades that have passed, she's hardly changed.

She takes a few steps in one direction, then turns and takes a few steps back again. She looks up and down Harbour Street, raising one hand to her mouth and lightly tapping her lips while pondering where to go next. And then she turns to face my office.

I leap back. After a few seconds, I step up to the window again. She's still facing my office, but she's taking in the businesses that line this side of the street. I can't take my eyes off her. She's still slender, with prominent cheekbones and dark shoulder-length hair worn short. Unlike me, she looks younger than her forty-two years. Though I still feel a trace of bitterness and anger in my heart toward her, I'm shocked to find she still moves me so much.

*She's still the most beautiful woman I've ever seen.*

I heard she was back in town, that her husband Luc died last March when his fighter jet crashed in Alberta, that Olivia and her teenage son moved back in with her mom in April.

I left the office the day I heard she was here, even though a voice in my head screamed at me not to do it. I jumped into my cruiser and drove by her mom's house. I saw a moving truck backed up to the open door, two men carrying boxes inside. In the driveway sat a green station wagon with Alberta plates.

After passing the house, I pulled into a secluded lane off the Lighthouse Road. I killed the engine and sat there, mind whirling. I cracked the window, breathed in deeply of the cool, salty air, and tried to calm down and think straight. I was still hurt, still angry, yet I couldn't stop a thrill of happiness from filling my heart, couldn't banish the surge of relief that flowed through my body. "Olivia's home," I said over and over.

I drove by the house three more times that same day. Since that day, I've probably driven past forty times, slunk down low in my seat. Lately, I've been driving by at night so Olivia won't see me. With the house lit up, I might catch a glimpse of her moving through the rooms. So far the curtains and blinds have always been drawn.

Each time I drive past, I tell myself I'm pathetic, acting like some kind of stalker. But then, to quell the lingering guilt and shame, I tell myself that I'm a police officer. I'm merely serving and protecting, making sure there are no prowlers lurking around Winnie McPhee's property. Never mind that in the past five years I can only remember two complaints being made in town about prowlers.

Even now, I can't seem to move away from the window. Twenty years have passed and seeing her still immobilizes me. But then, if I'm honest with myself, that's not really surprising. The truth is that in all this time, Olivia has never been far from my thoughts.

Outside my window, Olivia turns and starts walking down the sidewalk. I stare at her and watch her hair lifting in the breeze, her stride as lithe and graceful as ever. I watch until she turns a corner and disappears from sight. I rest my forehead on the cool window pane, my heart beating excitedly. I close my eyes and inhale and exhale a few times to slow it down.

I've dated other women since Olivia, yet I've never experienced the same connection, the same depth of passion. Olivia is unlike any of them, and no matter how long she's been away, just seeing her stirs my heart in a way no woman has ever been able to. Just as quickly, a jolt of bitterness passes through me. The old hurt comes back like a punch to the jaw. I loved Olivia intensely and she returned that love by choosing and marrying Luc Blanchard instead.

*Haven't you learned anything at all by what happened?* I chastise myself. *Olivia Blanchard never loved you as deeply as you loved her; she likely never loved you at all.*

I turn from the window and sit down behind my desk, disgusted with myself. I rest my head against the back of my chair and fold my hands over my abdomen. Do I really want to continue loving a woman who has never, will never, love me? Am I that pathetic?

I draw in a breath and let it out slowly. I resolve, for what has to be the ten thousandth time in the past two decades, to forget Olivia. To move on. I tell myself that I'm doing fine without her. I managed, whenever she and Luc were home on vacations, to avoid seeing her. I've managed not to bump into her in town or church since April. I can continue to manage.

I sit up, pick up a file folder, and pull out a document. I hold it up with shaky hands, read the same line five times, and then give up. I throw it down on my desktop and rub my face briskly. My mind is full of thoughts of Olivia.

## Chapter 7

## LOGAN

I stroll along the sidewalk of Harbour Street, heading to Fisherman's Wharf. The sun is high and the fog has burned away. Like the fog, my foul mood is gone. The air's warming up enough that I unzip my jacket. The wind is a light breeze now, gently lifting the leaves clinging stubbornly to the trees. It's turning into a gorgeous late-autumn day.

I'd never tell my mom this, but I spend a lot of time hanging around the town's two wharves. I like Fisherman's Wharf the most. I enjoy watching the fishermen check their equipment and inspect their diesel-powered engines before heading out to sea. Earlier in November, I was here watching them get their boats ready for the start of the lobster fishing season. The Department of Fisheries and Oceans set the start date for Tuesday, November 9, and in the days before the wharf bustled, the air filled with excited voices as fishermen called and joked to each other from the decks of their boats.

I like Galen's Wharf too. In the summer months, I enjoyed sitting on the wooden wharf facing town, the soft sea breeze caressing my face, the lights of Harbour Street's businesses shimmering on the dark water. Above the shoreline were the luxurious homes of summer residents. From their decks, where they sat out to escape the heat, the murmur of their voices carried over the water. Over the clatter of dishes and silverware, I heard the muted voices and laughter of tourists sitting at the outdoor patios of the bars and restaurants of Harbour Street. Clear lights strung around the patios faintly illuminated the customers sitting at tables. I was shocked at how many summer people flocked to town. From May to August, the population seemed to double.

At the harbour entrance is a tiny island called Seal Island. There's a red and white lighthouse standing in the centre of the island. On hot summer nights, its beam swept the sky, reminding me of the strobe lights over the runway at CFB Cold Lake, the weak similarity oddly comforting.

Today, I'm shocked at just how dead the town is. The tourists are gone. The summer people have left, their homes shut up tight for the winter. Town children are back in school, most of their parents either fishing or working at the fish-processing plant at Periwinkle Point. Shipwreck Cove is as quiet as a graveyard.

At the entrance to the wharf, I stop in front of a four-foot granite monument that honours all the town's fishermen lost at sea. With my fingertips, I trace the white letters of one name engraved in the stone, that of my grandfather:

Logan Q. McPhee. *The Olivia-Jayne.*
January 13, 1975.

He, his crew of three, and his boat were all lost in a savage snowstorm in the Bay of Fundy when my mom was a little girl. His thirty-seven-metre fishing boat was named after Mom and Gram. Gram's full name is Jayne-Winifred McPhee, but everyone calls her Winnie. I drop my hand, turn, and head down the planked wharf road. The wind is stronger and cooler on the wharf, the air heavy with salt and the odour of diesel.

I continue on. As I pass the empty berths, I find myself missing the bantering voices and laughter of fishermen. I stop at one empty berth, lean on the wooden railing, and look down at the water. The air reeks of brine, dead fish, and kerosene from the wharf pilings. The water around the pilings is murky and oil-slicked. My eyes follow a piece of blue foam from a fishing buoy as it floats by, slips between the pilings, and disappears under the wharf.

I move on to the southern end of the wharf. Twenty yards to my left, I see a blue and white lobster boat moored to the dock. I approach the boat, named the *Sea Predator.* I'm surprised by its name. Most fishermen in town name their boats after their wives or daughters. The name *Sea Predator* sounds so wicked. I love it.

A short, burly man is stacking lobster traps in the stern. He's wearing a green T-shirt, soiled blue jeans, and knee-high deck boots with the tops folded down and flopping around his calves. The T-shirt has large sweat marks on the front, back, and under both armpits. His portable radio blares country music.

I watch the man work. He has the dark, weathered face of a fisherman, but his scalp, visible through his buzz cut, is strangely white. I watch him leap off the boat and onto the dock. He lifts a trap and then carrying it effortlessly in his arms, which are bigger than my thighs, and jumps back over the rail and onto the deck of the boat. The tide's in, but his boat is a few feet lower than the wharf road. It bobs around on the water, yet he effortlessly and with perfect balance lands on the deck, carrying the trap to the stern and piling it on the stacks already there. For such a stocky guy, he's as light on his feet as a panther.

Almost the entire stern is filled with stacks of traps four feet high. I count seven bait bins, and the smell of dead fish wafting off them is sickening. I hold my breath. He's either purposely ignoring me or indifferent to my presence. I'm just about to move on when the radio suddenly dies.

"You want something?" he blurts, spotting me.

I look up into his brutal deep-brown eyes. His left cheek has a scar that looks like a thin white worm crawling over his face. Unnerved, it takes me a moment to find my voice.

"No," I say, finally.

He jerks his chin toward town. "Get lost, then. You're getting on my nerves."

He spins around, starting toward the wheelhouse. He squints up into the sun, then grabs a Toronto Maple Leafs ball cap from where it's jammed into his back jeans pocket and slaps it on his head. Now I understand why his scalp is so white.

Stopping abruptly, he whirls around again, observing me with the same rapacious stare as before. "What are you doing here anyway? Shouldn't you be in school?"

I lift a shoulder in a careless shrug. "Not today."

He sets his hands on his hips. "Uh-huh. You interested in making some cash then?"

"Doing what?"

He points to the piles of traps on the wharf next to the boat. "I need to work on the engine. I don't have time to load the rest on my boat. I'll give you twenty dollars if you finish loading them for me."

I take in the stacks of wire traps on the dock, then the larger stacks on the boat. There's close to a hundred and fifty traps in all, and about a hundred are on the boat. I frown. The traps are made of wire but I can see cement in the bottoms. "How much do they weigh, anyway?"

"Fifty pounds each. They've got concrete for ballast."

I nod, hiding my shock. I never imagined they were that heavy. The man lifted and stacked the pots like they weighed no more than a kitten.

He sneers. "Yeah, thought so. Forget it, kid."

"No, wait," I say, considering it. "I can do it."

He points to a long metal bar with a barbed spear on one end. It hangs from a hook on the back wall of the wheelhouse. "Nah, forget it. I don't know what I was thinking. You're almost as skinny as that gaffing pole. It'll be too much for you."

"I can do it," I snap back, "but not for twenty-five bucks. The job's worth at least fifty."

A gust blows in, whipping an empty pop can down the wharf road. The boat heaves and sways, the mooring lines pulling tight and groaning in protest. The man stays steady on his feet despite the boat's rocky movement.

I shove my hands in my jeans pockets, waiting him out.

Fat sea gulls swoop down to the boat's deck, lured by the bait bins before soaring again.

He puffs his cheeks and blows out a breath. "All right, deal. Fifty it is. Have at her, then. But you don't get the full fifty if you don't get them all on the boat."

The man picks up a long wrench and steps inside the wheelhouse.

I step over to the nearest pile. I put a hand on each side of the trap, grasp it firmly and lift it. Grunting from the weight of the trap, I stagger over to the wharf railing. I pause, drawing in a deep breath, and step up on the four-inch wide railing. I cautiously place my foot forward on the starboard railing. At that moment, the boat heaves and jerks away from the wharf. A two-foot gap opens between the wharf and the *Sea Predator.* I start to wobble, then glance down and see the oil-slicked water below and panic. I lunge for the safety of the boat's deck. I drop, lose my balance. The trap flies out of my hands as I crash to the deck.

The man sticks his head out the wheelhouse. He roars with laughter and shakes his head. "If you can't do it, kid, you can't do it. Just tell me and I'll find someone else who can."

"I can do it," I say, annoyed. "I'm fine. I just lost my balance."

He laughs again, then pulls his head back inside.

I stand unsteadily on the rocking boat, arms held out for balance. Once the boat's movement eases and I feel surefooted, I pick up the trap and lug it over to the stern. There, I heave it atop the nearest pile. I slap my hands together, thinking for a second. That's one trap, around forty-nine to go. If I can manage to pile twenty-five an hour, that's two hours of work, tops. Not bad for fifty dollars.

I work without a break under the hot sun for the next *three* hours. Sweat rolls down my face. My arms, back, and shoulders burn with pain, my thigh muscles cramping. But I continue, not wanting to give the man the satisfaction of seeing me quit.

Finally, I'm done. Clothes drenched with sweat, hair plastered to my skull, I look proudly at the stacked traps.

"I'm done," I call, turning to face the open door of the wheelhouse.

The man steps out. He stops, wiping his black greasy hands on a rag. His eyes move over the stacks of traps, all tied down with thick yellow bands that lock together at the ends. He glances at his watch, then gives me an approving look. "Three hours. Not bad, not bad at all. Small but mighty, hey?"

A surge of pride shoots through me, but I shrug like I pile lobster traps like this every day of my life.

The man reaches into his back pocket and pulls out his wallet. He lifts two twenties and a ten from it and hands them to me. When he does, our fingers inadvertently touch and something strange, rough, brushes against the flesh on my palm. I look at his hand when he pulls it back and see that tip of the pinkie finger on his left hand is gone from the knuckle up. It's just a stub. I barely hold back a shudder.

"Thanks." I take the cash and shove it in my jeans pocket. I grab my jacket from the hook on the outside wall of the wheelhouse where I hung it, then step up on the railing and jump over to the wharf road. I pull on my jacket as I start walking toward town.

"Hey kid, hold on there!"

I hear the slap of the man's rubber boots on the wharf road behind me.

I stop in mid-stride, turn around, and face him.

He's right behind me now, only a foot away. Once again, it hits me that he moves incredibly fast for such a stocky guy.

He eyes me. "How old are you, anyway?"

"Fourteen."

His eyes narrow.

I shrug. "I'll be fourteen next month."

The man nods, appraising me. He lifts his ball cap and scratches his head. "I don't know. Wish I wasn't so desperate. Nah, look, just forget it."

"Forget what?"

He slaps his cap back down and gazes off across the water. "I'm in a bit of a mess. Yesterday I got only a quarter of my pots set when the engine started giving me trouble. I need to get back out first thing tomorrow morning to set the rest, but it's too big a job for one man. I can't run the winch and set pots at the same time. I need another pair of hands."

I can't believe it. He wants me to work for him. My heart quickens. "I can help you."

The man laughs. "Actually, I was going to ask you if you had any friends, older and bigger."

My face falls. I shake my head, disappointed. "No, I don't. But listen, I can do it. You saw how I stacked your traps no problem."

The man regards me dubiously. "Well, you're not afraid of hard work, that's true. But you're young and skinny. Lobster fishing is dangerous, exhausting work. I can barely stand on my own two feet at the end of the day. Trust me, kid, it'd be too much for you."

I meet his gaze, hold it. "No, it won't. I can do it."

He squints at me and shakes his head. "Everyone says that. But I've been at this a long time and had young helpers before. It never works out. You'll just up and quit on me."

"I won't. I swear."

The man hawks up sputum and spits over the wharf railing. The phlegm disappears in the murky water. He lifts a sceptical eyebrow. "Fishing lobster is a lot harder than stacking pots. And this warm weather isn't going to last. It could turn like that tomorrow," he says, snapping his fingers. "The hardest thing to handle is being constantly cold and wet. It gets wicked cold out there. Nothing like you're used to, I'd bet."

"Cold weather doesn't bother me. I'm used to prairie winters."

The man falls silent. He regards me more thoughtfully, rubbing the scar on his cheek the whole time. Finally, he gives a reluctant nod. "Yeah, okay. I'm working myself to the bone here trying to keep things running by myself. I suppose I could try you for a day or two, just until I can find another helper. How's that sound?"

I'm not sure how I'll get away with skipping school for two days, but I want to go so bad I'd give my right arm. Still, I don't want to look too excited, so I pretend to think about it for a moment. Then, I say casually, "Okay, sure, I guess I'll take the job."

He holds out his hand. "All right, then. Name's Macklin Crocker, but only my wife calls me Macklin. You call me Crocker."

I shake his hand. "Logan Blanchard."

He cocks his head. "Blanchard? Are you Olivia McPhee's boy? She married an air force pilot named Blanchard."

My heart sinks, sure I'm about to lose this job before I even start.

"Yeah," I admit dismally.

"Your dad was killed over in Afghanistan or Libya, one of them places, wasn't he?"

I feel a sharp stab of pain like someone has shoved a bayonet through my chest. I want to say yes, my dad died a hero's death. I want to say yes, his plane was shot down while he flew a dangerous sortie over Libya, rather than the gut-wrenching irony that my dad actually survived the war in Libya only to die a year later when his fighter jet had engine trouble and careened into the ground. That secretly I'm deeply bitter that Jared's dad got out of the plummeting CF-18 while my dad was trapped inside.

I hesitate, unable to reply under the profound grief and desolation that darkens my heart whenever I speak of my dad, or of the accident that turned his fighter jet into a burning coffin, leaving his body nothing more than ashes for Mom and me to bury. Back in May, I admitted to Gram that I'm scared he didn't die instantly when his plane hit the ground, terrified he might have survived and burned to death in the cockpit. Gram's face filled with pain and sorrow, her chin trembling, when she said, "Oh, Logan, no, no, don't even think that." I vowed to never speak to her of it again.

"Yeah, too bad about that," Crocker says, his tone clear that he could care less. "I heard your mom moved back in with Winnie." He eyeballs me. "Yeah, now I see the resemblance. You look like the McPhees, especially your mom. But I guess you've probably heard that already."

"Yeah," I say flatly. In fact, I've only heard that about a thousand times since April.

Crocker looks lost in thought. "Yeah, I know Olivia well. We went to school together. She was a couple of grades ahead of me, but I always liked her. She's not a hypocrite or a phony like all the other Bible-thumpers in this town. Funny, I've seen her around town a couple of times, but I've always been in my truck. I haven't bumped into her in person yet."

I stiffen. For some reason, hearing my mom's name roll off his lips, with an almost intimate tone, really bothers me. And the look in his eyes, his almost obscene smile when he speaks of her, makes the hair on my neck stand up.

"Olivia comes from good stock. Her people, your people, are hardworking fishermen. It's in the blood."

I only nod. Shipwreck Cove is a small, close-knit community. People are either related to each other or know each other well. I never even heard the expression "your people" until moving here. On military bases, though they were a community unto themselves, everybody was from different provinces. Rarely was anyone related to anyone other than their immediate family. That always suited me just fine because I'm a bit reserved. But here, it's different. I'm not sure if I like everyone knowing who I am, or who my people are. I'm pretty sure I'll never get used to it.

"Well, now, I don't know about this after all," Crocker says.

I panic. "What... why?"

He winces and scratches his bristly chin. "I'm talking about your mom and what happened to her dad, your grandfather, on the *Olivia-Jayne*. Your mom took his death awful hard. She hates fishing. There's no way she'll let you go out. If she finds out I hired you, she'll skin me alive."

I look out over the harbour, experiencing a moment of disquiet. It's true. Mom despises fishing. She's warned me since I was a little boy that she'll die before ever letting me grow up to be a fisherman. I'm about to tell Crocker to forget it when suddenly a hot rush of anger and resentment surges through me. Mom moved us to this stinking fishing town, didn't she? Even after I begged her not to, she went right ahead, didn't she? She didn't care about my feelings, so why should I care about hers?

I look Crocker in the eye. "She can't mind something she doesn't know."

Crocker pauses, then gives me a long, calculating look. He grins slyly, relishing my deceit. "True enough, true enough."

As I look into Crocker's cold, devious eyes, I feel uneasy. When I was ten, I memorized the entire Book of Proverbs for a Sunday school contest, which I won. Right now, one of the verses fills my mind: *A righteous man is cautious in friendship, but the way of the wicked leads them astray.* I feel a prick in my heart, then drop my head and look at the ground.

*Don't do this. There's something not right about this guy,* I think.

Inexplicably, I lift my head. "How much does it pay?"

"Well, that depends on our catch, but it'll be a lot more than fifty bucks. And it's cold hard cash at the end of the day. You won't get that working at Mickey D's." Crocker hacks again and spits a wad of phlegm onto the wharf road.

I watch the phlegm slide down between the wooden planks. "Deal."

"All right, then. But listen to me. If your mom gets wind of this, you handle her. I don't want her coming after me. You understand?"

"Yeah, but don't worry. She'll never know."

Crocker points a thick finger at me. "Make sure of that. I want to get out to the fishing grounds before the others, so be here tonight by three-thirty or I'll leave without you."

# Chapter 8

## LOGAN

I wake to the sound of Mom's sobs. I don't bother glancing at my watch. I know it's around one in the morning. Since Dad died, Mom often wakes up at this time crying out for him. Since moving in with Gram, though, it's been happening less frequently.

Outside, a gust of wind slams into the front of the house, rattling my bedroom window. When it dies down, I listen again for her. Not that it matters. Even with the wind blasting the walls of the old house, each and every night I hear her. I don't know which is worse. The pain I feel from the loss of my dad or the pain I feel when I hear Mom crying. The weeping is agonizing enough; hearing her call out my dad's name is nearly unbearable.

I throw back the blankets and crawl out of bed. Groggy, I stumble out of my room and ease into the chilly hall to Mom's bedroom. I stand at her door and listen. A few seconds later, an anguished sob breaks the silence.

I tap lightly on the door. "Mom, are you okay?"

I hear the rustle of her sheets, a sniff.

"Mom, are you all right?"

She blows her nose softly, then replies in a trembling voice, "Yes, I'm fine, sweetie."

I sigh. She isn't fine. "Can I come in?"

"No, everything's okay. Go back to bed."

I close my eyes, letting out a breath. *Sure, Mom.*

"Do you need a drink of water?" I ask.

"No, thank you, I have a glass here on my nightstand. I'm sorry I woke you. Logan, please, go back to bed before we wake everyone up. We'll frighten poor Grace."

I glance down the long hall, dimly lit by two nightlights. The stairway divides the hall in half. My, Mom's, and Gram's bedrooms and bathroom are on one end of the hall. Audrey's, Shaye's, and Grace's bedrooms and bathroom are at the other. Maxine, because of her size, can't make it up the stairs, and has a bedroom and bathroom on the first floor right across from the kitchen.

*Right across from the pot of gold*, Maxine informed me happily the day we moved in.

Gram hates that Maxine is so close to the kitchen, but says there isn't much she can do about it. At least not until Maxine loses a good deal of weight and can climb the stairs to a bedroom on the second floor. Gram somehow remains hopeful, but I doubt this is likely to happen any time soon. For now, Gram keeps a small padlock on the main pantry door.

Heavy nasal snoring erupts from behind Grace's door. It sounds like a freight train roaring down the tracks. Despite her tiny stature, she snores so loudly I can feel the floorboards vibrating under my feet.

"Mom, trust me, Grace will never hear us."

"Doesn't matter," she says. "Please go back to bed."

"Not until I'm sure you're okay," I say gently. "Do you want a cup of tea? I'll make you a cup of tea and we can talk for a while."

"No, Logan. That's sweet of you, but you have school in the morning."

There's a terrible creak as a fierce gust of wind shrieks in from the Atlantic and explodes against the front of the house. The wind easily slides into the draughty old house. It slips through the rooms, under the doors, and into the hall where I stand, slithering icily over my bare feet. I shiver, wrapping my arms around my chest and tucking my hands in my armpits. I move closer to Mom's door, shifting my weight from one foot to the other to keep my toes from going numb. Once the wind has died down and the quaking old house falls silent, I try again.

"Mom, let me in, come on. I don't mind."

I hear the sound of a tissue being yanked from the box. She blows her nose again. When she finally speaks, her voice still carries a tremor. "No need, I'm fine. Go back to sleep."

I swallow hard against the lump growing in my throat. The first time I heard Mom crying and calling out for Dad, I went into her room, intending to comfort her. Instead I broke down and cried like a baby while Mom comforted me. Later I burned with shame. I resolved to never let that happen again. Dad would want me to be a man, to take care of Mom. So the next time Mom tried to comfort me, I pushed her away, gently at first, and then, when she tried again, more forcefully.

From then on, despite my own crushing heartache, I held back my own tears and eased her pain and grief. In time, repressing my emotions grew easier.

"Mom, you're not okay. Open the door and let me in."

"No, Logan. You need a good night's sleep. You have to get up early for school. Go back to bed. I mean it."

Giving up, I walk back to my room, climb into bed, and pull the covers up to my chin. Sure enough, not more than thirty seconds later, another muffled sob reaches my ears and I know Mom is holding her pillow over her face to keep me from hearing. Soon the sobs turn to soft, heartbreaking whimpers. It takes everything in me to stay in bed and not go to her. A few minutes later, all is quiet. She's fallen back to sleep. Relieved, I let out a weary breath, roll over, and fall dead asleep.

## Chapter 9

# LOGAN

My alarm goes off an hour later. I reach out to shut it off before it wakes anyone. I lay on my back for a moment. The room is damp and chilly and I don't want to crawl out from under the warm covers. But then, remembering why I set the clock, I toss the covers back and slide out of bed.

I dress quietly but quickly. I grab my backpack and knee-high rubber boots from where I hid them at the back of my closet. I shoulder the pack, full of clean clothes to change into after fishing, and carry my boots into the hallway. I pad in sock feet past Mom's and Gram's closed bedroom doors.

I stop at the top of the stairway, facing the long hallway. I tilt my head and strain to listen. Only silence. I slip down the stairs to the kitchen and move toward the fridge. A dark figure standing at the counter suddenly turns and I jump about a foot in the air.

"Who's that?"

I recognize Maxine's voice and feel a surge of relief. Not Mom or Gram. I set my backpack and boots down on the floor around the side of the stove.

"Maxine, what are you doing?" I whisper.

"Nuffin," she mumbles.

I walk over to the stove and turn on the exhaust fan light, which casts a dim light. She stands facing the counter, her body turned away from me. She swings her head sideways, giving me a furtive glance, and turns her face away again.

I study her more closely. Maxine has a double chin and hypertensive red cheeks. But not tonight. Tonight her moon face looks bloated and her cheeks are a bloodless white under the glow of the fan light.

She sees me staring at her and scowls. "Take a gander, why don't you?"

"Are you eating something, Maxine?"

She shakes her head angrily at me. "No."

I scan the countertops for evidence. I step over to the corner of the room and lift the lid on the garbage bin, looking inside for empty cookie bags or chocolate bar wrappers.

"What are you rooting around in the garbage for?" she hisses at me. "Stop that. You're getting as bad as your grandmother."

I lift an empty bag of frozen corn and peer at the garbage under it.

"Is there something wrong with your hearing? I told you to stop that," she says, looking insulted. "I think your mother needs to get your ears checked."

I let the lid drop back on the bin and turn to face her again.

She turns and stands with her back pressed tightly against the counter. Just behind her, I spot a white napkin on the counter with dark crumbs on it.

"What's that?" I ask. "Are those cake crumbs?"

Maxine edges her body sideways to try to hide the napkin.

I dart over to the counter and peer behind her. On the napkin is a tiny piece of chocolate cake and a lot of crumbs. "Oh no, don't tell me. Are you eating cake?"

"No, why would you even ask me that?"

I study the crumbs closer. "Maxine, you are eating Audrey's birthday cake."

Maxine is the crankiest human being I've ever met. She takes offense easily and is often angry. When she's angry, she glares at you and speaks in the snarkiest tone I've ever heard. She shoots me an acid look. "I am not eating cake! Tragically, mister man, I can't eat sweets. In case you haven't heard, I have the diabetes."

*No danger of that, Maxine, since you tell me and everyone else in the house about a hundred times a day.*

A floorboard creaks overhead, and Maxine and I both freeze, listening for a footfall on the stairway. But there are no further sounds.

I turn back to her, lowering my voice a notch. "How much cake did you eat, Maxine?"

She lifts her chins indignantly. "What cake? I don't know what you're going on about."

I step over to the fridge and look inside. My jaw drops. There's only an eighth of the cake left. After supper, I saw Gram putting it away with at least half a cake on the plate. I shut the fridge door.

"Maxine, there's hardly any of Audrey's birthday cake left."

"Well, don't look at me."

"Who else would I look at?"

"Haven't a clue. I need to sit down now." She shuffles unsteadily across the floor to the table. Maxine's feet and ankles are so swollen that she always wears open-toed pink slippers with thick rubber soles. Because she doesn't lift her feet, they drag noisily across the oak floor. The sound is like sandpaper against a piece of rough wood.

"Pick up your feet," I whisper.

She pauses, glares at me. "I am," she barks, and then shuffles on again.

When she finally reaches the table, she places her hands on the back of the chair to catch her breath. She slides the chair out, carelessly scraping the legs across the floor. She falls heavily into it, and the chair lets out a harsh creak.

I go still and tilt my ear toward the stairs, listening hard. It's quiet upstairs.

Maxine's colour is still off, and a bead of perspiration leaks out of her hairline and rolls down the side of her face. The veins on her swollen feet are dark and knobby under her white skin. With the amount of cake she's just eaten, there's a good chance her blood sugar levels are dangerously high. I know I should go wake Gram, but how will I explain what I'm doing up and dressed? How will I explain the backpack and fishing boots? I chew my bottom lip, thinking. Finally, I decide to put the backpack and boots back in my closet and wake Gram. I'll just tell her I'm dressed because I couldn't sleep and was going to go down to the cove for a while. Gram knows I often go there just to be alone. It's not the best excuse, but it's all I can think of right now.

"I'm going to wake Gram."

"No, don't! I'm fine. And stop gaping at me like a sea bass, will you? It's getting on my nerves something awful."

"If you're fine, why is your face all sweaty?"

She swipes the perspiration away with the heel of her hand. "It's too hot in here. Your grandmother puts too much wood in the furnace at night. You know that. For goodness' sake, you run around the house in nothing but your boxers half the time."

"They're not boxers. They're pyjama shorts. And I wore them once, okay?" I retort, remembering the night in May when I walked into the kitchen wearing pyjama shorts and Shaye whistled and swatted me on my bottom before Gram could stop her. I never made the mistake of wearing those shorts again outside my bedroom.

"Whatever. The fact is that it's too hot in here and that's why I'm sweating. It doesn't mean my sugar is high."

"I don't know, Maxine," I say doubtfully.

"I'm fine, I said. But arguing with you about it half the night isn't helping my sugar levels any, I'll tell you that."

"Are you sure you're okay? Your eyes look funny. Glassy or something."

"I've had the diabetes for twelve years now, so I think I know whether I'm fine or not. Okay, maybe I ate a sliver of cake. But I had to. My sugar hit bottom, and when that happens I have to eat something sweet fast. It's a medical emergency. There's no fooling around or I could die. You know, I'm really starting to wonder if there's something wrong with you." She raises an index finger and taps her forehead twice. "Upstairs, if you get my drift."

I ignore that. "You can't keep sneaking sweets all the time. You're going to kill yourself one of these days."

She glowers at me. "I *do not* sneak sweets all the time. Anyway, what do you know? Last time I checked, you weren't a doctor."

The wind gusts and hammers a side wall of the house. The window rattles. Seconds later, a loud creak resounds right above the kitchen—Gram's bedroom.

Maxine and I go completely still. I look out the open doorway of the kitchen to the dark hall, heart pounding. I hold my breath and hear a rumbling snore from Grace's room, but nothing else.

I turn back to Maxine. Her lips tremble slightly and a lone tear squeezes out from her eye and slips down her cheek.

I soften my voice. "I'm sorry, Maxine. You're right, I'm not a doctor. What do I know about diabetes?"

"Nothing much, I'd say," she snorts. "So feel free to leave anytime."

She squeezes her eyes shut, and they nearly disappear into the flesh of her face. Another tear slips down her cheek.

"Why don't I stay here until you feel better?" I say gently.

She pulls a tissue from the pocket of her bathrobe, dabs at her eyes, and then waves the tissue at me. "You don't have to do that."

"I don't mind, Maxine. I want to make sure you're all better."

She eyes me suspiciously, dubiously. "Up to you."

We fall silent. The refrigerator kicks on with a rumble, then runs noisily. Over it, I hear Maxine's wheezy breathing. Behind me, the clock on the wall ticks off the seconds. My heart drops. It's nearly three. I'm going to be late. Crocker will leave without me.

"I know I shouldn't eat sweets, Logan," she says forlornly, "but it's when you can't have something that you want it most." She rocks back and forth in her chair. The chair creaks frighteningly. "It's difficult watching everyone else in the house eat whatever they want all the time, especially sweets. I always had the worst sweet tooth. And you may not believe this, but I'm a brittle diabetic. A lot of times, even when I stick religiously to my diet, my sugar goes way up. That discourages me and then I figure I might as well eat something tasty if it's going to go up anyway."

I reach out and pat her hand. "I understand, Maxine."

"I know people in town make fun of us, with me eating enough for a fishing crew. And that poor old loon, Audrey, putting on that phony English accent and believing she's Helen Mirren. And pretending she's smoking… nuttiest thing you ever saw isn't it? And Shaye pinching men's butts whenever we go out to town, oh my." She shakes her head. "Try not to let it bother you, Logan."

I nod.

She gives me a small, sad smile. "You understand. You've suffered a terrible grief yourself, losing your dad so young."

The familiar pain squeezes my heart. It's like a festering wound that won't heal.

She takes my hand in hers and gives it a gentle squeeze. "It'll get better, Logan. You have your mom and Gram and they love you. I know it may not seem like it to you right now, but Shipwreck Cove is a good place to live, a good place to heal."

I nod again, but I don't really believe that at all.

"Please don't tell Winnie I ate some of Audrey's cake," Maxine pleads.

I'm pretty sure Gram will notice the missing cake without me telling her, but I keep that to myself. "I won't. Just promise me you'll try harder to stick to your diet. I wouldn't want something to happen to you."

"You mean that?"

"Yes, I do."

She smiles and her face lights up. "All right then. I promise I'll try to stick to my diet just for you. *And* I promise I won't tell your grandmother you're sneaking out of the house to go lobster fishing, either," she says, with a small, conspiratorial smile.

I try to hide the shock from my face. I say evasively, "Lobster fishing?"

She leans ahead and points to my boots, partially visible by the side of the stove. "My Arnold, God rest his soul, fished lobster for forty years. I think I know fishing boots when I see them, mister."

Face hot, I can only nod.

"Did you pack a lunch?" she asks.

"Not yet. I meant to."
"You might want to do that now."
I nod again and head for the fridge.

## Chapter 10

# LOGAN

I run through dense fog down the Lighthouse Road. It's quiet out. Only one car went by so far, and I hid behind a tree at the side of the road when it passed. The fog is so thick it coats everything—the trees, my clothes, my hair, and my face with salty droplets. I doubt the driver would have seen me even if I had stayed on the shoulder, but I don't want to risk it.

I hear the wind in the pines that grow along both sides of the road, the sound of the water crashing into the rocky shore, my boots squeaking with each footfall. The streetlights cast a weak yellow glow that barely reaches the two lanes and I have to watch my step so I don't stumble in one of the many potholes in the asphalt.

Close to town, the Lighthouse Road gives way to Harbour Street. There, I slow to a jog as I make my way along the sidewalk. The streets and sidewalks are deserted. The shops are closed, their parking lots empty. Most of the homes I pass are silent, their windows dark. There's only one house with the blue flickering light of a TV in a living room window. As I continue through town, soft yellow lights come on behind the curtained windows of two homes.

*Fellow fishermen*, I think and pick up my pace, heart thumping eagerly.

The pre-dawn fog covering the wharf is even heavier, the air colder, laden with the mixed odour of fish and diesel oil. As I jog down the wharf road, I glance at the moored lobster fishing boats. There are no empty slips. The moored boats are all dark and silent. I glance at my watch. It's 3:35. I sprint now, hoping Crocker will still be here, and if he is, my being late won't put him in a bad mood. As I run, I scan the far right side of the wharf. I hear the low rumble of the *Sea Predator*'s big diesel engine start up and the boat's running lights come on. In the haze, I can just make out a yellow light in the wheelhouse.

*Yes!* I run full-tilt now, arms pumping. When I reach the *Sea Predator*, I skid to a stop and face the boat. Exhilaration prods me forward; guilt freezes me to the spot. If Mom finds out about this, she'll be devastated. And I hate that my deceitfulness will add to the sorrow that daily clouds her face. Then my dad's face flashes to mind. He was a brave military officer, a man of integrity. If he could see me right now, he'd be terribly disappointed.

The thrill evaporates. What was I thinking? I can't do this. I'll go back home and go to school today. I'll be the man my dad would have wanted and expected of me. I turn around and start back down the wharf toward town.

Suddenly, the harsh blast of a horn sounds behind me. My heart jumps into my throat. I whip around and see Crocker's head poke out of a window of the wheelhouse.

He's laughing hard. "Scared the crap out of you, didn't I?"

I smile a bit sheepishly. "A little."

"Where were you going anyway? The boat's this way. Hurry up, untie the dock lines, and get your butt on here."

I look at him with uncertainty, then turn sideways and take in the homes and businesses along Harbour Street. With their curled, weather-beaten, grey cedar shingles, they look forlorn and shabby. A hot rush envelopes me. It's not like Mom gave a rip about me or how I felt about moving here. She went right ahead and made a decision I felt unalterably ruined my life. Facing the town, my heart grows colder, harder. I have little, if any, compassion for my mom.

Crocker yells at me, jerking me from my thoughts. "Come on, move it! Unmoor us and jump aboard. Let's get this show on the road!"

"Coming," I yell back.

I run over and lift the bow and stern mooring lines from the bollards. I toss the lines onto the deck of the boat and jump in after them. The boat rocks on the water and I hold out my arms for balance. Once steady, I look in through the open door of the wheelhouse. Crocker stands at the helm, his back to me. He eases the throttle forward and guides the boat away from the wharf. Once safely clear, he increases the throttle and we steam across the harbour.

As we approach Seal Island at the harbour entrance, the red and white unmanned lighthouse looming above us, my heart pounds so strongly with excitement that I'm afraid it might explode. As we speed past, parallel to the island, I catch a sudden movement in the corner of my left eye. I peer hard at the rocky sea barrier that circles the island and make out the black silhouettes of seals moving over the large boulders. Unexpectedly, a group of big ones rise up and let out shrill barks over the roar of the engine. Startled, I jump and then laugh aloud at myself. At one point, I fear we'll crash on the rocks—we're so close to them that my breath catches in my throat. Seemingly at the last second, Crocker steers the boat away and we roar safely past and out of the harbour.

To my left, I see Gram's house. My heart falters, all happiness draining away. Gram's house faces the sea, quiet. The windows all dark. I think of Mom and Gram asleep in their beds, trusting that I'm asleep in mine. Once again, guilt fills me. For a moment, I regret my decision. I wish I was in the house with them. But soon Gram's house fades from sight, and so too fades the remorse. My heartbeat escalates again, my stomach's all butterflies. Nothing could get me off this boat right now.

Soon we're in the bay, steaming to the lobster grounds. The wind intensifies out here and the seas grow increasingly volatile. The swells rise to five feet, hammering the hull, sending a wall of water up over the bow. Crocker increases the throttle some more and the sea gulls, lured by the blood and guts scent of the bait barrels, speed after us to keep up.

The wind gusts rock the boat and I grip the railing. The cold sea wind batters my exposed flesh, salt spray soaking me. I have to wipe it from my eyes. The darkness this far out at sea takes me by surprise. The sky and the water are so black I can just barely tell where one ends and the other begins. Our running lights shimmer on the water and the moon, at times obscured by clouds, casts down a thin ray of silver light on the surface of the water. But that's it.

Out in the open water, the waves grow more powerful, exploding against the hull with a deep pounding that shakes the boat. I feel the vibration under my feet and right up into my tailbone. It feels like the water's bashing us to pieces. It frightens me at first, but before long the fear is replaced by an extraordinary rush of excitement.

The engine fades. "Logan, get your butt in here. I need to go over some things with you," Crocker calls from the wheelhouse.

I turn from the rail. "Be right there."

My words are drowned out by the growl of the diesel as Crocker throttles the engine. Grinning, I go inside.

# Chapter 11

## LOGAN

"Thermos of coffee's on the shelf over there. Grab a mug if you like," Crocker says, nodding his chin to a wooden shelf on the wall of the wheelhouse. "Get me one too, will you? Black for me. Just fill it halfway."

The shelf is deep and has high sides, which I realize are to keep things from sliding off in rough seas. It holds white ceramic mugs, sugar, spoons, and a stainless steel thermos. The insides of the mugs are stained brown, as are the spoons. Next to the shelf is a cabinet that Crocker told me holds survival suits, life jackets, rubber and wool gloves, and the like.

I pour two mugs, leaving one half-full, adding lots of sugar to mine. I hand Crocker his mug and stand next to him at the helm. He nods, then, to my surprise, pulls a stainless steel flask from his jacket pocket, unscrews the lid, and pours some of the liquid into his mug. The smell of alcohol fills the air. He holds the flask out so I can read the initials etched on the front.

"Nice, hey? Wife gave me this for my birthday a few years ago."

He slips the flask back into his pocket and gives me a wink before taking a long drink. He sets the mug down on the dash.

"Fairly good swell this morning," he says, pointing out the windshield to the water as the *Sea Predator* climbs a high wave and glides down it again.

I nod as I take a sip of the hot, strong coffee.

He sticks a cigarette between his lips. "Don't mind if I smoke do you?" Without waiting for my reply, he takes a disposable red lighter from the same jacket pocket and lights up. He takes a drag, exhaling right in my face.

There's a small bathroom—or head, as Crocker calls it—at the back corner of the wheelhouse and the door's open a crack. Rank urine fumes drift out of there and mix with the cigarette, coffee, and alcohol already filling the wheelhouse. Stomach churning, I take a small sip of the bitter coffee.

The bow dips low into each wave, sending a spray of water into the air, splashing onto the windshield. At times, the bow sinks so low that I'm afraid we'll go down and not come back up again. Other times, the boat pitches and rolls so sharply from one side to the other that I'm afraid we're going to capsize. A mixture of fear and exhilaration fills me. My pulse thuds hard in my chest.

I survey the wheelhouse. Three foul-weather suits hang from wooden pegs on the back wall next to the head. The overalls hang from the pegs by their suspenders. The jackets are draped over the pants. The name *Sea Predator* is printed in bold black letters on the back of each jacket. Crocker's wearing a yellow foul-weather suit, the jacket open and flopping at his sides, the suspenders of his overalls hanging down by the sides of his legs. His Toronto Maple Leafs ball cap is on his head.

Crocker follows my eyes to the suits. "Go ahead, put one on. One of them's a small."

I grab the small overalls and pull them on over my jeans. Then I slide my arms into the jacket. The sleeves hang over my hands and I have to roll them up. I rejoin Crocker and pick up my coffee mug from where I had set it down in the deep shelf.

Crocker cuts his eyes sideways at me. "You should eat more, lift weights or something. Get some muscle on you. The first time I saw you, I figured you were about twelve years old."

My cheeks burn a little, but I nod in agreement. I'd give my right arm to hit six feet and beef up to one-eighty like my dad. I hate that I take after Mom's side of the family with their short, slender statures. I'll be fourteen soon and I'm only five-three and weigh one hundred twenty measly pounds. With my clothes on.

Crocker shoots me an annoyed look. "Don't be late again. I don't like waiting. I won't wait for you next time."

"I won't be late."

"Why were you late anyway?"

"Someone was in the kitchen, so I couldn't leave right away."

Crocker frowns. "Your mom?"

"No, it was one of the residents."

Crocker grins. "In the kitchen, ha. Bet it was old Maxine, wasn't it?"

I nod.

He slaps his thigh and howls with laughter. "I knew it."

I wish I hadn't told him that now.

Crocker shakes his head. "I don't know how you can live in that house with those crazies. Do you know what people in town call your gram's place?"

"What?"

"McPhee's Mental Asylum. And they're right. If you ask me, that place is a nothing but a glorified loony bin.

*Nobody asked you,* I think, feeling suddenly protective of Gram, Mom, and the four residents.

"It's not that bad," I say, surprising even myself.

Crocker snorts a laugh. "Sure it isn't." He puts his cigarette to his lips, leans into my face, and says in a fake English accent, "Do you have a light, love? I mean, if the crazy old thing wants a cigarette, why doesn't she just smoke a real one?"

The disgust in his tone bothers me, a lot. I don't respond.

As if he can sense my anger, Crocker cuts his eyes sideways. I keep my face neutral, and after a few seconds he shifts his eyes forward again.

We fall silent, staring out the windshield. The rumble of the engine and the steady pounding of the water against the hull are loud in the wheelhouse.

"All right, let's get down to business," Crocker says a few minutes later, his face serious. "You ready to learn how to fish lobster?"

And with that, my irritation dissolves. "Sure."

"Then listen up," he says, eyes flicking from the windshield to me as he steers toward the fishing ground. "You don't need a college degree to fish lobster. But you do need to be alert or you can get hurt. Worst case scenario, you get killed. You need to listen to me all the time. That's number one. You got it?"

I nod eagerly.

"Good. I'll tell you about the boat first. She's eleven metres in length," Crocker says with pride, gesturing with his arm from the bow to the stern of the vessel. "Someday, I hope to get a bigger boat, one with a steel hull, but for now, this will do. I'm not working for someone else. I'm master of my own ship. That's the most important thing, you understand?"

I nod, swallow another mouthful of coffee. It's still half-full and so strong I don't know how I'll finish it.

Crocker points above the dash. "This is the VHF radio. It's usually set to channel 16, which is the local VHF channel. That's so us fishermen can talk to each other and anyone on shore. Also, if one of us runs into trouble, we can send a distress call over the local channel and the other fishermen will hear it and come and help." He smirks at that. "Not that I'd help anyone even if their boat was sinking and I was closest to them. Too bad, let them all drown. I've never wanted to be a hero, never wanted to save anyone, especially not one of those idiots from town. If I ever hear one of them calling for help, I'll turn this boat around and head the other way as fast as I can."

I'm shocked. I think of my dad and Jared's father, both Christians who volunteered with the airbase's search and rescue unit. Believing strongly in Jesus' teaching that a man should lay down his life for another, they risked their lives to search for their fellow downed and missing pilots. Often they were called in to help search for lost civilians, hunters, hikers, or young children who wandered out of their backyards into the forest around Cold Lake.

Crocker doesn't notice my shocked expression. "That's the Loran, the radar, GPS unit, the compass, and the fathometer. Cost me a fortune, but she's all decked out with state-of-the-art technology. You don't need to worry about any of that yet, but if you keep working for me, in time I'll teach you what each one does. Got it all so far?"

I nod again, concentrate hard, repeating the name of each piece of equipment in my mind so I'll remember them all.

"Right now, all you need to worry about is baiting the traps and laying down the lines. Later on, you'll be pulling them up, removing the lobster, and baiting them again before dropping them into the sea. I'll show you how to do that when we get out there." He lifts his brows. "So far so good?"

"Yes."

"Good, I don't like repeating myself. Oh, and another thing you should know: each fisherman has his own designated fishing area. We mark our trap lines and territory with coloured buoys. Mine are bright orange and have my registration number on them. Every fisherman in town knows those are mine. The red ones are Guy Hendrickson's, purple ones are Kurt Thomason's, green ones are Gage Kelly's. Can't stand any of those morons," he says with disgust. "When we reach the fishing grounds, I'll show you all that too, got it?"

"Yes," I say, nodding.

A half-hour later, we reach the fishing grounds. Crocker slows the boat and we idle for a moment in the roiling swells. Then he cuts the engine. In the sudden hush, the sound of the waves hitting the hull comes as a surprise.

Crocker drains his coffee, slams the cup down on the shelf, and turns to me. "Okay, time to make some money," he says, smiling and draping an arm around my shoulder.

I smile back, forcing down the last of my coffee. I walk out onto the deck with him into the cool morning air. My heart lifts. My dad used to do that all the time, put his arm around me. I didn't realize how much I missed that.

The sky is just beginning to lighten in the east. The early-morning sea air is chilly and thick with salt, but feels good on my face. It's revitalizing and snaps me wide awake. The boat's stern lifts up and then slides down on the troughs and crests of the waves.

I brace my feet and lift my arms out from my sides a little, struggling to keep my balance in front of Crocker who's watching me with an expression of amusement. Once I'm steady, I look around the boat. My eyes stop on the hydraulic winch.

Crocker removes his arm, following my eyes to the winch. "Don't worry. I'll be the one operating the winch. You'll use the gaffing pole to snag the buoy line, haul it up, and then slip it around the pulley. Once you do that, I'll winch the pot up. When the pot gets high enough, you grab it and pull it over the side of the boat. Got it?"

"Okay."

"Good, then listen up. There are two things you *do* need to worry about. Number one is paying attention every second you're working so you don't get hurt. Look at this." Crocker holds up his left hand and wiggles his pinkie finger in the air. Or rather, what's left of it, which is only a stub. "I lost the top of this finger when I was about your age," he says with a rueful smile. "I was working on my dad's boat, the *Amelia-Anne*. Filet knife slipped on me."

"I'll be careful."

Crocker nods curtly. "You do that." He notices my eyes on the scar on his cheek and reaches up and runs a finger along it. "I got this one fishing with my dad too. He sewed it up himself out at sea. Used a regular sewing needle and thread. Hurt like the dickens, I can tell you that."

"Oh," is all I say.

He drops his hand again and waves it around the boat. "The second thing you need to worry about is falling overboard. That happened to my last helper. The seas were big and rough, the wind turned wicked, and he was washed right over the side. He was gone before I could turn the boat around and throw a line to him. But even in calm seas, bad things can happen. A rogue wave can come out of nowhere. Or you can get a foot caught in one of the ropes on the trap line as it's going over the side. That happened to another one of my helpers a while back."

I stare at him, wide-eyed. That's what he meant when he told me yesterday on the wharf that he'd lost his helper. It hits me that Crocker's helper is the guy who Mom and Gram were talking about, the young guy named Jeremy who fell off a fishing boat at sea during the first week of the season.

He doesn't notice my expression. "It was a calm day. The seas were so smooth, they looked like a mirror. Suddenly, I couldn't believe it. Cullum was standing on deck one minute working the line and gone the next. All I heard was his scream. At first I thought it was a sea gull. By the time I got the anchor up and the boat turned around, he'd vanished. He got his foot caught in the trap line and the weight of the traps hauled him over the side and took him right to the bottom. They dragged the seabed for his body for a few days, but all they found was his Montreal Canadiens ball cap. That's what you get for being a Canadiens fan."

My mouth falls open.

"What? Don't tell me you're a Canadiens fan."

His callousness staggers me. His smile creeps me out. I don't reply to that—*can't* reply.

Doesn't matter, he doesn't notice. "Neither guy was paying attention when he should have been. Couple of slackers, those two. Both of them went around in a daze half the time. Coast Guard never did find their bodies. So you stay alert unless you want to end up like them, not a brain between them."

I don't say a thing, but the realization that I don't like Crocker too much takes hold. I tell myself it's only for a day or two, and then I'm done.

He continues, sweeping his hand out toward the water. "I've got a hard-shell life raft aboard and a couple of survival suits. But still, you don't want to be in the water in November. Trust me. As we get closer to winter, you won't last longer than twenty minutes without a survival suit. And even if you do have time to get a suit on, if it's not zipped up properly, or doesn't fit right, got a leak, anything like that, it won't keep you alive for more than a few hours in below-zero water before hypothermia gets you. Do you understand?"

"Yes."

"Make sure you do." He suddenly reaches out and cuffs me on the side of the head.

I grimace and touch my head. "Hey!"

Crocker hawks up sputum, turns his head, and spits it over the side of the boat. Then he looks back at me, twisting his mouth up into a sneer. "Hey what?"

Shaken by how fast he can change, all I can manage is a quiet, "Nothing." But it hardly matters. Crocker has his back to me and is already walking towards the winch.

My eyes boring into his back, I take in a deep breath and let it out again to dispel my anger. I pull my gloves on tighter and walk over to the railing.

# Chapter 12

## LOGAN

"Now, watch closely, because this is the last pot I'm doing. After this, you're on your own," Crocker says.

"I'm watching." But my eyes are looking out to the horizon where the sun is rising, filling the eastern sky with streaks of crimson and lavender. It's the most beautiful sunrise I've ever seen.

Crocker snaps his fingers in my face. "Hey! Wake up!"

I pull my eyes away and give him my full attention. "I'm listening."

We've just pulled up a line of pots set by Crocker and his helper, the one who fell overboard. Using a gaffing pole, I snag the buoy line and lift it up. Next, I grab the line and run it over the wheel of the winch. Once that's done, Crocker winches up the trap. Once it gets high enough, I lean over, grab it, and pull it into the boat. Now Crocker is showing me how to remove the lobsters inside, and replace the bait in the traps.

Crocker is wearing thick, dark orange rubber gloves. He reaches inside the trap and hauls out a lobster. Using a tool called a bander, he slips a red rubber band around its big claws.

He holds the lobster out to me. "See that? It's got both pincher and crusher claws. You want to rubber band them right away. Don't fool around or you'll lose a finger. These rubber gloves won't protect you from something like that. So haul them out like that, rubber band them fast. Got it?" He gently drops the lobster into one of the three holding tubs at the aft of the boat. "Measure them if they look undersized. If they are, throw them back in. I don't want a fine for bringing in undersized lobsters. Got it?"

"Yes," I say, but feel a bit anxious. It seems like Crocker expects me to do everything exactly like him, but he's been doing this since he was a kid working on his dad's boat. This is my first day.

"Go ahead, give 'er a go then."

Crocker watches as I remove the lobster from the next trap. After a slight fumble with the banding tool, I slip a band around its claws and toss it into the ice-filled tub.

"Drop it in more gently. Don't want them damaged." He reaches out and ruffles my hair. "But good job, Logan. You pick things up fast. I think you just might have the makings of a fine fisherman."

I don't say anything but feel my chest swell with pride. All my doubts about working for Crocker instantly fade.

Crocker points to one of the plastic bait tubs next to the wheelhouse wall. "There's fresh dead herring and mackerel in there." He reaches in and pulls out a long silvery fish. "Watch me." Using his filet knife, he slices the fish down its belly and into chunks. He places the chunks of bait into the trap. "*Never* forget to put fresh bait in the pot before we reset it."

I grab a herring, and using a fileting knife I do exactly like him. The bait smells nasty and at first I hold my breath, but by the tenth trap I don't even notice the stink anymore.

Watching me closely, Crocker nods in approval.

We work the strings of traps steadily. At ten o'clock, we take a break. We stand at the rail and down the coffee and blueberry muffins Crocker's wife packed for him. Crocker can talk. He talks almost nonstop as we eat. The whole time I can see mashed blueberry muffin in his mouth. As soon as we're done, we go right back to work.

By eleven, the sun has burned off the fog. The wind dies away; the seas grow mild and slap lightly against the hull. The sun's rays glare off the flat water directly into my eyes. Wincing, I make a mental note to bring a ball cap and sunglasses tomorrow.

Lines of perspiration pour down my face and my clothes are damp. I constantly wipe the sweat off my brow with the back of my gloved hand. The air, even out at sea, is so much heavier than out west. I thought the ocean breeze would be as cool and fresh as Alberta's mountain breezes, but rather the wind carries such humidity that I feel like I have a damp towel over my head. Crocker removes his foul-weather suit and the flannel shirt he's wearing over a T-shirt. Dark circles of sweat are visible on his T-shirt at the chest, back, and under the armpits.

I quickly peel off my foul-weather suit and hoodie and work in a T-shirt and jeans too. Within minutes, my T-shirt is damp with sweat and sticks to my skin. The sweat runs down my nose, dripping to the deck like rain.

Crocker smiles wryly. "It's not usually this warm in November. Enjoy it while you can, because it's going to change. You'll be freezing your butt off before too long."

At noon, we stop to eat lunch in the wheelhouse. I brought two chicken sandwiches, a handful of chocolate chip cookies, and a banana. I'm starving and shovel it in, washing it all down with some water Crocker brought in a big plastic jug. The food doesn't even put a dent in my hunger. I make another mental note, this time to bring water and a bigger lunch along with my sunglasses and ball cap tomorrow.

As we eat, Crocker stops talking finally and silence reigns. The waves grow more placid. Even the gulls are quiet. Normally shrill and cross, diving down to the deck, battling each other for every scrap of food, they glide peacefully down to the water. The only sounds are the soft flutter of their wings, the gentle lap of the sea against the boat. I find the tranquillity of being out on the water, so far from land, incredibly calming. It brings a sense of peace to my heart like nothing else has been able to do since my dad died.

After lunch, we step out of the wheelhouse into the warm fall afternoon. We continue laying down Crocker's trap lines, baiting the last fifty I stacked on the boat myself yesterday before we drop them over the side and into the sea. Every now and then, I hear the low rumble of other fishing boats in the vicinity, but not once do I ever see one.

Around mid-afternoon, grey clouds move in. The wind picks up and carries a chill. The temperature drops and I shiver as I work. My nose runs and my eyes tear almost nonstop. My hair feels damp, dirty, and matted with salt. I stop only long enough to put my sweatshirt and foul-weather jacket back on, but I still feel slightly chilled. I'll wear two shirts tomorrow.

Close to four o'clock, I drop the last pot over the side. I watch the line of pots follow it, twisting down below the surface of the ocean to the seabed. Only the bright orange buoy bobbing on the water marks the location of Crocker's trap line.

"Well, that's it for the day," Crocker says, wiping the sheen of sweat from his brow.

I exhale a tired but happy breath. I'm sweaty, bone-tired, and my clothes stink of fish bait. Despite all that, I feel great. I'm crazy about lobster fishing. I enjoy the gruelling work. I love standing on the deck and looking all around and seeing nothing but the bluish-green sea stretching endlessly before me. The serenity out here soothes my inner turmoil. I decide fishing is in my blood, passed down from Mom's side, a long line of fishermen.

Crocker slaps my shoulder. "You did great for your first day, Logan. You pick stuff up quick. You're fast and steady on your feet, you work hard, and you're not a yapper. You've got the makings of a fine fisherman."

I beam, nodding back at him. "Thanks, Crocker."

He stands on the deck facing the sun, which is in the west now and beginning to descend. "Well, we'd better get back. Unusually warm or not, the days are getting shorter."

He walks over to the port rail and takes a long look out to the water. He cocks an ear, then walks over to the aft side and does the same thing.

"It looks like we're the last to go back in. That's good." He goes into the wheelhouse and starts the engine, but instead of heading back toward the harbour, he steers the boat to the northeast. We skim along the water for a time before he eases back on the throttle.

Across a hundred yards of water, a cherry-red buoy bobs lightly on the water. Crocker steers the *Sea Predator* toward it, then stops and kills the engine. The boat drifts a little on the light swells. In the silence, I hear the buoy tapping lightly against the boat's hull.

Puzzled, I watch as Crocker steps out of the wheelhouse again, eyes gleaming. He draws a six-inch filleting knife from a leather sheaf on his belt and crosses the deck to the railing. He leans over the portside with a gaffer in one hand and knife in the other. He snags the buoy marker, pulls it over, and holds it against the hull with the gaffer. Grunting, his elbow moving in and out, he saws away at the rope that holds a string of traps that lay on the bottom of the seabed.

Shocked, I step over to him and look down at the water.

"Crocker."

"Mm?" he grunts.

"What are you doing?"

He pauses, then starts sawing again, cutting the line in two. "Don't worry about it."

"Crocker, wait—"

"Leave it alone," he says with an edge in his voice.

"But what are you doing?"

He straightens up, turns and faces me. "What?"

"Aren't the red buoy lines Guy… ah…"

"Hendrickson's."

"Yeah, right. Hendrickson."

"They are."

"You just cut his lines," I say, appalled.

He lifts his hand up, palms out. "So?"

"Why did you do that?"

He shakes his head, dismissing me. He starts for the wheelhouse, brushing past me. "Leave it alone, boy. It doesn't concern you."

"That's a dirty thing to do, Crocker."

He stops, then turns slowly around, cocking his head. "What did you say?"

My heart lurches a little, but I don't back down. "I said I think it's a dirty thing to do."

Crocker's face darkens. He stares at me for a long moment, then strides directly toward me. He leans into my face and speaks in a voice that's frighteningly quiet. "Is that right? Well, I don't give a rip what you think."

I give him a disgusted look and shake my head.

Crocker cocks his fist and feigns a punch at my face. I duck, stumble back a little, and hit the railing. I look up at him, stunned. Crocker throws his head back and laughs raucously.

My face burns with humiliation. He was just having fun with me. He wasn't really going to hit me, and here I'd gone and flinched like a coward. I straighten up, but don't hide the revulsion from my face. He's got a mean streak.

His eyes narrow. "Hey, get that look off your face."

"What look?"

He leans in even closer. He's unshaven. His eyes are bloodshot. I smell alcohol mixed with coffee on his breath. I suspect he has emptied his flask into the four mugs of coffee he's drunk today.

"The look that says because you and your family are Christians. Because your dad was some hotshot fighter pilot, you think you're better than me."

I jerk my head back. "What? I don't think that."

"Yeah, you do. Lose the superior attitude, I mean it."

"Crocker, no, that's just stupid. I don't think I'm better than you."

"Oh, so now I'm stupid too."

I shake my head, wondering if it's the alcohol talking. "I didn't mean that. I just don't understand why you would cut another fisherman's lines. It's his territory, and he's just trying to make a living."

"Is that right? One day out at sea and now you're the big expert on fishing," he sneers.

I exhale heavily and look away. It seems impossible to reason with the guy.

"Hey, Logan, look at me."

I turn my head and meet his gaze. There's a tic in the corner of his mouth.

"If you don't like it, then you're done working for me."

His words are like a boot to the gut. "No, Crocker."

"Yeah, you heard me. This is my boat. I do things my way, not yours. If you've got a problem with it, you're done. As soon as we get back in, get off my boat."

I don't speak, but can't seem to take my eyes off his. His stare is cold, malicious, unblinking. He's dead serious. My heart pounds so forcefully that the blood roars in my ears. I love fishing. I can't believe this is happening.

Black clouds slide across the descending sun. The chill wind gusts off the water. Seagulls circle overhead, shrieking as they dive to snatch something from the water. I start to shiver, hating that Crocker sees this.

"Well?" he says, darkly. "You got a problem with it or not?"

"I guess not."

"You guess not?"

"No, I don't have a problem with it."

"Good, now listen up." He lifts his ball cap and gives his scalp a hard scratch. "This is between me and that idiot Hendrickson. I got my reasons, and you don't need to know the why, where, or how. All you need to worry about is doing your job and keeping your mouth shut, you understand?"

"Yes," I agree, hiding my reluctance.

He slaps his cap back on and moves toward the wheelhouse. "All right, then. Get back to work. Clean up the deck."

I start picking up loose gear and stow it for the trip back in.

Crocker stops at the wheelhouse door. "Logan?"

I glance over my shoulder at him. He's standing with his back to me. "What?"

"We're good, aren't we?"

After a couple of seconds, I say, "Yeah, we're good."

He turns slightly, grins and winks. "That's my boy."

A verse I memorized in Sunday school comes to mind: *"He who winks with his eyes is plotting perversity; he who purses his lips is bent on evil"* (Proverbs 16:30). I feel a jab in my heart, but I ignore it, pushing the verse out of my mind.

As I watch him go into the wheelhouse, I think there's something seriously wrong with this guy. His mood swings are scary. I've never seen anyone go from compliments to insults, from calm to rage so fast. I'm not sure how I'm going to deal with it, but I know I'm going to have to be very careful around him.

# Chapter 13

## LOGAN

Back in the harbour, we dock at the weigh station and sell our catch. Crocker gives me two hundred dollars. For one day's work! That's more money than I've ever made in my life. I calculate how much I'll make if I work for Crocker for the entire lobster fishing season and feel my heart lift with hope. Soon I'll have enough for a plane ticket to Alberta. Soon I'll be seeing Keltie and Jared again.

After that, we ease away from the weigh station, slip around to the far side of the wharf, and tie up at Crocker's slip. I stand on the stern quarter of the deck and look around. The sun is gone and the streetlights on the wharf are on, but anything outside their yellow orbs is cast in shadow. All the other lobster boats are already tied up in their slips. I watched the sun rise out of the sea, and now the sun sinks back into it. Crocker told me he likes to be the first out and the last in so he can catch as much lobster as possible, but I think it's also so he can cut other fishermen's lines without being seen.

It's been a long day, and other than the line-cutting incident, I loved every minute of it. I can't wait to go out again tomorrow. With renewed energy, I stow all the gear and clean out the bait tub. I wash the deck down with a citrus-scented dish soap Crocker keeps on board.

That done, I change from my stained clothing into the clean jeans, sweater, and running shoes I brought with me in my backpack. I stow my dirty clothing and rubber boots in a cupboard for tomorrow. When there's enough dirty clothing, I'll take it home and wash it secretly in the laundry room. This way when I leave the house each morning, I'll be dressed in school clothes and carrying my backpack of textbooks. If Mom or Gram catches me up and dressed in the middle of the night, I'll just say I'm thinking of my dad and can't sleep, that I need to go out for a walk. Neither Mom nor Gram would like the idea of me walking around town in the dead of night, but they'd probably let it go if they think I'm overwhelmed with grief.

I go out on deck and look around the wharf for Crocker. I don't see him, but his truck is still parked next to his berth. Then I spot him. The weigh station office faces the wharf and he's standing in front of the lit window with two other fishermen, talking heatedly. Crocker shouts something I can't make out, then raises his arm and shakes his fist in one of the fishermen's faces. He spins around and stomps in my direction.

I leap over the boat railing to the wharf road and walk to the weigh station. I slide a toonie into the pop machine against the front wall and hit a button. I take a long drink and then join Crocker. Just as I do so, he whirls around and stomps down the road toward his boat.

I hustle over to him. "What's going on?" I ask.

Crocker shakes his head. "Nothing, don't worry about it."

I look over my shoulder to the weigh station and see the two men eyeing us, their expressions furious. One is in his early twenties, the other in his late forties. With their similar sharp, angular facial features and red hair, they must be father and son.

"Is one of those men Guy Hendrickson?"

Crocker's eyes narrow at me. "You're a clever one, you are. No, neither of them are Hendrickson. That's Rupert Bowness and his son Bradley."

The men's angry voices carry across the wharf. I make out the word *jumpstart*.

"They seem mad at you. What's jumpstart mean, anyway?"

Crocker gives a quick, dismissive shake of his head. "They think I set my traps before the season started. You know, getting a jumpstart. Pay no attention to them. They're a couple of morons. This town's full of them."

"Oh."

He loops an arm around my shoulders. "Hey, come on. How about a burger before you head home? It's my treat."

I'm starving and know I'll have no trouble eating supper even after a burger or two. "Sure."

"That's my boy. We got to put some meat on those bones."

Grinning, I let Crocker guide me over to his pickup truck.

# Chapter 14

## LOGAN

"How are you today, Lucky?" Crocker asks the middle-aged waitress as she steps over to our booth.

"Fat and sassy," she says, yanking her order pad from the pocket of her white blouse.

"Yeah, how's that working for you?"

"Just fine, Crocker." Then she looks at me, smiling and lifting a curious eyebrow. "So who do we have here?"

"I'm Logan Blanchard," I say, suddenly shy.

Her voice goes soft. "Blanchard? Winnie's girl, Olivia, married an Air Force pilot by the name of Blanchard. So, are you Winnie McPhee's grandson?"

"Yes." Privately I'm astonished how everybody knows everybody in this town.

Her smile broadens. She holds out her hand. "Well, I'm pleased to meet you, Logan Blanchard. There's no other woman in this town with a heart as big as your grandmother's. I just love her to death."

I shake her hand and smile back.

"One of the women your grandmother cares for is my aunt, my mom's sister," the woman says. "Audrey Piper."

"Audrey, sure." I try not to think of Audrey pretending to smoke an imaginary cigarette.

"Yes, your grandmother takes such good care of her. Poor Audrey has never been the same since she lost Floyd and young Ian. The shock nearly killed her. I think that's why she sort of, um… reinvented herself?"

I nod and relax a little knowing that the waitress is so comfortable with the whole thing.

"I don't know what Audrey would do without your grandmother. But I do know one thing. There's a special chair in heaven just for Winnie. When she gets there, she can just sit down and rest those feet while the angels wait on her for a change."

"A special chair in heaven," Crocker snorts. "What a bunch of codswallop."

I frown at Crocker, puzzled.

He flicks his eyes to me. "A bunch of crap," he explains, chuckling.

The woman waves her hand in the air, dismissing Crocker's words. "Oh, don't you listen to him, Logan."

I nod, then notice the gold nametag over her blouse. It reads *Lucky Ducky*. I quickly bite down on my bottom lip to smother a laugh.

She sees me and grins. "Oh, go ahead, let it out. You look like you're about to burst a blood vessel. My mom loved the name Lucky, but she never in her wildest dreams imagined I'd end up marrying a man with the last name of Ducky. So it's Lucky Ducky for me for the past sixteen years."

I laugh softly. She laughs along with me.

"But I've been lucky in marriage," she adds. "I can tell you that."

"Lucky in marriage," Crocker echoes with a derisive snort. "Give me a break."

Lucky only smiles. "Yes, Crocker, I'm very happily married."

"Don't kid yourself, Lucky. Nobody's happily married."

She sets a paper placemat and silverware down in front of me. "Speak for yourself, Crocker. I am and have been happily married from day one."

Crocker raises his eyes from the menu. His lips curve into a sly, thin smile. "Oh, I know you're only speaking for yourself, Lucky. Believe me, I know."

I stare at Crocker, not sure if he's joking or not.

Lucky pauses, holding a second placemat and set of silverware in the air. She frowns at him. "What are you saying, Crocker?"

His smile turns cruel, his eyes harden. "I've seen that big dork you married walking around town. His face is always hanging like he's the most miserable man in the world. Maybe you should ask him if he's as happily married as you. From the look of him, I'd put my money on no. I bet he wants out so bad it's all he ever thinks about."

"Stop it, Crocker," says Lucky.

"Stop it, Crocker," he mimics in a soprano voice.

She goes quiet, pressing her lips together.

"In fact, from the way he's always hanging around pretty little Patsy Boyle over in Merrill's, I'd say he's probably already gone and you don't even know it. He's a typical Christian fraud, just like all the rest of them in this town."

Lucky's face goes white. "You just shut up, Crocker. You hear me?"

The diner goes deathly silent. I flick my eyes around the room. Customers are either watching us or pretending to be absorbed in their food or menus. No one's talking or moving.

"Yeah, thought so," Crocker says loud enough for everyone in the room to hear. "Like they say, Lucky, the truth hurts,"

He shifts his eyes to me and winks. I find the look of pleasure in his eyes revolting.

Lucky shakes her head slowly orth. "Oh you hateful little man, I should—"

"Careful, Lucky," he cuts her off, his voice a whisper.

Murder in her eyes, Lucky slaps the placemat on the table in front of him. Then she bangs the silverware down. "You go ahead and try something. You don't scare me one bit, Crocker."

He jerks back against the seat. "Hey, watch it with that knife."

She stares at him without speaking. She doesn't back off, either.

Crocker's nostrils flare. Finally, he flicks his eyes to me, laughing at Lucky under his breath. "Lucky needs to take our order and get back to work. She's always been too chatty. So, what'd you want, anyway?"

"Nothing, I'm not hungry," I say flatly, reaching for my jacket on the seat next to me. "I'm heading home."

"What? No way. Stay put. Burger and fries for the kid. Same for me."

"I said I'm not hungry," I repeat, then look at Lucky, shaking my head in apology. "I don't want anything, Lucky, thank you."

She nods at me with a softening expression. When her eyes shift back to Crocker, though, she gives him a scathing look. "He doesn't want anything. And I won't serve you, so you might as well leave too."

Crocker leans back against the booth and sets his arm along the top, tapping the edge with his fingers. "No, I'm starving actually. And the boy's hungrier than he realizes, so two orders of burgers and fries."

I start to get up. "I'm leaving."

He reaches out and grabs my arm, yanking me back down. "Sit down!"

I hit the seat with a thump.

He glares at me, then turns his eyes to Lucky. "Get a move on, Lucky. We're in a hurry here."

Lucky gives him a knowing smile, one that says she sees through his bluster to the true coward inside. "Fine, but I won't be your server."

She nods at me and turns away.

"Suit yourself, you stupid cow," Crocker calls after her.

Lucky stops dead in her tracks. Then she whips around, picks up Crocker's glass of water, and throws it in his face. She slams the glass back down on the table and spins on her heel. I watch Lucky walk over to another table, admiring her. I'm shocked by Crocker's meanness, but her bravery in the face of it fuels me with courage.

"That witch," Crocker grumbles, wiping the water from his face with a paper napkin, his right arm still draped casually over the back of the booth. Then he looks at me. "What?"

I release a sharp breath in revulsion. "That was rude."

"So?" He barks a laugh. "What's it to you?"

"It's embarrassing sitting here while you talk to her like that. Lucky seems like a nice woman. You're disgusting, Crocker."

"Is that right?" he says softly.

I stiffen in my seat. When he's angry, his voice is usually loud, harsh. I find his soft, quiet voice unnerving. But I manage a nod.

In the diner, silverware rattles, ice clinks in glasses, and the low drone of the other diners' conversations continues. A twitch begins at the corner of his left eye. He drops his arm from the top of the booth, leaning across the table so close I can smell his breath, which stinks like a brewery. His breath whistles in and out of his nose.

"Don't ever talk to me like that again."

I don't reply. My heart thuds in my chest, but I keep my face cool, keeping my hands still on the tabletop.

After a minute, his lips twist into a peculiar smile. He drops his eyes, then looks around the diner and calls out to a fellow fisherman at a table across from us. The fisherman, a burly old man, glances at Crocker with a look of disgust. It hits me that there are a lot of fishermen in the diner, sitting in booths or on stools at the counter talking and laughing together. But none of them have spoken to or acknowledged Crocker in any way.

I move my eyes back to Crocker. He's playing with his cell phone now. He knows I'm looking, but won't meet my gaze.

I barely hold back a smile, thrilled that he'd backed down first. Still, it's not a nice feeling to realize that the man I work for, the man I'm friends with, is a cowardly bully disliked by the other fishermen in town. In fact, he's so disliked that when they enter or leave the diner and have to walk by our booth, which is nearest to the entrance, they steer away like he has the bubonic plague. When he stupidly calls out to them, they either ignore him or look right through him.

And that depresses me, because they're also ignoring me, looking right through me like I too have the plague.

## Chapter 15

# CADE

It's Wednesday, at 3:00 a.m., and I'm in my cruiser, parked in a secluded lane facing the Cutter River. My sister Bridget died here four years ago, and when I'm on patrol I often stop her for a moment, watching the river, my heart heavy with her memory.

I let out a long, slow breath, start up the engine, and pull back onto the highway, heading back to town.

Minutes later, I'm patrolling the quiet street.

Drowsy, I lower the window, inhale deeply, and hope the salty sea air will wake me up. It feels damper and chillier than usual. Tendrils of fog slither like snakes over the streets, making them hard to see even with the cruiser's fog lamps. I proceed slowly. Anyone could be lurking in the shadows of buildings and houses, and I'd never see them.

Right where the Lighthouse Road becomes Harbour Street, I spot a small figure walking along the sidewalk. As my headlights find him, he flinches. I accelerate before he can duck into an alley, the revving of my engine filling the silent night. As I approach, I turn on my car's spotlight.

He pauses and turns, wincing against the brilliant light. He starts walking faster with his shoulders slouched, head down, and eyes fixed on the sidewalk. It's a boy, maybe twelve or thirteen. Way too young to be out walking the streets in the middle of the night.

I hit the gas, keeping the light fixed on him. He shoves his hands in his coat pockets and ducks his head down into his collar. I flick the emergency lights on and pull over alongside him. When he still doesn't stop, I give a quick whoop-whoop of the siren.

He jumps at the sound, then stops. He turns to look at me, lifting one hand to shield his eyes. I kill the spotlight, but leave the revolving red and white emergency lights on. They eerily illuminate the buildings on both sides of the street. I open the door and climb out, clicking on my flashlight and pointing the beam at him.

He starts walking again.

"Hello, there," I call out. "Hold on."

He keeps going.

"Stop, now," I say sharply, moving around the front of the cruiser, ready to sprint in case he takes off.

He stops and turns, then shoves his hands back into his coat pockets, trying to appear nonchalant. Like it's normal for him to be out in the dead of night, like he didn't just almost decide to bolt on me.

I step up on the sidewalk and stand in front of him. I run the beam of my flashlight over his face, studying him quietly for a few seconds.

He squints and turns his head to hide his face, but it hardly matters. I've seen Olivia's boy over the years at church and around town when his family came to visit.

"Let's move over here under the streetlight," I say, moving over a few steps. He joins me. I click off the flashlight. "Bit late to be out, isn't it, Logan?"

He gives a cool shrug, but not before I catch the startled look when I say his name.

"What's going on?" I ask. "Is there some reason you're out at this time of night?"

His eyes meet mine. He stays silent, his expression guarded.

A dog barks from the backyard of a house a few streets up. I hear a door open, a man calling it in, a door banging shut.

"Why are you out this late?"

He doesn't respond. That doesn't faze me one bit. I've been a cop for almost twenty years.

I glance at my watch and prod him a little more. "You must have a good reason to be walking through town at three in the morning."

"I couldn't sleep."

"You couldn't sleep?"

He shrugs.

I understand that it's going to be like pulling teeth with this kid. I drop my head, rub my temple with my fingertips, then look at him again. "Does your mom know you're out this late?"

Looking pained, he shifts his eyes and stares at something behind me. I know the only thing behind me is the post office with its unlit windows. I watch him, waiting him out.

"No," he says finally.

I nod. We are quiet for a spell.

"I'm Constable Cade Stone," I say, holding out a gloved hand.

He hesitates, stares warily at my hand, but in the end he shakes it.

"I'm sorry about your dad, Logan."

His face closes down completely. Though his grief is raw, intense, he keeps it private. He's not about to talk about it with me, a cop and a complete stranger.

"Do you mind if I have a look inside your backpack?" I ask.

"I guess not," he says, though reluctantly, and hands it to me.

I check the outer pockets and find a twenty-dollar bill, a small jackknife, and four energy bars. Inside I find two bottles of spring water, three thick sandwiches, a package of peanut butter cookies, two apples, and two bananas. More interestingly, under all that is a pile of clothing: a sweatshirt, pair of wool socks, and stained ball cap.

"So, Logan, who are you going fishing with?"

He jerks his head up, clearly shocked.

"The clothing," I say, running the beam over the sweatshirt and socks. "You clearly packed extra clothing to stay warm and dry, but your sweatshirt and ball cap have old bait stains. You've packed a big lunch and you're headed in the direction of Fishermen's Wharf."

He nods, biting his lower lip.

"Who are you going out with?" I prod.

"Macklin Crocker."

I let out a soft breath, deeply troubled. Mack Crocker is a ruthless, cruel man. I've been dealing with him since he was ten years old and working on his growing reputation as the town bully. He preys on the young and vulnerable, the old and weak.

"I see." I keep my voice casual. "How long have you been fishing with him?"

He cuts me a sullen look. "Why?"

"Well, for one thing you're too young to go fishing." He only watches me. "So how long has it been?"

"A week and a half or so."

"Does your mom know?"

He looks at me with a shrug, seeming to understand that I'll stand out here all night waiting for an answer if I have to. I have years of experience at this.

He sighs. "She knows."

I keep the doubt from my face. "Really?"

"Yes."

I give him a long, speculative look. "I'm surprised your mom is okay with this. I know how much she despises fishing, not to mention missing school."

"It's just till Crocker finds another helper."

"I see." I stroke my chin while I think this through. I seriously doubt Olivia knows or would allow this, but I let the lie pass for now. "Fishing is extremely dangerous work, Logan. Do you know that more people die from fishing than any other job in the world?"

"Yeah, I know, but I'm careful."

I let out a light breath, wondering how many young, eager fishermen have said the same and then died at sea.

He decides we're done and takes a step to leave.

"Ah, Logan, hang on. One more thing. Do you have a cell phone on you?"

He looks at me with a wary expression. "Yeah, why?"

"Where do you keep it when you're out fishing?"

"In the wheelhouse," he replies. "I can't keep it on me unless I'm wearing rain gear, because my clothes get too wet."

"Listen, do me a favour. Put your cell phone in a waterproof bag and keep it on you at all times while you're fishing. You can pick one up at Morse's Fishing Supplies. Most fishermen in town do it in case they run into trouble and can't use their radio. Maybe Crocker already told you that."

Understanding fills his eyes. "No, he didn't."

*Of course he didn't,* I think but keep my irritation hidden.

I smile at him, kindly, with concern. "We've lost a couple of young fishermen this year. Maybe you've heard?"

The boy nods.

"One got his foot caught in a trap line and was pulled over the side. The other fell overboard, we think. The first boy didn't have a cell phone on him and the tide carried him away. The second boy had his cell phone on him but it was in his jeans pocket, so we figure the seawater ruined it. We never did find their bodies. Who knows? If they had both had cell phones stowed in a waterproof bag, they might both be alive today."

The boy nods with a serious expression on his face. "Sure, I'll do that. Is that all?"

I hesitate, uneasy. "And your mom knows you're fishing?" I ask again.

"Yes," he says irritably.

"All right, then. I guess that's all. Have a good day. Be safe out there."

He quickly steps around me and heads in the direction of the wharf.

I walk over to my cruiser and open the door, but stand there watching him. At the entrance to the wharf road, he stops under a streetlight. In the pool of yellow misted light, he glances back and sees me. He flinches, then turns and hustles away, clearly wanting to get out of my sight as fast as he can. I tap the roof of the cruiser with my fingers, deeply troubled. Bridget was only seventeen when she died, not much older than Logan. At his age, Logan likely thinks it'll never happen to him. But I know better.

I didn't tell Logan that the two young fishermen who died both worked for Crocker. I wonder now if I should have, if it would have made any difference. The latest young fisherman to die was young Jeremy Tanner, who only worked for Crocker for a few days before falling overboard. I blame Crocker for that. He takes risks no other fisherman in town would, and the results speak for themselves. Four years ago, he lost a helper after going out in a horrid winter storm. That day, Crocker's boat was the only one out at the fishing grounds.

And Crocker is a ruthless coward. I know he regularly drinks and drives both his truck and his boat. He cuts his fellow fishermen's lines, and steals traps and expensive equipment off these same fishermen's boats. But he's so sly, he rarely gets caught. He's been in many fistfights on the wharf over the years, each one worse than the last. In the last one, he punched Ned Worth in the face and broke Ned's jaw. I charged Crocker with assault, but because of his pleas to stay out of jail to support his wife and kids, the judge gave him probation. I believe he's capable of much cruelty, of far greater violence. It's only a matter of time before he kills someone.

When I found out Jeremy Tanner was working for Crocker, I drove right down to the wharf and found him on Crocker's boat. I tried to warn him, but he wouldn't listen. He was twenty-one, an adult. There wasn't anything I could do. But Logan Blanchard is a minor. I can and will put a stop to this.

I sigh heavily and climb behind the wheel, hating that my first conversation with Olivia is going to be about this.

## Chapter 16

# LOGAN

I walk briskly along the sidewalk, anxious to get away from the cop. The air is so sharply cold that the hair in my nose feels like wire, the crunch of my boots on the frosty ground sounds like I'm walking on seashells. I hear the sound of the cruiser door opening, but not shutting. I glance back over my shoulder. He's standing at the open door, watching me. I flinch a little, hating that I did and hoping he didn't see it. I walk faster but feel his eyes boring into my back.

It strikes me that he has a way of asking questions he already knows the answer to. He isn't the kind of cop I expected. He seemed to really get how deeply I miss my dad. In fact, his calm, kind manner reminds me of my father.

Still, it's disarming in a cop. I need to be careful around him. He might be a nice guy, but he's a cop. Though his eyes, with their penetrating stare, didn't betray it, I'm sure he knew I was lying about Mom being okay with me fishing. I'm certain he's going to talk to her about it.

I wonder if I should turn around and go home right now, but the very thought kills me. I want to go fishing so badly. I love lobster fishing. And Crocker isn't looking for another helper anymore, he's that happy with me. I decide to risk it, and jog the rest of the way down the wharf.

Twenty minutes later, Crocker opens up the engine and we head out. I cross to the portside railing and face the sea. The only illumination is a narrow band of silver moonlight across the water. I flex my arm and my biceps pops out. I feel it with my left hand and grin. It's definitely getting bigger. My knuckles are red and my palms covered in thick calluses. I carry a tube of chap stick in my pocket to dab my wind-chapped lips throughout the day, but that's only because of Mom. Otherwise, I'd just do like Crocker and chew the dead skin off my lips. Chapped lips or not, I'm beginning to look like a fisherman. Crocker says all I need is a tattoo of his boat, the *Sea Predator*, like he has on his left forearm.

I've always wanted a tattoo. In fact, I begged Mom to let me get one since I turned thirteen. I even promised her I'd get one of a cross, so it would look Christian, but so far she has refused. She hates tattoos, thinks they're ugly.

The thought of getting one of the *Sea Predator* is too great a temptation. It would be such a cool tattoo. Anyway, she didn't care about me or my feelings when she decided to move to this dumpy town, so I don't care about her feelings about tattoos.

I agree with Crocker and plan to get one soon.

Soon we're in open water, steaming for the fishing grounds. The sky is a cold hard blue, the moon shining down, the water glistening under its rays. The boat scuds across the water, easily riding the swells.

Suddenly the boat lifts and tilts on its starboard side. I plant my feet down and hold my arms out, quickly regaining my balance. I grin again, proud that I now have *deck legs*. I'm in a great mood, more relaxed than I've been since I began fishing for Crocker. Not only do I look like a fisherman, I am a natural fisherman.

The engine slows. Crocker bellows at me from the open wheelhouse door, telling me to get inside.

"You were late again," Crocker says when I enter the wheelhouse.

I pour myself a cup of coffee. "Sorry about that. Want a coffee?"

"I got one already. Listen, I told you I don't like you being late."

I step up to the dashboard, blowing on the hot coffee. "I couldn't help it. A town cop stopped me on Harbour Street."

Crocker turns to look at me, narrowing his eyes. "Who was it?"

"Constable Cade Stone."

Crocker snorts, amused by this. "Don't worry about it. That guy's an idiot."

"I don't know, Crocker. He seems sharp to me. He went through my backpack and knew right away I was going fishing. I had to tell him I was going out with you and that Mom is okay with it. But I don't think he believed me. I'm pretty sure he's going to tell her."

Crocker scowls, stewing over that for a while. He slams his hand palm down on the dash. "Oh, I hate that guy. Always sticking his nose where it doesn't belong. Well, look, I know Cade Stone. He'll forget all about it."

"I hope so, but he doesn't seem like the type to forget anything."

"He'd better, if he knows what's good for him."

I look at Crocker, wide-eyed. "What's that mean? You'd go after a cop?"

Crocker fixes a cold stare at me. "Yeah, I would. I'm not afraid of a cop. They're only human. Don't forget, even cops can disappear."

The rumble of the diesel engine, the thump of the waves and static from the radio fill the wheelhouse. I'm not sure if Crocker's threat is bravado to impress me or if he really means it, but either way I'm shocked. And as I look into his cold eyes, Proverbs 12:6 comes to mind: *"The words of the wicked lie in wait for blood..."*

We fall silent, sip our coffee, and look out to the water.

"I think it'll be better if I pick you up from now on," Crocker says after a time. "Don't want him catching you again."

"What? No, you can't pick me up at the house."

Crocker reaches out and cuffs me on the head. "Course not. You think I'm stupid or something? Meet me down the road, at Puffin Point Lookout. There are a couple of picnic shelters there. Wait in the one closest to the road. If you see headlights coming, stand out of sight until you know for sure it's me."

I frown at him, annoyed. It was a light cuff, but still, I feel like cuffing him right back. "I'll be there at three sharp to pick you up," he says. "Don't be late, you hear me?"

"I'll be there."

Before long, we reach the fishing grounds. Strangely, the early morning air is mild, almost balmy. The fog is thinning, almost as sheer as a veil and quickly dissipating. Crocker passes his own territory. He steers the boat southeast, pointing the bow toward neon pink buoy markers. After a few minutes, he eases off the throttle and pulls up alongside the markers. He stops the boat, leaves the engine idling.

He emerges from the wheelhouse, drawing his filleting knife from the leather sheaf on his belt. As he steps past me, he gives me a sly wink, putting an index finger over his lips. Like before, he leans over the portside and pulls up the buoy line.

"See this pink buoy? Well, it belongs to a moron by the name of Andy Coldwell. And not too far to our south is his buddy, Kurt Thomason's purple buoy markers. I can't stand either one of those guys."

"Crocker," I say. "Don't, come on."

"Come on, what? They're always mouthing off at me, accusing me of poaching their lobsters. This'll teach them to keep their big mouths shut."

I open my mouth to protest again, but he glances over his shoulder and gives me an icy look. I think better of it and shut my mouth again. I watch in despair as he leans over the railing and saws at the rope, laughing under his breath.

After he's cut the purple buoy markers as well, he points the fileting knife at me and grins. "Now, I want you to steer the boat. We're going to head to the southeast, where some yellow buoy markers are located."

My heart plummets. I remember him saying that the yellow buoys mark a fisherman named Chance Murray's trap lines. I met Chance the first time I walked along the wharf back in May. He was young, in his mid-twenties, and a real nice guy. He introduced himself and shook my hand, even offered me a tour of his lobster boat.

Then it registers that Crocker is telling me to drive the boat. He's never let me drive the boat before. Excitement surges through me, tempered by the fact that I'll be aiding him in a crime. I pause, glance into the wheelhouse and eye the steering wheel, but still don't move.

"Go on," he says, squeezing my shoulder.

"I don't know."

"You can do it," he says, mistaking my hesitation for doubt about piloting the boat. "Just go easy on the throttle. Don't give it too much gas. Go ahead now, quarter-speed ahead."

"But Crocker, I've never driven a boat before."

"So what? You're a bright kid. I've never seen anyone pick stuff up so fast. I know you can do it."

His comments, whether genuine or not, and the appeal of piloting the boat are too much for me. I head for the wheelhouse, telling myself I'll do it this one time but never again.

"Logan?"

I pause, glancing back over my shoulder.

He smiles with approval. "That's my boy. You make me proud."

A rush of pleasure mingled with pride passes through me. I smile back. My dad used to say that to me all the time. I didn't realize how much I missed hearing it.

I step up to the helm and put my hands on the steering wheel. My heart leaps in my chest. I reach out my right hand and throttle up just a little. I carefully, slowly, guide the *Sea Predator* across the water, eyes fixed on the yellow buoy marker ahead.

"That's it. Nice and slow, nice and slow," Crocker yells encouragingly from the deck. "Turn the helm a little to the starboard side."

I ease it just slightly to the right.

"Another couple feet, easy, easy, keep her coming."

I have never been so excited in all my life. I can hear my heartbeat in my ears. My guilty conscience is eased by the power of piloting the vessel. I look out the starboard window and position the boat alongside the buoy.

"Slow, slow, that's it, stop! Just let the engine idle now."

I put the engine in neutral and step over to the open wheelhouse door. I watch as he slides his filleting knife back out of his sheaf and leans over the starboard side railing. Instantly, my happiness vanishes, my heart sinks. I'm a liar and a criminal. It has to be the lowest of crimes for a fisherman to cut a fellow fisherman's lines.

"Let's go find some puke green buoy markers," Crocker says merrily as he stands again, wiping his wet hands on the thigh of his jeans.

My conscience won't allow it. "Crocker, no."

"Excuse me?"

"I don't want to cut any more lines, okay? I hate doing it."

He gives me an exasperated look and nods to the wheelhouse. "Did we already have this conversation once, or am I wrong?"

"Yeah, but come on."

"Listen to me, boy. I'm done talking about it. Now get your butt back in the wheelhouse and steer the boat where I tell you."

I turn and walk heavily back into the wheelhouse.

## Chapter 17

# LOGAN

We arrive back at the wharf a little past four o'clock. We unload our catch at the weigh station and then moor the boat in Crocker's slip. He heads back to the weigh station office angry, because he thinks he got ripped off. When I'm finished, I stow the hose, grab my backpack, and jump onto the wharf road.

As I walk past the weigh station, I hear heated voices inside. Crocker's standing under a street light with two other fishermen. Their heads are bent toward each other, their posture stiff and their voices loud. One man abruptly lifts his arm and points a finger in Crocker's face. With a sneer, Crocker slaps the man's hand away.

I wonder if I should go over and see what's going on, but it's getting late and Mom will be wondering where I am. I have to get home fast so she'll believe I'm returning from school.

I slide my backpack on my shoulder and walk in the middle of the road and out of the glow of the streetlights. I pretend not to see Crocker and the men. As I near them, one of the men says something about *cut lines*. My stomach does a little flip-flop. I drop my head and walk faster.

"Hey, Logan, come over here for a second, will you?" Crocker shouts out.

I halt. My heart rate triples. I nervously draw in a deep breath to slow it down as I join the three men.

Crocker claps a hand around my neck. I feel heat rising in my neck and face. These men must be two of the many fishermen whose lines Crocker cut in the past couple of days. I stand frozen, my eyes locked on Crocker's, unable to look at the two men.

Grinning, Crocker gives my neck a squeeze, his fingers like nails piercing my flesh. He looks me dead in the eye and gives me a sly wink. I know it all means: *Keep your mouth shut.*

Crocker changes the subject. Quickly, cunningly. "Boys, this here's my new helper, Logan Blanchard. He's Logan McPhee's grandson. And just like his granddad, he's one fine fisherman, let me tell you. He got his sea legs in no time at all. He's a good worker and he's quick and always alert."

Both men shift their eyes from Crocker and look at me in surprise and, it strikes me, obvious concern. In the silence, a sea gull dives down to the wharf with a scream and snatches an apple core before soaring away with two more gulls on his tail.

The tall, red-headed fisherman's face softens. He gives me a small smile and extends his hand. "Yes, yes, I remember seeing you at church with your grandmother and your parents. I'm Andy Coldwell. I'm sorry about your dad, Logan. I spoke with him a few times in church and he struck me as a good Christian man."

I swallow. "He was. Thank you."

Andy smiles kindly. "I knew your granddad too. I was just a kid then, but he was a fine Christian man too, and a great fisherman."

The second fisherman is short and in his late thirties. Despite being younger, he's bald, with a round face and stocky build. His face is flushed. He hesitates, still angry. After a few seconds, he nods brusquely and holds out his hand too. "Kurt Thomason. I'm too young to have known your granddad, but I heard enough about him to know he was well-respected, well-liked. I did meet your father two summers ago. He was a good man."

Again a verse fills my mind. This time I don't feel a jab of guilt, but rather love and pride as I recall Proverbs 10:7: *"The memory of the righteous will be a blessing..."*

I nod my thanks at their kind comments about my dad and granddad and shake hands with them. I can't look them in the eye, though. My face is hot with shame. I feel no pride in Crocker's praise. I find the scorn in his voice and the laughter in his eyes appalling.

"Now Logan, these two men have rudely accused me of cutting their trap lines yesterday," Crocker says, his eyes dancing with hilarity. "You were with me. Did you see me cut their lines?"

The two fishermen return their gazes to me.

My stomach twists. I feel sick as I draw in a small, quiet breath, forcing myself to meet and hold their gazes. I fight to keep my expression cool, my voice steady, and somehow manage to shake my head.

"No," I say, feeling a fresh swell of guilt.

Andy narrows his eyes. "Are you sure about that?"

I nod yes, unable to voice the word.

*I didn't see him cut their lines yesterday,* I say to myself in a pathetic attempt to appease my conscience. *It was today, so I'm not actually lying.*

It doesn't work.

*You're still lying,* my guilty conscience screams back.

Crocker curls the corners of his mouth up into a smug smirk. "You heard him. I didn't cut your lines."

"Yesterday, anyway," Andy says in a dry, cold tone.

"Yeah. We know it's you who's been cutting them since the season started," says Kurt, so angry there's a visible tic in the corner of his left eye. "And you've been poaching lobsters too."

Crocker's eyes flash at the insult, but he just gives a loud, malicious laugh. "Yeah, well, prove it, boys. Prove it."

"Don't worry, we will," says Andy, angrily pointing a long finger at him. "Count on it, Crocker. With lobster prices at rock bottom and the price of fuel going up all the time, the last thing we need is you cutting our lines and stealing our catch."

"You think I don't know that? Are you deaf, Andy? You just heard the boy tell you. It wasn't me who cut your lines." He places a hand over his heart. "I have never cut a fellow fisherman's lines or poached a lobster in my life."

I keep my expression neutral, though I'm so nervous my hands are shaking. I slide them in my pockets so the two fishermen won't notice.

The men release disbelieving snorts.

"You don't want to work for this guy, Logan," Andy says softly.

Kurt nods grimly. "Yeah, he's a bad fellow. Go home."

"Shut your traps before I shut them for you!" Crocker shouts, raising a clenched fist.

Andy and Kurt look at me, then exchange a glance. Andy tilts his head in the direction of a brick-red GMC pickup parked at the end of the wharf. "Let's go, Kurt."

They turn away, heading for the pickup. If I wasn't here, I think things might have escalated to a fistfight.

"Nice talking to you, boys," Crocker sneers at their backs. He drapes an arm around my shoulders. "Good job, Logan. I knew I could trust you to keep your mouth shut."

I hate this, supporting his dark lies.

He nods approvingly. "You're a good man."

He's remorseless. I just shake my head, too exhausted to say anything to him.

As I stand next to Crocker on the wharf, watching the two fishermen walk away, shame burns through me. I despise Crocker. I despise myself. The cash in my pocket burns like a piece of hot coal against my thigh.

"Hey, you hungry?" he asks. "Want to grab a burger at Lucky's?"

"No."

"What do you mean, no? What's wrong? Is it Lucky? No worries. I promise I'll be nice to her today," he says, cutting me a wink.

I watch Andy and Kurt climb into the truck. Both men sit in the cab, watching us through the windshield, their lips moving silently.

"I can't. Mom will be looking for me."

"Tell her you went to the library or went to a buddy's house or something. Come on and keep me company." He wraps an arm around me. "I'm starving and I hate eating alone. Once you smell the food, you'll change your mind quick."

For some reason I can't fathom, I decide to join him. As I walk with Crocker over to his pickup truck, I feel the men's eyes on me. I drop my eyes to the ground so I don't have to look at the two fishermen.

## Chapter 18

# LOGAN

When I walk in the house, I find Mom and Gram in the kitchen making supper. Maxine's sitting at the table working a crossword puzzle in the local newspaper. Grace sits on Maxine's right knitting a pair of men's size-ten wool socks for me, even though I told her oh so many times I wear an eight. Audrey's holding up a sheet of paper, reading aloud as if she's rehearsing lines for her next movie. Shaye sits with her chair back from the table, legs crossed at the knees, painting her toenails a garish red.

"Hi sweetie," Mom says, turning from the stove where she's stirring a big pot of spaghetti sauce. "How was school?"

"Good." I shift my backpack on my shoulder. The delicious aroma of Mom's spicy sausage and pepper sauce makes my stomach growl. She makes the best spaghetti sauce I've ever eaten.

She raises an eyebrow. "You were up and gone before anyone else was even out of bed. In fact, you've been up and gone before breakfast for over a week and a half. What's going on?"

I shrug carelessly, fake a yawn. "Oh yeah. Sorry, Mom, I should have told you. I'm working on a science project with a guy from class. I've been going over to his place to work on it before school."

Maxine raises her head from the newspaper and looks at me, but remains silent.

Mom smiles. She thinks I have a friend. "Oh, that's great, Logan. So who's the friend? What's the topic of your project?"

I step over to the kitchen table and grab an apple from the fruit bowl. I take a big bite, chewing slowly to buy time. "He's not a friend. He's just a guy I got picked to work on it with. The project's in the beginning stages, but the subject's tornadoes, the unbelievable destruction they can cause. I'll let you know more once we really get going."

"Wow, you're getting to be a keener," Mom says happily, believing that I'm finally adjusting to my new school, the new town.

Maxine gives a soft snort. I catch her eye to give her a warning look. She gives me a small evil grin, then drops her eyes and fills in a word in the puzzle.

Gram, loading dishes in the dishwasher, turns and glances at Maxine and me, then looks away. She has better hearing than me!

"Still, what's the boy's name?" Mom says. "I might know his family."

I return my gaze to Mom, thinking fast. "Shane Orson."

Shaye's head snaps up, the brush frozen in the air over her big toe. "Is he hot?"

"Shaye," warns Gram without turning around.

Mom frowns, tapping an index finger against her lips. "Mmm, Orson, Orson. Oh yes, I remember now. They moved to town a few months ago. His father is a marine biologist at the Oceanographic Institute and his mom's an investment broker."

"Bring him over sometime. I'd love to meet him," says Shaye, giving me a lewd wink. "I'll be his personal welcome wagon."

Gram whips around. "Shaye, stop it right now!"

Maxine throws the pencil down on the newspaper. "Olivia, have mercy here. You've been stirring that sauce forever. When is it going to be ready? I'm so hungry I could eat my own leg."

"It should only be another half-hour or so."

"I have homework, Mom. I need to get at it," I say, starting out of the room.

"All right, I'll call you when we're ready to eat," Mom says, her back to me as she moves away from the stove and reaches into a top cupboard for plates.

"Wait, Mom. I'll get that for you." I hurry over and pull out a stack of plates.

"Thanks, sweetie."

I set the plates down on the table, then head out of the room again, but pause at the doorway. "I'll probably be leaving early every morning for another week. Don't worry if I'm gone when you get up. I'll grab some breakfast before I leave."

She smiles. "All right."

"Why don't you call Shane and invite him over for supper?" says Shaye, running her tongue across her bottom lip.

"Shaye!" Gram's voice rises a little. "That's enough, I mean it. You're going to traumatize poor Logan."

"But we never have company," Shaye complains.

"Male company, you mean," snorts Maxine. "Could somebody please have a heart and put some food on this table before I pass out?"

"Oh, Logan," Gram says quietly. "We're all going to prayer meeting tonight. I wonder if you'd like to join us."

"No, I would not," I reply harshly, then regret it at once, because it's Gram.

"Are you sure?" she asks.

I release an exasperated sigh. "Gram, I don't believe in prayer anymore, so what would be the point in attending your church?"

Gram lifts a brow. "It's your church too, sweetheart. And there *is* power in prayer. Don't forget that."

I choke back a laugh. "Yeah, well, all the praying I did for Dad didn't help him a bit, did it? Where was God then, Gram? Tell me that."

Gram's eyes moisten, her expression heartbroken. "Logan, we can't always understand—"

"Forget it, Gram." I keep my bitterness out of my voice. Her sorrowful expression is killing me. "You guys can save the sermon for someone else. I gave up all the crap!"

"Tsk," I hear Grace murmur.

I bolt out of the kitchen and run up the stairs, taking them two at a time.

In my room, I stash three hundred dollars in the zipped side pocket of my tennis bag. I never use the bag, haven't even played tennis since Dad died, so I know Mom won't touch it. So far, I've made nearly a thousand dollars. Unbelievable money for a couple of weeks' work. And there's more to be made. Crocker got his wife to call the school and pretend she was my mom. She told them I had the flu and would be out for at least another week. And Mom believes I'm working on a science project. So I'm covered for now.

As I look at the five-by-seven photo of my dad I keep on my nightstand, my heart sinks. I look at the Bible Gram gave me when I turned ten. I could just cry. I pick up the Bible and carry it over to my dresser, shoving it in the back corner of the bottom drawer. Next, I lay my dad's picture facedown on the nightstand. Just for tonight, I tell myself.

From downstairs, I hear the murmur of the women's voices and can tell they're all gathered around the kitchen table, praying. For me, of course. Who else?

I release a groan and then cover my ears with my hands.

# Chapter 19

## LOGAN

On Friday, I trudge home after another long day at sea.

"Your grandmother's sick, so you and I are going for groceries," Mom informs me when I step into the kitchen. "And we're taking the girls with us."

"No way, I'm not going," I say, horrified.

Mom narrows her eyes at me. "Oh yes you are."

"Mom, I'm staying overnight at Shane's, remember? I told him I'd be there by 7:30."

She glances at the clock on the wall. "I remember, but if we leave right now we'll be back in plenty of time for me to drop you off at Shane's house. So go call the girls and help them get ready, now."

Annoyed, I roll my eyes as far back in my head as possible.

Mom frowns. "What was that for?"

"In case you haven't noticed, they're not girls, Mom. They're old women. They're practically ancient."

She laughs softly. "Oh, they are not. And that's just what we women call each other."

"And another thing," I add spitefully, because I'm exhausted and I don't want to go grocery shopping with Mom and the loons. "Do you know what people in town call this place?"

Mom picks up a spoon and turns to the stove, stirring a pot of soup. "I have no idea."

"I'll tell you then. They call it McPhee's Mental Asylum."

Mom only smiles at me, unfazed. "Do they? Well, don't let it bother you. We both know it's nothing of the sort. It's a special care home."

My mouth drops open. "Wake up, Mom. This is the local nuthouse, loony bin, whatever you want to call it. But it's not a special care home."

She narrows her eyes at me. "Do *not* let me hear you say that ever again. Your grandmother is a wonderful nurse and she works hard for her patients, and you know it. This is a well-run, highly respected special care home. Think of your grandmother. What if she heard you saying that?"

Gram steps into the kitchen. She's wearing blue flannel pyjamas and a white bathrobe. Her nose is red and she's dabbing at it with a tissue. "I've heard it before, Olivia. McPhee's Mental Asylum. McPhee's Loony Bin. I know that's what some people call it, but I wouldn't call them my friends, either." Gram gives me an admonishing look. "No one in this house needs to repeat it."

Mom nods in agreement. "Did you hear your grandmother? Don't ever say that again." She turns her eyes back to Gram. "Mom, go back to bed. I just made you a cup of tea and some soup and toast. I'll bring it up in a minute."

"You have enough to do tonight, Olivia," Gram says. "You don't need to wait on me."

Mom points upstairs. "Back to bed. I'll bring it up shortly."

Gram frowns, doesn't move. "I don't like feeling like a patient here."

"Too bad. Go to bed." Mom turns to me. "We'll be leaving soon. Call the girls and help them get ready."

"Call the loons, you mean," I say.

Gram gives me a disappointed look. I see the strain in her face, the dark shadows of fatigue around her eyes, and I feel bad.

Mom steps forward, angrily pointing the soup spoon at me. "Logan Blanchard, go get Grace and the others right now or you're going to be grounded until Christmas."

I let out a disdainful laugh, but don't push it any farther. As I walk out of the kitchen to collect the four women, I feel both Gram's and Mom's eyes burning into the back of my neck.

An hour later, I'm standing behind a display of baked goods in Cleary's Grocery, observing Maxine. She's hanging around the bulk candy bins, looking suspicious. I watch as she takes a furtive look around the store. When she sees the coast is clear, she steps up to one of the bins, over which the sign reads "Bulk Candy—3 for a Quarter." Below it is a cash box. Maxine slides a nickel into the slot, then opens her purse wide, reaches into the bin, and scoops two huge handfuls of candy into her purse. She snaps it shut and lumbers away.

I let out a breath and give chase. Maxine hears my footsteps and glances back. She pauses, lifts a clenched fist, and shakes it at me in warning before ambling off again.

"Maxine," I call out.

"Go away," she says over her shoulder.

I come up alongside her and grab her coat sleeve. "Hold it, Maxine."

"Go on with you," she says, huffing alarmingly.

She's shorter than me, so it's awkward, but I manage to hang on to her sleeve. But she keeps moving, a sour look on her face, dragging me with her.

"Maxine, stop, will you?"

"Leave me alone, stupid boy."

"Put that candy back."

"What candy?"

"The candy you just stole from the bulk section," I say, holding on to her arm tightly, but still she drags me along.

"What are you, a cop now?"

I hang on as my running shoes slide along the floor. "Maxine, stop!"

She takes two more steps, then leans over, badly winded. "What is your problem?" she gasps.

"You're not supposed to eat candy. Put it back."

She shoves her purse way up on her arm and holds it snugly against her chest in case I make a move for it. She gulps in two big breaths. "I need them for when my sugar's low. Doctor said."

"Sure, but he meant one or two candies. Not fifty."

She glares at me so fiercely her eyes are just two slits in her face. I can't see her pupils at all. "I didn't buy fifty, okay? I only bought a couple."

"Actually, you didn't buy any since you only put a nickel in the box."

"Oh, listen to him talk. You're a bold one, you are."

I frown. "What?"

She purses her lips and puffs out a laugh. "You're all worried about me being dishonest? Ha, pot calling the kettle black, don't you think? What was that story about leaving the house early to work on a science project with a friend? Oh, what was the boy's name now? Oh yes, Shane Orson. You forget I was in the kitchen the first night you were sneaking out to go fishing?"

My face burns.

"You can lie like nobody's business, I'll give you that." She juts out her chin. "Oh, look, here comes your mom. Say, I know, you go tell her where you really were today, and I'll go put the candy back."

I follow Maxine's eyes and see Mom heading our way pushing a full grocery cart. Audrey, Shaye, and Grace are with her. Audrey's wearing a faux fur coat and big black sunglasses; she's puffing on an imaginary cigarette. Every few seconds, she stops to slide her sunglasses onto the top of her head and pretends to sign an autograph for a fan. One shopper, a woman around Mom's age, pretends to accept the imaginary piece of autographed paper from Audrey, then turns and pushes her cart away, shaking her head.

Grace tightly clasps the cart rail with one hand as her eyes close and then pop open seconds later. I watch Shaye come up on a man in the aisle who just set his basket on the floor and is bent over reading the labels on cans of soup. As she passes him, I hear her say, "Ooh-la-la," and then she reaches out and pinches his behind.

The man whips around and stares at Shaye, open-mouthed. Shaye looks up and gives the man an approving nod. His face turns bright red. He lifts his basket and takes off at a near sprint.

Mom, who missed the whole thing, looks over and spots me. She smiles and gives a little wave.

"Well, what's it going to be?" asks Maxine.

I don't move. Can't move.

Maxine smiles triumphantly. "Ha, that's what I thought. Here's some advice, mister. Try minding your own business for a change." She turns away. "Now what do we have here," she says eagerly, heading for a booth where a woman in a white lab coat is handing out free samples of chocolate.

"Good day, ma'am, care to try a sample of artisan chocolate?" the woman asks her.

Maxine looks delighted. She steps over to the booth, but then sees Mom approaching. Maxine skids to a halt, gives the woman a horrified look. "Would I like a chocolate? What are you trying to do, kill me? I've got the diabetes. I have to be careful. I could die if I eat that stuff. I can't believe you even offered it to me."

The woman, hand over her mouth, watches Maxine shuffle off.

An elderly couple farther down the aisle stares with pity at Audrey as she puffs away on her imaginary cigarette while pretending to write her autograph on a box of cereal, then hands it to a bewildered woman whose basket she took it from. Eyeing Audrey warily, the woman accepts the box, tosses it back into her basket, then hurries away as fast as she can without looking like she's running.

A toddler standing up in a young mother's cart hurls his toy car and it smashes to pieces on the floor. This sets the toddler off bawling, his face turning a fierce red. The noise jolts Grace, who has nodded off while standing beside

Mom. She lets out a bloodcurdling scream that makes me and everyone else in the store jump.

A hot rush of embarrassment shoots up from my toes to the top of my head. Even my ears feel like they're on fire. Before anyone realizes that I came in with Mom and the loons, I spin around and flee the store.

## Chapter 20

# LOGAN

"And we're off like a herd of turtles," shouts Grace, clapping her hands together. "Like a rafter of wild turkeys," adds Maxine. "Gobble, gobble, gobble, turkey with mashed potatoes, stuffing, gravy and peas."

I lean my head against the cold glass of the passenger side window and close my eyes, wanting to just cry. Nine times out of ten, whenever Maxine speaks, food's involved.

It's 6:15 now. Mom sits in the driver's seat of the van. Behind us are the four loons. Mom is super-stressed because it's her first time caring for the women without Gram's help, and she's finding it harder than she thought it would be. And it's snowing. Just a light dusting, but enough to make the roads slick.

"Speaking of turkeys, Olivia," Maxine calls to Mom. "If I don't get home soon and eat supper, I'm going to slip into a diabetic coma here."

"I seriously doubt it," I mutter under my breath.

Maxine hears and leans over to tap me so hard on the shoulder that it feels like a punch. "I could too, Mister Smart-Aleck. Diabetes is life or death, and don't you forget that."

I lean sideways so she can't hit my shoulder again, gritting my teeth in irritation.

"Hey, this isn't the Indy 500, you know, Olivia," Grace calls out nervously.

"I'm only doing thirty, Grace," Mom says, keeping her eyes on the road as she steers the van down the highway.

Grace puffs out a disbelieving breath. "So you say. It feels faster than that to me."

"Oh shut up, will you, Grace," Maxine grumbles. "Olivia, don't you dare slow down. If I don't get something to eat *tout suit*, I'm going to drop dead here. I'm serious."

"And I'm going to miss my show," puts in Shaye, an avid *Grey's Anatomy* fan.

"Fascinating, Shaye, dear," says Audrey snootily from the back of the van. "More importantly, Olivia, I have an early-morning dress rehearsal. I really do need to get to bed speedily."

"Hang on, girls. We'll be home soon," says Mom wearily.

*Girls.* I roll my eyes but don't comment. I'm sick and tired of the whole bunch of them and just want to get home.

As we speed down the highway, the van's headlights briefly light up the huge snowflakes drifting down. I rest my brow against the cool glass and stare out the side window at the pine trees whipping past in a black and green blur.

Suddenly, only a couple of miles outside Shipwreck Cove, there's a thump and the van begins veering back and forth on the road.

"Oh no," says Mom. "Great."

I look over at her. "What is it?"

Mom grasps the steering wheel tightly and brings the van back under control. "I think we've got a flat."

I groan loudly. I can't believe it. We'll be even later getting home now, and that could blow my pretend sleepover at Shane's house. It's Friday night, so there's no school tomorrow. I need a good excuse to be up and gone out of the house in the morning.

Mom taps the brakes and eases the van onto the shoulder. She leaves the engine idling, lights on, and flicks on the four-way emergency lights.

"Sorry, girls, we've got a flat tire," she says to the women.

Grace jerks her head up and cries out, "Fire, fire! Oh no, help, help!"

Mom flips on the interior light and turns around in her seat. "It's all right, Grace. I said tire, not fire. We've got a flat, that's all."

Grace's eyes dart to the window. She peers out. "Still, there are bad men out there, robbers and murderers."

Maxine grins evilly at Grace. "That's right. They're hiding in the bushes right outside your window just waiting for the right moment to come into the bus and kill you."

Grace's eyes widen. She covers her mouth with her hands.

"Oh, for goodness' sake, Maxine," says Mom, shaking her head. "What a terrible thing to say. Grace, listen to me, there's nothing to be afraid of. There's no one out there."

Grace nods, but her breathing grows rapid, her eyes dart wildly from Mom to the window and the darkness outside.

"Oh, what's that? Is that footsteps I hear outside?" Maxine gasps, looking at Grace.

Mom looks back sharply. "Maxine! Stop it right now!"

Maxine looks out her own window, but I can see her shoulders shaking with silent laughter.

"I can't believe you'd even say something like that, Maxine. Where does that nastiness come from?" Mom puts a hand on Grace's thin shoulder, speaking in a soothing voice. "It's all right, Grace. Logan and I will change the tire and we'll be back on the road shortly. Try not to worry."

Grace nods nervously. "Okay, Olivia. But change it as fast as you can, please."

A minute later, Mom and I stand on the shoulder of the road in the falling snow, staring at the flat tire on the back passenger side of the van.

"Awesome," I mutter. I scoop up some snow, make a small ball, and hurl it across the road. It hits the trunk of a birch tree and disintegrates. As we retrieve the jack and spare tire from the back of the van, a woman's voice cries out from inside.

"That's Grace," Mom says. "Maxine must have said something to scare her. Oh that woman, honestly, what brings out that mean streak in her?"

"When she goes five minutes without eating, Mom," I say dryly.

Grace lets loose with another shriek.

Mom sighs. "I'd better go check on her. You start on the tire and I'll be right back."

As I squat down, I hear a car coming around the bend in the road. Its headlights find me as it approaches. The driver hits the low beams and pulls up behind me. I stand and turn to face the car, shielding my eyes from the glare of its headlights. The emergency lights on the car's roof glitter under the moonlight. It's a police cruiser.

The headlights go out and the emergency lights on the roof come on, lighting the road and the trees around us in shades of white and red. The engine idles quietly over the snowy asphalt. The door opens, and as the dome light comes on I recognize Constable Stone.

I blow out a heavy breath, unable to believe my bad luck. I forgot about him catching me going fishing with Crocker the other night. It hits me that he didn't tell Mom about it after all.

*Probably forgot about it like I did,* I think. But I'm sure he'll remember now.

He climbs out of the cruiser, shuts the door, and walks toward me.

"Well, hello again, Logan," he says with a smile.

I look up and nod. A shot of relief passes through me that Mom isn't out here to hear him greet me by name.

He squats down and shines his flashlight on the back tire. "Got a flat, I see."

I barely keep my eyes from rolling. Mom and Gram do it all the time too. Why do adults always state the obvious?

Mom steps out of the van and moves up alongside me, her eyes on the police cruiser. "It was Grace. She's upset, so I left the interior light on. Let's get this tire changed and get her home fast." She draws a quick, sharp breath. "Oh, Cade! I saw the cruiser pull up, but I wasn't expecting it to be you."

Cade stands and clicks off his flashlight. "Hello, Olivia," he says flatly.

Their eyes lock and hold. Mom opens her mouth slightly, then closes it again. He doesn't speak either.

I look at Mom, then to the cop, then back to Mom, mystified.

"It's been a long time, Cade," Mom finally says with a clear tremble.

"Yes, it has. Nearly twenty years."

Mom bites her bottom lip. Apparently she's lost her voice again.

I study Mom curiously. Despite the cold air, in the red and white light of the cruiser's emergency lights her face looks hot, flushed. Her hands shake. I look at the cop more closely. He's watching her intently with that same cool expression.

"It's good to see you, Cade," says Mom with a smile, but her voice still quavers.

"It's good to see you too, Olivia."

She looks at him, seeming suddenly sad.

I tense, on guard, not understanding or liking Mom's reaction to this guy. I slide her a look. "Mom?"

"Hmm?" she says absently, eyes still on Cade.

"Mom," I say louder.

She slowly shifts her gaze from Cade to me. "Yes?"

I lift my brows in a gesture that asks, *Are you all right?* She nods and gives me a smile, but she's still acting all weird. I frown, unconvinced.

Mom's eyes return to the cop. "Cade, this is my son, Logan."

My heart thrums in my ears. Our eyes meet. I hold my breath, waiting for him to tell her we've already met.

But after only a slight hesitation, he smiles at me and says, "Well, Logan, why don't I give you a hand getting that tire changed?"

I nod, letting out my breath.

He's quiet while we change the tire. Mom is strangely quiet too. The wind has kicked up and the sound of the creaking limbs and branches on both sides of the road is loud and constant. The air around us is charged with whatever is going on between them. The whole thing leaves me confused and uneasy. Still, when he does speak to me, he smiles a lot and is pleasant. At first I chalk it off to Mom being there, but by the time we're finished changing the tire, I realize he's genuinely nice.

As I'm putting the tire iron away, Mom and Cade stand by the van talking together quietly.

I hear a tapping on the van window and look up to see Grace's white face peering out at me. I motion that we're all done. Her eyes close, her chin drops, and her forehead hits the glass with a muted thump.

*Ouch,* I think.

Next, Maxine puts her hand over her heart, closes her eyes, and slumps forward, her chin on her chest, pretending to have fallen unconscious from lack of food. I ignore her and turn back to Mom and Cade.

Suddenly, Grace releases a hair-raising screech that makes all three of us jump a little.

Cade looks up. "What was that?"

"That's just Grace. She has narcolepsy," Mom explains. "Sometimes she falls asleep and hallucinates. It scares her awake."

"Oh, right, I knew that. Wow, she's got quite a scream. That must take some getting used to."

"No one in the house has yet," Mom says with a smile.

Cade smiles back at Mom, then seems to catch himself. His smile vanishes.

There's another tap on the van window. We all three look up and see Shaye looking out at us. She jiggles her finger at Cade, silently mouthing for him to come and join her.

Cade quickly returns his eyes to Mom, a slightly embarrassed smile on his face.

"Oh, Shaye, no," says Mom, shaking her head.

Shaye whistles at Cade so loudly it carries easily outside.

Mom looks at him. "I think I'd better get them home. It was nice to see you, Cade."

"You too," he says, but his voice has gone flat again.

"Thanks for the help with the tire," I say.

"You're welcome."

His eyes shift back to Mom and remain on her as she walks around the front of the van to the driver's side door.

## Chapter 21

# LOGAN

"So you know that guy?" I say to Mom later in the van.

"Cade?" she says vaguely.

"Yes, the cop."

"The cop." She looks and sounds like she's a million miles away.

I scowl. "Yes, Cade Stone, the cop! Who else would I be talking about?"

That snaps her awake. She gives me a pointed look. "Watch your tone, Logan."

"Yeah, watch your tone, mister!" says Maxine, getting hungrier and grumpier by the second.

I glance back and scowl at her before turning back to Mom. "Do you know him or not?" I ask, but lose the sarcasm.

"He's an old friend," she says. Her voice trembles, though she tries to hide it.

"An old friend, really?" I say. "Because it seemed like something more."

"No, there's nothing more. We're just friends. We go a long way back."

I snort. "Oh right, Mom. Must be why you're so upset."

"I'm not upset."

"Then what's with your hands?" I point to her hands, which are shaking despite being wrapped around the steering wheel.

Mom glances briefly at her hands and then smiles sadly. "It's a long story. I don't think you really want to hear it."

"Yes, I do. Tell me."

Her eyes back on the road, she lets out a soft breath. "Cade and I dated in high school. We were pretty serious for a while. Engaged, in fact."

I make a face, mortified. "You were going to marry him?"

"That's usually what engaged means."

I cringe imagining Mom and Cade Stone as a couple, picture them kissing. "So what happened?"

Mom glances briefly at me, but doesn't respond. She turns her eyes back to the road, but before she does I see that she's fighting back tears.

I frown, at a loss. "Mom, what is it?"

She shakes her head. "After graduation I went to Halifax for nursing school. I waited tables at Salty's on the waterfront on weekends. Your dad was taking a course at CFB Greenwood in Nova Scotia and he and some fellow pilots came in for lunch one Saturday. You know the rest. I think everyone in town was shocked when I broke off the engagement. Cade more than anyone else. I hurt him deeply, Logan. He was devastated."

I shrug. "Well, he doesn't seem devastated now."

"That's just Cade. He's reserved, not one to show his feelings. But I know him. He was hurt and angry back then. I'm sure he still is, although, as you say, you couldn't tell that by his expression. Being a cop all these years has likely helped him become even better at hiding his emotions."

I remember the flat, slightly cool tone he used with Mom, the tinge of hurt I caught briefly in his eyes when he looked at her. *Maybe not all his emotions, Mom.*

Grace wakes up, confused.

Mom looks into the rear-view mirror. "How are you doing, Grace?"

"Not good," she says, eyes jumping from the darkness outside the window to me. "Where are we? I want Brogan to sit with me."

*It's Logan,* I correct her silently.

Mom gives me a forced smile, her face pale and drawn in the glow coming off the dashboard lights. "Would you sit with her, please?"

"No," I say irritably. "Why can't Maxine or Shaye do it?"

"FYI, mister, I'm too weak from hunger to move," says Maxine, sulking.

"I'm kinda busy." Shaye fidgets with her clothing at the back of the van.

Mom's temper goes up. "I asked you to do it, so you get back there right now and sit with Grace. I mean it!"

I release a long breath, glancing over my shoulder at Grace. Sensing my eyes on her, she turns her head from the window and meets my gaze. She gives me a brave little smile, but her chin quivers. She's badly frightened. My heart softens.

"Try not to worry, Grace," I say gently. "We'll be back in Shipwreck Cove soon."

Grace frowns. "Shipwreck Cove?"

"Yes, Shipwreck Cove," Shaye tells her. "That's where you live."

"I do?"

"Yes, you do," says Shaye. "You live in McPhee's Special Care Home in Shipwreck Cove, Nova Scotia. I've told you a thousand times, woman."

Grace snorts a disbelieving laugh. "News to me."

Shaye gives up and continues fumbling under her coat.

A few seconds later, I smell toffee. I flick my eyes to Maxine. She's chewing away, eyes closed in ecstasy. I know she's eating a candy she pilfered from the grocery store.

She swallows and opens her eyes. "Doctor said," she whispers to me. She looks up at Mom. "Olivia, any chance we can stop at Mickey D's for a snack when we reach town?"

Mom glares over her shoulder. "Over my dead body, Maxine."

Maxine presses her lips together. "If you don't keep your eyes on the road that might just happen."

"Logan, please sit with Grace," Mom turns to me, pleading. "Falling asleep and waking up in the dark van can be scary. I can't sit with her, I have to drive. I need your help, please."

Mom's expression is stressed and her eyes are wet with tears. She's at the end of her rope. It's heartbreaking. I take a breath and release my seat belt. I touch her shoulder softly.

"Okay, Mom," I say as I make my way back to Grace's seat and sit down next to her.

Grace reaches out and grabs my left hand in hers, holding on for all she's worth. "Thank you, Brogan," she whispers. "You're a good boy."

I want to pull my hand free, but hers feels so fragile, so frail in mine. And I see that she's shaking. I give her hand a gentle squeeze. "It's all right, Grace. There's nothing to be afraid of. I'm here with you."

She edges over in the seat so that there's only a half-inch between us. She nods, gripping my hand even tighter.

Behind us, Audrey and Shaye begin whistling and whooping. "Grace loves Logan, Logan loves Grace."

My mouth drops open, my cheeks flaming bright red.

"That's enough, girls," Mom says sternly, coming to my rescue. They stop.

We speed down the highway, the drone of the engine the only sound for a time. Grace falls asleep with her head resting against my upper arm. Mercifully, this time she doesn't let out one of her awful screams.

Behind me, Audrey places another imaginary cigarette between her lips. She runs her thumb over the top of a pretend lighter and holds it under the cigarette. She takes a deep drag of the fake cigarette and exhales the imaginary smoke. When she sees me watching, she holds up the cigarette. "I am not smoking a cigarette, love."

My face brightens. There's some hope in this moving lunatic asylum after all. "That's right, Audrey," I whisper so as not to wake Grace. "Now you get it. That's not a real cigarette."

"Precisely, I am not smoking a cigarette. I am, however, smoking a cigarillo," she says, and blows imaginary smoke at me.

"Since when does a refined English actress smoke a cigarillo, Audrey? Think about it."

"Since this refined English actress is preparing for an upcoming starring role in a western that requires that I smoke cigarillos," she informs me, her voice holding an imperious tone.

I spend the rest of the drive fighting the urge to jump out of the van to my death. The only thing that stops me is the fear that I'd only be badly injured, maybe a quadriplegic, and end up one of Gram's patients.

## Chapter 22

# CADE

I watch the van pull away and proceed down the highway in the direction of town, white exhaust trailing out of its tailpipe. I sit behind the steering wheel, thinking about Olivia. I haven't seen her for almost two decades and I'm amazed by how little she's changed. I thought the same thing seeing the back of her head and neck from the last pew in church the other day, seeing her from my office window. Up close, it's even more apparent. She has some grey in her hair, lines around her eyes and mouth, but still she doesn't look her age at all.

I turn the rear-view mirror down and check my reflection. I flip it back up, groaning aloud. I look older than my forty-five years. I could easily pass for fifty.

Then a thought hits me hard, like a punch to the nose. I was so rattled to see Olivia that I completely forgot about her son fishing with Mack Crocker. I planned to talk to her about it since the night I caught him, but each day has been too busy. This morning there was a serious car accident. A drunk driver in an SUV drove through a stop sign at an intersection a few miles outside town and smashed into a minivan carrying a young married couple and their six-year-old son. All three were injured and taken to the hospital. The drunk driver walked away with just a minor laceration on his cheek. I was so busy at the accident scene, and then the hospital later, that I forgot all about her son.

I shake my head in disgust. *Some cop you are,* I tell myself. Olivia needs to know her son is fishing with Mack Crocker. If something happens out at sea and it ends badly, Olivia will never forgive me. I have to tell her.

I tap my fingers on the steering wheel and think about it some more. What if the boy isn't fishing anymore? He did say it was only until Crocker hires another helper. I think about the acute pain and anguish I saw in Olivia's eyes. She's already trying to cope with unspeakable grief. She doesn't need me adding to it.

I glance at the clock on the dash. Ten minutes after nine. I'm on shift until seven in the morning. I know Crocker is always the first to leave the wharf. He's almost always gone by three. If Logan's still working for Crocker, he'll be walking to the wharf in four or five hours. I decide to drive up and down Harbour Street at that time to watch for the boy. If I don't see him, I'll drive right down the wharf to see if he's on the *Sea Predator*. If I don't find him on the road, and if he isn't on the Crocker's boat, I'll just keep my mouth shut about the whole thing. If he's on the boat, I'll take him off and drive him home to talk to Olivia. I'll have to wake her in the middle of the night, which I dread, but it's necessary.

I start the engine, hit the gas, and speed down the highway until I see the red taillights of the van up ahead. I reach it and then ease off the gas, staying about a hundred feet back as it moves down the highway.

Someone in the back window is waving something bright red, frantically trying to get my attention. Concerned, I accelerate and move in closer. I lean over the steering wheel to get a better look.

And then promptly sit back.

"I don't believe it," I say aloud.

My headlights have clearly lit Shaye, sitting in the van's back seat, facing me, smiling broadly while waving a lacy red bra back and forth in the window. She's wearing a white winter parka and it's zipped up, thankfully. I figure she must have somehow slipped off her bra under her coat and sweater so Olivia wouldn't see her.

I fall back a few hundred yards so that I can't see Shaye anymore. I follow the van all the way into town and then along Harbour Street toward the Lighthouse Road. I tell myself it's not because Olivia's in the van. After all, it's my duty as a police officer to make sure all six people on board get home safe and sound.

## Chapter 23

# OLIVIA

Later that evening, the four residents are all in the living room and I'm in the kitchen, having just finished putting the groceries away. I'm about to plug in the kettle to make a cup of tea for my mother when Logan steps into the room and walks past me wearing a red T-shirt and jeans. He's carrying his backpack in one hand. I stop what I'm doing and stare in shock at his right biceps.

"I'm ready, Mom. Can you drive me to Shane's now?"

"Logan, what's that on your arm?"

He looks at his arm and his face turns read. "Umm…"

For a moment, I'm dumbstruck. I can only stare at it, lips parted.

"Awesome, isn't it?" he says, his initial fear replaced by defiance.

My temper rises. "Awesome? You think that's awesome? No, it is most certainly not awesome. What it is is ugly."

He studies his tattoo, snorts a breath out. "No way, Mom, it's great. Look at it."

Right then, my mother enters the kitchen, dabbing at her red nose with a tissue.

"Will you please stay in bed?" I implore her.

She just waves my words away and heads for the sink.

I turn back to Logan. "I'm looking at it. And I don't remember giving you permission to get a tattoo."

He drops his arm. "You would have just said no."

"That looks new. When did you get that?"

"This afternoon."

I shake my head in disbelief. "I can't believe you went behind my back to get that done."

He makes a face. "Mom—"

"Mom, what?"

"Chill out. You're acting like I robbed a bank or something. It's just a tattoo. It's not a big deal."

Heat shoots up my neck. My face is so hot that it feels on fire. I know I'm too angry and need to calm down before I say something I'll regret. I look out the window, draw two quiet breaths, and then face him again. "Not a big deal? You listen to me, Logan Blanchard. It may not be a big deal to you, but it's a huge deal to me. Why would you even have that tattoo? That looks like a lobster boat. Is it? Is that a lobster fishing boat?"

"Yeah, it's a lobster boat from town called the *Sea Predator*."

From the sink, I hear my mother gasp quietly under her breath.

I stare at Logan. "Why did you get a tattoo of *that* boat?"

His expression turns suddenly guarded. "No reason."

I glance over at my mother, who's watching Logan closely. Her eyes linger on him and then she looks at me, shaking her head worriedly.

"Whose boat is it?" I ask Logan.

"A guy named Mack Crocker's," he says warily. "Most of the fishermen in town name their boats after their wives or daughters. But this name was different, so wicked that I loved it. I got a tattoo of it, that's all." He grabs a can of soda from the fridge and heads out of the room.

"Freeze, Logan," I say.

He stops and sighs loudly. "Mom, relax, you're overreacting."

I open my mouth and quickly close it again, furious. I take in a quiet breath, regaining my composure. "Overreacting? You went ahead and got a tattoo, something you know I would never have allowed, and I'm overreacting?"

He glances at his grandmother, looking for help. My mother meets his gaze, but doesn't speak. She doesn't have to. Even I sense quiet disapproval.

"Gram," he pleads.

"I'm sorry, sweetheart, but your mother's right. You shouldn't have gotten that tattoo without asking her first. You deliberately disobeyed her."

His grandmother's disapproval is too much for him. "Fine, I'll get it removed. Will you guys be happy then?" He storms out of the room and down the hall to the front door.

"Removing a tattoo isn't that easy to do," I say to his retreating back.

"I'll be waiting in the car," is all he says.

"We aren't finished talking about this." But my words are drowned out by the sound of him slamming the door behind him.

I look at my mother and she shakes her head, her face glazed with dismay too.

Late that night, I'm unable to sleep. The tattoo thing has upset me tremendously. And meeting Cade earlier has left my mind whirling with memories of him. I recall when he looked up from the flat tire and saw me. Did I imagine it or did I hear his breath catch in his throat a second before his expression turned stony?

I think back to the first time I saw his face, the first time I looked into his warm blue eyes. Even now, twenty years later, I remember it. It strikes me that I've always loved Cade's face, his eyes, his shy smile. Then I think of Luc, and a wave of guilt sweeps through me. My beloved Luc is dead less than a year and here I am thinking of another man in this way? Appalled with myself, I force Cade from my mind, flip the pillow over, and settle down again.

My mind flies right back to Cade. How when our eyes met tonight for the first time in years we just stood and stared. But then, it had always been like that between us. Whenever we saw each other, we would stand and stare, not moving, not speaking, hearts thumping.

After all these years of telling myself I was over him, of believing that, I have to wonder if I've been deceiving myself all along. Have I been pretending that my love for him doesn't exist? I know I loved Luc deeply. He was a good husband and a wonderful father to Logan. But seeing Cade again has brought back all these old feelings. I have to wonder if I ever loved Luc with the same intensity and passion I had loved Cade.

After Cade and Logan changed the flat tire, I thanked him and he gave me a cool nod. Then a small smile slipped out. On the highway driving through town, I saw his headlights behind me. And to my shock, my heart quickened. I couldn't stop a tiny thrill from passing through me at the thought that he was following me, making sure I got home safe. That he still has feelings for me.

Then I told myself to stop being so foolish. I wasn't alone in the van. I had four disabled women and a boy with me. Cade's a police officer. He was only doing his duty. After what I did to him, after I hurt him so terribly, he can't have any feelings left for me.

A sudden gust of wind shudders in off the water and pummels the house, jarring me from my thoughts. I pull the covers up to my ears and close my eyes.

Before I drift off to sleep, I remember something that's been niggling at me all night. I was so rattled by seeing Cade that when I introduced Logan to him, I didn't react when I got the feeling they already knew each other. I make a mental note to ask Logan about it in the morning.

I make another mental note to ask him more about his friend, Shane Orson. I've been meaning to do, but I've been so busy helping my mother out that it keeps slipping my mind. Too late, I realize that I missed a good opportunity to do it earlier when I dropped him off at the Orsons'. I should have walked up to their front door and met Shane and his parents.

I let out a weary sigh and try to go to sleep.

## Chapter 24

# LOGAN

Mom pulls over in front of Shane's house. I get out and walk right up to the Orsons' front door, my things in my backpack. I turn and wave to Mom, who smiles out the windshield, looking thrilled that I've been invited to stay the night.

Once she drives away, I creep off the step to the sidewalk and make my way along the dark sidewalks to Fishermen's Wharf. I jump aboard the *Sea Predator* and make a bed in the wheelhouse out of blankets I find in a storage cabinet. I use my backpack for a pillow. I read by flashlight until 10:00 p.m., then curl up under the blankets and go to sleep.

I wake at midnight, chilled from sleeping on the damp boards. It's so cold that puffs of my breath swirl around my head like smoke. Shivering, I wrap a damp blanket around my shoulder, grab my backpack, and leave the boat. I walk toward the weigh station, hoping the heated bathroom is open so I can wait inside until Crocker arrives.

I just reach the small building when headlights appear at the entrance to the wharf. I run around the side of the station and try the washroom door. It's locked. I peer around the side of the building to the approaching car. As it passes under a streetlight, I see that it's a police cruiser. My heart nearly stops. There's no way to explain what I'm doing on the wharf with a blanket and my backpack at this time of night.

I bolt out from the side of the building and, keeping to the shadows, run as fast as I can to Crocker's boat. I leap aboard and hurry into the wheelhouse. I watch from an aft window as the police cruiser drives slowly up to the *Sea Predator*. It stops and the driver directs the spotlight onto the boat. My stomach lurches when I see Cade behind the wheel. I drop to the floor and crouch below the window, heart pounding, until I hear the car drive away.

When it's safe, I crawl under the blankets. But it's no use. I'm too jacked up to sleep. At 2:30 a.m., I hear a vehicle speed down the wharf road. I relax, recognizing Crocker's pickup truck by the thunderous rumble of its missing muffler.

Crocker laughs when he steps into the wheelhouse and sees me shivering under my blanket. "You look nearly frozen to death. Well, no better way to warm up than by working. Get out there and unmoor us and I'll get the beast started."

Only seconds after stepping out on deck, I see the bright headlights of a vehicle coming down the wharf road; I catch the glitter of the police cruiser's emergency rack. Its spotlight is on and the driver is probing the dark shadows of the wharf as he moves toward the *Sea Predator.*

I leap aboard and hustle into the wheelhouse. "Cops are coming."

Crocker waves off my words. "Relax. They're just doing their job, patrolling the wharf, keeping an eye on the boats."

I shake my head. "I think it's Cade Stone. He was here earlier. He shone his spotlight all over your boat like he was looking for someone. He hasn't talked to my mom yet, so maybe he's trying to see if I'm still fishing with you."

Crocker goes to the side window and looks out. "Yeah, it's him." He turns his head and swears, then storms out of the wheelhouse, tossing orders over his shoulder. "Get down out of the light before he sees you! I'll get rid of him."

I squat on the floor beneath a window, listening as the cruiser pulls up alongside the boat. I can't resist. I stand and peek out the window. Cade is behind the wheel, directing the spotlight at the boat. The bright light catches Crocker standing on the stern deck and stays on him.

"Shut the light off before you blind me, Stone, you moron!"

Cade shuts off the spotlight and engine, then climbs out. He turns on the long flashlight in his right hand.

I'm so nervous that I feel my pulse throbbing in my temple. If Cade catches me in here, I'm done for. He'll take me home and tell Mom everything. I hate the idea of that, of how sad Mom will be. And I'm not sure I can handle another one of Gram's disappointed looks. They just about slay me. I breathe in and breathe out, putting a hand on the wall to steady myself.

Crocker, his stride fast and angry, jumps onto the wharf road and meets Cade, blocking his path.

I slide the window open a quarter-inch, listen hard.

"What do want, anyway, Stone?" Crocker barks.

"I'm looking for Logan Blanchard," Cade says. "Is he on board?"

Their voices fade. I hear Cade ask something else about me, but I can't make out the words. Crocker replies that I'm not on board, that I only worked for him once and was so useless he had to let me go. My mouth drops open. I sure don't like Crocker telling Cade that, but there isn't a thing I can do about it.

Their voices grow more muted, so I ease the window open a little more. Crocker tells Cade if he doesn't believe him, he's welcome to come aboard and have a look around, but in a tone that reveals he doesn't mean it. I crane my head sideways and see Cade start for the boat. My gut squeezes so violently I feel sick.

I look around, panicked. I considering hiding in the head, but I'm sure that's the first place Cade will look. I hurry over to a big storage cabinet under the dash. I ease the door open and crawl inside, shutting the door softly behind me. I sit hunched over, knees drawn up to my chest, palms sweaty. I hear the thumps of the men's boots hitting the deck. Cade's footsteps are easy to make out; his regulation boots make a light thud while Crocker's rubber boots smack the deck as he stomps behind Cade, muttering curses and insults the whole time.

I bite my lip hard as the wheelhouse door opens and the two men step inside. The cabinet door is a little warped and doesn't shut tightly. Through the thin gap, I see Cade standing in the middle of the wheelhouse. He clicks off his flashlight and taps it against his thigh as he looks around. He steps over to the head, opens the door, peers, in and shuts it again. Then his eyes fall on the cabinet. My breathing grows loud and ragged. I'm so scared he'll hear me that I bite down on my knee to kill the sound.

"All right, Crocker," Cade says after a long, tortuous moment. He turns to leave.

"Told you he wasn't here," Crocker snarls, following him out to the deck. "Now get off my boat. Some men have to actually work for a living."

I wait until I hear the sound of the cruiser's engine start up and then fade as it drives away. I crawl out and join Crocker on deck. Crocker, rubbing his face viciously, is staring at the red lights of Cade's cruiser as it proceeds down the wharf road toward town. Within seconds, the cruiser's red lights are swallowed up by the thick fog rolling in.

"Oh, I hate that guy. I hate his guts. Why can't he mind his own business?" Crocker says through clenched teeth.

I can't think of a response to that, so I just shrug.

"He comes back nosing around my boat like that again and it'll be the last time he'll do it," he says in a quiet, unnerving voice. "And you can believe me on that."

I look into his cold, cruel eyes and believe him.

He starts up the diesel engine and the *Sea Predator* pulls away from the wharf, moving sluggishly through the heavy winter fog. It's as though a dense blanket of grey has settled on the town and harbour. But once we pass the lighthouse at the mouth of the harbour, Crocker throttles up to full speed and the boat thunders over the water.

I stand at the helm beside Crocker, looking out the windshield. I try not to think of Mom, who believes I'm at Shane's house right now. But I can't dispel the heaviness in my heart that I know is a result of my deceitfulness.

## Chapter 25

# LOGAN

Once at the grounds, I go out on deck and look up at the starry-filled sky. The temperature is below zero. The icy wind slices through my clothing to my skin, and a weird freezing fog that Crocker calls "ice fog" has moved in. A layer of ice coats everything on the boat. The deck is like a skating rink. I tie my hood tighter, then carefully make my way over to the stern and get right to work. It's the only way to make the time pass faster, to keep warm.

By daybreak, the temperature comes up and the ice fog disappears, but the sky is overcast, a dense grey blanket overhead. Then rain begins: a cold November rain that continues all morning. We work steadily, not talking much. I don't know if it's because of the miserable weather or his run-in with Cade this morning, but Crocker's extra impatient and bad-tempered. He's been barking at me all morning.

Just after lunch, I do the unthinkable. I slip on the wet deck and drop an empty lobster trap. The weight carries me forward and I fall on top of it.

"Wake up!" Crocker screams from behind the winch.

Usually, when I'm fishing I love it so much I get in a tranquil zone, but today I'm tired and cold and in a bad mood myself. I'm sick of his constant screaming and criticism.

"I am awake. I just slipped on the deck!" I yell back.

"I am awake. I just slipped on the deck," Crocker mimics in that sardonic tone I despise.

I glare bullets at him.

As usual, my anger is lost on Crocker. He only points to the railing. "Get moving, will you? I don't pay you to stand there gaping at me all day."

Now I'm really ticked, and I've had it with his mood swings. He'll be good-humoured, slapping me on the back and praising me up one minute, then mean-tempered, cuffing me in the head and ridiculing me with a cutting remark only seconds later. Even after working for him for almost two weeks, I still never see it coming. It's like a bolt of lightning out of a clear blue sky. What really unnerves me is the hint of violence toward me I catch in his eyes at times.

Close to two o'clock, the clouds disappear and the sun shines down with its welcome, warming rays. For the first time all day, I feel comfortable.

Crocker steers the boat toward a green buoy marker. I let out a breath. He's going to cut a fisherman's lines. But when Crocker emerges from the wheelhouse, he heads for the winch.

"Get over there and grab the pot line when it comes up," he orders.

I close my eyes and feel my shoulders slump. He's not going to cut the trap line, which I recognize by the maroon colour as belonging to Rupert Bowness. It's worse. He's going to steal Rupert's catch.

I'm immobilized by shock and disgust. *How low can the man go?*

He's standing only an inch from me, furious. "What's your problem now?"

"You're stealing someone else's catch, Crocker."

"So what?" he shouts right into my face, spittle hitting my cheek. "Look, I need these lobsters bad. I need the money. If I don't catch lobster, my family doesn't eat. Do you understand that? So get over there and grab the freaking pot."

*You're not catching lobster, you're stealing them, and I'm pretty sure Rubert needs his lobsters so family can eat too,* I think silently, disgustedly.

I walk across the deck and stand at the port side. I watch as the winch lifts a pot from the bottom of the sea. The engine grinds noisily and the line whines by my ear. The pot breaks the surface of the water and begins its climb to the boat, the sunlight glinting off its wire sides and top. The trap line squeaks, the pot swaying as it ascends. I pull my rubber gloves on tighter and lean over the side, making ready to grab the pot.

My heart jumps into my throat. I cry out, stagger back. I stand frozen, staring at the trap line. The wind kicks up and the pot swings forward and hits the hull.

"What's wrong? Grab the line!" Crocker shouts.

The winch's motor whines in my ears like a cloud of mosquitoes. The pot continues to rise. I tell myself it's a mistake, a trick my mind has played on me. I draw in a deep breath and try to will my body to move.

"Logan, get over there and grab the pot!"

Crocker's scream works. I step over to the railing, leaning over the side as it rises. I freeze with my arms outstretched in the air, the blood in my veins turning to ice. Under the pot, tangled in the trap line, is a body. Its bloodless white face is turned up toward me. No eyeballs, just holes in the face.

A strong gust of wind pushes the pot and body and they hit against the boat's hull with a loud thud. The impact sends the corpse's right arm up in the air, its fingers splayed as if reaching out to me for help.

Horrified, I stumble back and fall to the deck.

Crocker jerks his head around the side of the winch. He levels his dark, raging eyes at me. "You let that happen one more time and I'll throw you right over the side. You hear me?"

I look at him, eyes wide with horror, mouth opening and closing but no words coming out. Blood rushes to my head. I feel like I'm going to pass out and have to place my gloved hands palm down on the deck to steady myself.

Crocker swears, shuts down the winch, and stomps over.

In the sudden silence, the trap line creaks and groans in the wind.

Crocker glares down at me. "What are you doing? Get up and grab that pot!"

Too shocked to speak, I only manage a weak jerk of my chin to the body.

"Get up!" he leans over and spits at me. "Get up now!"

I stagger to my feet. "It's a… a—"

Crocker stares at me. Before I can react, he lifts a hand and cuffs me hard on the head. "You're useless, a complete waste of skin," he hisses, then turns and leans over the side, reaching for the pot. I hear his breath catch. "What the!"

He too rears back, flinging his arms and hands into the air. After regaining his footing, Crocker stands on the deck, face stunned. He stares in silence at the twisting buoy line. The top of the corpse's head is visible now. The line sighs and moans eerily as it twirls in the air. There's a soft thunk as the wind pushes the body against the hull. Gulls circle and screech overhead.

"Now who do we have here?" Crocker sets his hands on his hips, leans over the side of the railing, and eyes the corpse more closely. He swivels his head around to me with a cold smile, thumbing to the dangling body. "This boy's been in the water for a while, wouldn't you say?"

Our eyes meet and hold for a few seconds. I remain silent, shivering in the sunlight, as though a sheet of ice fog has suddenly enveloped my body.

Crocker gives a short, callous laugh. "What's your problem? You never seen a dead guy before? Come on. Don't just stand there. Give me a hand. Start the winch, you can work it yourself. Go ahead, I'll pull the pot in and get this thing untangled from the line."

I take in a deep breath of air and nod. On shaky legs, I step over to the winch and turn it. My heart slams against my ribs. Even though I don't want to look, I can't seem to turn my eyes away. The winch line moves with a harsh grinding noise. The pot ascends. I watch in horror as the body slowly rises above the railing.

"All right, shut it down and come over here and give me a hand. I can't do it myself."

I shut off the winch and come alongside Crocker. Together we lift both the pot and the body over the rail. I try to hold the body steady and gently lay it down onto the deck. The flesh is mushy, rotting, and slides right off. Even through my glove, the texture feels like cottage cheese. I panic and frantically flick a few pieces of it off my glove.

Crocker laughs violently.

Sudden, hot acidic bile rockets up my throat and I vomit onto the deck.

Crocker stops laughing. He eyes me in disgust, shaking his head. "You're puking over a dead body? No way. What a wuss."

I straighten up and grit my teeth to hold the bile down.

"Come on. Get a hold of yourself."

I draw in a deep breath. We stand on deck, staring down at the gruesome sight at our feet, silent. It's clear the body has been in the water a long time. It's horribly decomposed. It's wearing blue jeans and nothing else; the current has stripped away the rest.

Crocker chuckles softly and flick my eyes over to him. He's moved nearer to the body. As I watch, he leans over and eyes the corpse's face with a strange, almost intimate expression. "Well, hello there, buddy."

A vicious shudder runs through me. His crazy-sounding voice and words are frightening, revolting.

I can't look at him anymore. I study the corpse. From his bare chest, I can tell it's a male, but not his age. He could be twenty. He could be forty. His short brown hair has green seaweed tangled in it. What's left of his rotting flesh is a mushy, bloodless white, reminding me of cooked oatmeal. His eyeballs, eyebrows, eyelids, nose, lips, and left ear are all missing. And there's a deep gash in the left side of his head that reveals his white skull.

A second, more violent shudder rips through me. When it passes, I feel my entire body trembling, partly from cold, partly from shock.

Just when I think Crocker can't do anything more to shock or disgust me, he does. He toes the side of the body, nudging it. "Is buddy really dead, do you think?"

His callousness is deeply disturbing. "Crocker, don't."

He abruptly lifts a foot and kicks the corpse's bare foot with his boot, sending a piece of decayed flesh flying through the air. It lands on the side of the bait barrel. "Yep, he's dead," he laughs.

I can't take my eyes off the piece of slimy flesh sliding down the side of the plastic barrel. Another wave of nausea wracks my gut. Before I can stop it, I vomit the rest of my lunch.

Crocker slaps his thigh, roaring with laughter. "You wuss, you big wuss."

I sprint over to the railing and retch over the side into the water. When I'm done, I turn around and he's right there, right in my face.

"You're puking again? I don't believe this. What a wimp."

I wipe my mouth with the back of my hand.

Smiling cruelly, he cuffs me on the side of the head. "Man up, I mean it. It's just a dead body."

He smiles slyly and steps over to the body. With one eye on me, he lifts his foot again.

"Crocker, no," I say, in mounting horror.

"Crocker, no," he mocks as he kicks again, dislodging another piece of mushy skin. It lands on the toe of my rubber boot.

Horrified, I shake it to remove the rotting flesh. It won't come off.

The engine is still idling and the wind carries the diesel fumes and stink of decomposing fish from the bait tub into my face. My stomach lurches. I clamp my lips together to keep from vomiting, but end up gagging. I drag the toe of my boot along the wooden deck boards to scrape off the bit of flesh.

Crocker pauses to study me. He shakes his head in anger. "What's your problem?" He grabs my arm and squeezes it, looking right into my eyes. "You need to get a hold of yourself, right now. I'm serious. You hear me?"

I nod but yank my arm free.

His face goes cruel as he returns his eyes to the body. "What a nuisance. I wish we never found him. It would have better if he'd been caught on something else down there. At least then the fish and eels would have finished eating him and there'd be nothing left but bones."

I'm so unnerved by the decomposing corpse before me, and by his cold-hearted indifference, that all I can do is stare at him.

"Get... a... grip," he says, pointing a finger at me. "Let's go. Move your butt. Let's pull up some pots."

My jaw goes slack. "What? Aren't we going to bring him in?"

Crocker scowls at me. "No, we aren't going to bring him in. Man, you can be stupid. Think about it. How would we explain that we found him tangled up in Rupert's lines? Besides, he's dead, bringing him in won't help him now. Cover him up with a tarp if it bothers you so much. And hose off that puke from my deck before the stink makes me lose my lunch."

I stand firm. "Crocker, we have to bring him in. We have to call the cops, or the Coast Guard. We need to let someone know about this. His family needs to know. We can just say we found him tangled in your lines. No one will know the difference."

Crocker looks at me with curiosity. "Are you serious?"

I swallow audibly, but don't back down. "Yes, of course I'm serious."

He gives a quiet, derisive laugh. "Unbelievable. Well, tough. We're not stopping. We've got pots to pull up."

"What are you talking about? They're not even your pots. They belong to Rupert Bowness!"

"Yeah, well, too bad for Rupert Bowness. And like I said, it's not going to matter to this guy if we keep working." He looks down at the corpse, smiling bemusedly. "He's not going anywhere, is he?"

With that, he turns and stalks over to the winch and starts it up again.

I stand in place for a full minute, knowing there's nothing I can do or say to change Crocker's mind. I force my feet to walk over to a wooden storage bin built against the side of the wheelhouse and pull out a blue polypropylene tarp. My hands shake as I drape it over the body, laying the tarp down crooked, leaving the corpse's horrible face uncovered. Trying not to look at him, I pull the tarp over the rest of the way.

I pick up two buoys and set them down on the corners, but then a gust sweeps over the deck, revealing the corpse's bloodless white hand. I find it so disturbing that I quickly grab two more buoys and set them down.

We pull up pots for the next hour, working carefully around the body. Each trap holds five or six large-sized lobsters, and this elates Crocker. He works steadily with unflagging energy, casually chattering the whole time as though these are his pots, as if a corpse isn't lying on the deck. I don't speak at all. As usual, my silent anger and disgust goes unnoticed by the man.

At three o'clock, I hear the low drone of another fishing boat and it sounds close.

Crocker hears it too and instantly shuts down the winch, motioning that we're done. "Time to motor out of here," he says, hurrying toward the wheelhouse. As he passes me, he stops, reaches out, and slaps me jovially on the back. "Good work, Logan."

I hate him right now. I hate him touching me. I move out of the way so he can't do it again.

He looks at me, canting his head to one side. "What's your problem now?"

I avert my eyes, repelled.

"Give me a break here, Logan. Rupert's not going to miss a couple of lobsters."

"That's a lot more than a couple," I counter.

"Look, you know full well I lost a couple of days at the beginning of the season. I have to make them up somehow."

"By stealing from a fellow fisherman? We don't have to do that. Let's just work longer and harder to make up the lost time."

He throws his hands up in the air. "We already are! We're the first out and that last in as it is. The price of bait and diesel has gone way up. Lobster's selling for less than five dollars a pound now. I have a boat payment, a mortgage, a family to feed, your wages. I have to make a living here. You don't know what that's like, the kind of pressure that puts on a man."

"I do understand, Crocker. I heard some of the other fishermen talking about it on the wharf yesterday. I know the cost of fishing is high, but I also heard them say they aren't making a lot of money, either. They're under a lot of pressure to feed their families too, so the last thing they need is us stealing their catch."

Crocker's face goes completely still. His eyes narrow. He observes me with a frightening gaze. "I don't give a rip about them. I look out for me and my family. I don't care if every one of those idiots lose their boats and go bankrupt. In fact, I hope they do. Get that through your thick head."

I keep my eyes on the water. He's remorseless, without a conscience. There seems to be no bounds to his cold-blooded, thieving behaviour.

"Now clean up the deck. We're heading back in." He turns and stomps back into the wheelhouse.

I stow the gear, trying to keep from looking at the lump under the blue tarp. When I'm done, I stand at the port rail. The short-lived red sun is dropping on the horizon. I glance at the body, then up at the crimson and maroon streaks that fill the sky. It strikes me that death, ugly and heartbreaking, seems so incongruous in the magnificence of this glorious sunset.

The engine starts, revs, falters, and stalls. It starts again and Crocker guns it a little.

"Logan, come on in," Crocker shouts from the wheelhouse over the sound of the engine. "No sense standing out getting wet and freezing your butt off."

"Over my dead body," I whisper to myself. With a sickening lurch of my stomach, I realize what I said.

"Logan!" he bellows. "Get in here."

I wonder how I ever let myself get so mixed up with him. I glance at my upper arm and regret ever getting the tattoo of the *Sea Predator*. It'll be a lifelong reminder of how I let him have such a hold over me.

"No!" I scream back.

He swings around from the helm, furious. Lifting his coffee mug, he throws it hard against a side wall, shattering it. He stomps over to the wheelhouse door, glares at me with furious eyes, spittle forming at the corners of his mouth.

"Fine," he says in an ominous whisper, then slams the door in my face.

I stand with my back against the wall of the wheelhouse to avoid getting soaked. The water sprays up over the rails and finds me, the icy wind cutting through to my bones. I press even further against the wall, shivering violently. I'll freeze to death before I go in there with him.

We roar over the water in the direction of town. Just thirty seconds later, the engine dies. The door rips open and Crocker bursts out. He stares at me, his whole body tight, his face crimson with rage. A thick blue vein pulses in his neck.

"I've had enough of your attitude. Get in the wheelhouse, that's an order."

I ignore him and walk over to the port side railing. I listen for footsteps, uneasy that my back is to him.

And here he comes. His footsteps on the cold deck boards crack like thunder. In a split second, he's right beside me. "Look at me," he says quietly.

I gather my courage, turn meet his gaze and hold it.

He bounces on his toes now, his hands opening and closing so tightly his knuckles are milk white. "Get in the wheelhouse."

"Leave me alone, Crocker."

"Leave you alone? You want me to leave you alone? All right then." He steps over to the corpse, bends over the body, and slides his hands under it. He lifts it up, carries it back over to the railing, and with a loud grunt heaves it over the side. I hear the splash as it hits the water.

I can't believe what I've just witnessed. I look down just in time to see the body sink below the surface. I can't speak. I can only stare at him, mouth open, paralyzed by horror.

Crocker eyes me, his expression cruel. "Now you're alone." He jabs me in the arm with his index finger. "And you keep your mouth shut about this."

I shake my head, find my voice. "No, Crocker. I won't stay silent."

"Yes, you will. Don't forget, if you tell anyone, your mom will know you've been fishing with me. She'll know you've been lying to her." A drop of saliva shoots out of his mouth and hits my cheek. His breath stinks of whisky, cigarettes, and teeth that haven't been cleaned for a year.

"I don't care about that."

He leans in close. "No? Then you give deep thought to the consequences of going against me." He tilts his head toward the water. "If you want to join buddy there at the bottom of the sea, just go ahead and tell someone about this."

He is so still. His voice is terrifyingly quiet. His eyes are like two pieces of glittering ice. Behind them, a black rage is building. They make my blood run cold. I truly believe he will toss me over the side. Numb with fear, I can't even swallow my own spit.

"You just went as white as a ghost. Are you frightened, Logan?"

"No," I say.

He smiles maliciously. "Oh, I think so."

I shake my head, but focus on a coil of rope hanging from a nail on the wheelhouse wall. If I look at him, he'll see how scared I really am.

A seagull shrieks overhead. An airliner flies by, a big 767, its low rumble reaching our ears. The fumes from the bait barrel fill my nostrils. A tiny blob of white flesh remains on a corner of the blue tarp. My stomach churns with nausea.

"So what's it going to be?"

I feel dizzy and weak. I swipe at my runny nose, taking in a deep breath to steady myself. "I won't tell anyone."

He nods. "You make sure of that. If you get the sudden urge to say something, think of your mom. She wouldn't want to lose her boy so soon after losing your dad, would she? Probably couldn't go on living, I'd say."

A chill slithers up my back. The sudden roar of my heartbeat drowns out the seagulls and airplane. I can't seem to take my eyes off his.

He gives me a thin, ominous smile. "Stow the tarp and then get in the wheelhouse."

I fold the tarp, my hands trembling so bad I make a mess of it as I put it away. Crocker watches me, cold and calculating. Then, on shaky legs, I walk into the wheelhouse with him following, his rubber boots smacking hard on the deck boards right behind me.

# Chapter 26

## LOGAN

In the rapidly fading light, we enter the harbour. I leave the wheelhouse and Crocker doesn't stop me. I stand at the railing and watch the dim rocky shore roll past. Night fog clings like gauze to the tops of the trees along the shoreline. Even the bell in the tall steeple of the Baptist church my family attends, which sits on the highest hill in the centre of town, is shrouded in grey mist. But through the fog, the lights of Shipwreck Cove glow.

I think of Gram's house, by now lit warmly from inside. All six women are likely in the kitchen, Mom and Gram making supper. Audrey smoking a fake cigarette, Maxine complaining she's hungry, Shaye grumbling about the lack of men in the house, and Grace asleep. Yet for the first time since moving here, I can't wait to get home.

After unloading our catch at the weigh station, Crocker shifts into low gear and swings the boat back around the wharf and toward his slip. As we pull into the berth, I look over to the squat fish-and-chip takeout stand, now closed, which sits next to the weigh station office. Next to the stand, under a streetlight, three fishermen huddle together, all looking toward the *Sea Predator*. From their postures, they seem angry.

I leap over the railing onto the wharf road and secure the mooring lines around the bullock. Crocker looks out the port window and I give him a stony nod. Seconds later, he kills the engine.

I go back on board and change my insulated coveralls and fishing clothes for the clean set I brought with me. Crocker's working on his books, tallying the lobster catch as if it's all ours. As if we didn't steal half of it from Rubert Bowness. I look at him and he lifts his eyes from the books to meet my gaze, but there's a chill silence between us. I don't give a rip. I don't wait for him to pay me. I don't want the money. I'm done working for him.

I jump off the boat and walk toward the weigh station's washroom. I could use the head on the *Sea Predator*, but I want to get off the boat and away from Crocker as fast as I can. As I pass the three fishermen, they all fall silent and stare at me. I recognize Kurt Thomason and Andy Coldwell, but don't know the third man. I nod at them and they nod back. It's clear they're upset. The air is electric with their anger.

I wash my face with cold water, rinsing out my mouth five times to wash away the taste of vomit. I'm still badly shaken by finding the body, by seeing Crocker toss it overboard as casually as if it was an undersized lobster. I'm still rattled by his threat to throw me overboard. I stop at the doorway to steady my nerves and then head back out.

I see a town police cruiser parked beside the fishermen. Cade and a young constable are standing by. Angry voices carry easily to my ears. I remember that another fishing boat was very close when Crocker stole Rupert's lobster. Someone might have seen us poaching. Or maybe, I think, my stomach sick at the thought, someone saw us pull up the body, or later, saw Crocker throw it back in. I'm about to bolt down the wharf road when Cade looks over and sees me. He lifts a hand and beckons me over.

I take a big breath and walk on wobbly legs toward the group. I can feel Cade's eyes on me. I'm a wreck. I shove my hands in my jeans pockets to hide the tremor. I have bigger worries now than the fact that Cade Stone has caught me fishing with Crocker and will tell Mom. Poaching is a criminal offense. And who knows what kind of trouble I'll be in if this is about the body Crocker threw back into the sea.

I join the group of men, my gut clenching.

Andy Coldwell, Kurt Thomason, and the third man who's rail thin with coal black hair and a hawkish nose all turn their eyes on me. Cade and the young constable observe me closely.

I want to look them in the eye, but instead I turn away, ashamed, embarrassed.

Cade addresses the constable. "Austin, why don't you take Andy, Kurt, and Gage over to the cruiser while I talk to Logan?"

The constable nods and gestures to the men.

The three fishermen give me disappointed looks before reluctantly turning their backs and following the constable. They're fellow fishermen and I respect them. Their expressions and the way they turned their backs to me wound me deeply.

Once they're out of earshot, Cade turns back to me. "Let's talk over by the *Sea Predator*." He cups my elbow with his hand and steers me back to Crocker's boat. The wharf road's cold wooden boards creak loud as we walk past the other boats moored in their berths.

At the *Sea Predator*, we stop. A bitter wind whisks up the harbour. I stand in the cold and growing darkness, unable to stop a shiver from running through me.

"You look upset, Logan. Are you all right?"

"I'm good," I reply, trying to banish the image of the decomposed corpse swivelling from the trap line. It rushes unbidden to my mind every couple of minutes. The corpse looked like some kind of ghoulish puppet dancing on a string. The picture is so distinct, the stink of seaweed tangled in its hair so powerful, that I feel like a character in a never-ending horror movie.

"You guys just get back in?" Cade asks.

I want to say I wasn't even out at sea, but that would be ridiculous. I just shrug, glancing over at the wheelhouse. I don't want to deal with this alone.

Cade follows my eyes to the boat. "Is Crocker aboard?"

I nod, trying hard not to look nervous.

"You're as white as cottage cheese, Logan. Feeling a little seasick today?"

His question triggers the image of Crocker kicking the corpse and the piece of white cottage-cheese-like flesh sliding down the bait barrel. As much as I'm trying, I can't seem to come to grips with the horror I saw lying on Crocker's deck. I don't respond, partly because of the nightmare and partly because I'm sure he already knows the answer anyway.

"Logan, are you sure you're all right? You seem troubled," Cade says in a gentle tone.

I know he's around Mom's age, but the deep, craggy lines around his eyes make him look older. His eyes are soft and kind, betraying his serious cop's expression. It's easy to understand why so many people in town like him, trust him. I nearly blab the whole story, but catch myself in time.

"I'm fine, just really cold." I pull my hands from my jeans pockets and stick them into my armpits as if to warm them up.

Cade rubs his face, watching me carefully for a long moment. "All right, then. I need to ask you some questions."

I'm sick, exhausted, and scared. "Shouldn't you be asking Crocker?" I say irritably.

My tone doesn't faze him. "I'll do that when I'm finished talking to you."

I nod, averting my gaze to the police cruiser. The three fishermen look like they're arguing with the young constable. The odd word carries down the wharf road. They don't want to leave without talking to Crocker.

"So where were you guys fishing today?" Cade asks.

I bring my eyes back to him. "At his fishing grounds. Why?"

"Because one of the those fishermen," he nods over to the group, "claims he saw—"

Crocker emerges from the wheelhouse. "Stone!" he shouts, interrupting Cade. "What's going on?"

I still jump a little, but Cade doesn't even flinch. He stands coolly with his back to Crocker.

Crocker strides briskly across the deck, his eyes never leaving Cade's back, a furious expression on his face. He catches my eye and gives me a menacing look that says, *Keep your mouth shut.* He hops over the railing and lands on the wharf road without losing his balance. He moves up alongside me, faces Cade.

"I repeat: what's going on here, Stone?"

Cade looks at Crocker, his gaze unperturbed. "Good day, Crocker."

Crocker leans right into his face. "What… do… you… want?"

"I'm just having a conversation with Logan." Cade's voice has a slight edge.

"He's a kid. Leave him alone. You got questions, you ask me," Crocker shouts, spittle flying out of his mouth.

Cade holds a hand up. "Step back and calm down, Crocker. Logan can speak for himself. I'll talk to you after I'm finished with Logan."

Crocker smirks. "No, sir, not if it's to do with my boat. He's a minor and he works for me, so you talk to me, not him."

Cade silences him with a warning look. Then he turns his gaze back to me. "As I was saying, one of the fishermen reported seeing you guys fishing in Gage Kelly's territory. Did you see any green buoy markers in the area where you were fishing today?"

My heart gives a wobble and I recoil a little. Despite this, I feel immense relief that this isn't about the body.

"What, fishing in Gage Kelly's territory? No way," says Crocker, slipping a hand around my neck. He gives it a squeeze.

I jerk away, and his hand falls to his side. He fixes a venomous, cautioning stare at me and shakes his head almost imperceptibly. I see a thick vein pulsing in his temple.

"I'm asking Logan," Cade says without taking his eyes off me. "Logan? Andy Coldwell says he saw you and Crocker on the *Sea Predator*, close to three o'clock this afternoon, anchored at Gage Kelly's territory. He claims he saw you guys pull up a line of Gage's traps."

My heart booms in my chest. It's getting colder by the minute, but I feel a drop of sweat leak out of my hairline. I swipe it away with the back of my hand.

"Andy Coldwell's been smoking something he shouldn't be if he thinks he saw that," Crocker snorts. "If you had a brain, which you clearly don't, you'd be over there checking his boat for dope instead of harassing us. So why don't you take off now, Stone, and go do some real police work for a change?"

Cade holds a hand up at Crocker, keeping his gaze fixed on me. "Be quiet, Crocker. Stop talking before I put you in the back seat of my cruiser. Do you understand me?"

Crocker just waggles an eyebrow at Cade, false humour in his eyes. "Loud and clear."

"Logan, you're new at fishing and you may not have understood what Crocker was doing," Cade says. "Did you see any green buoy markers when you were pulling up trap lines this afternoon?"

I shake my head. "No."

My guilt eases a bit because I'm not really lying. The buoys were maroon and belonged to Robert Bowness.

"You're sure about that?"

"He just answered you!" Crocker blurts.

"Crocker," Cade warns him again. Then he looks at me. "Are you sure, Logan?"

"Yes," is all I manage.

Cade gives a slow nod, as though he doesn't believe me.

We all fall silent. The only sound is the strong wind churning the water, rocking the *Sea Predator* and the other fishing boats in their slips. Cade and Crocker both watch me intently, one wanting me to tell the truth, the other warning me to stay silent.

Finally, Cade says, but in a kinder tone. "I see. Well, did you see any other boats out there, a boat not from town maybe?"

I shake my head again, then realize I'm shaking it too fast. Nervously. So I stop.

"You heard him the first time, didn't you?" Crocker snaps. "He said no. Now unless you got some concrete proof it was us, and that's impossible, since we fished all day in my territory, get lost. Leave us alone."

Cade goes silent, watching Crocker for a moment. Then he nods. "We're done for now, but this isn't over, Crocker. Not by any means."

"Whatever, Stone, you idiot," Crocker says, half-laughing.

Cade's jaw tightens with anger, but he sees me watching him and turns his head and looks out at the dark water of the harbour. All anger has gone out of his face and posture. When he speaks, his voice is mild. It triggers another verse from my memory: *"A man of knowledge uses words with restraint, and a man of understanding is even-tempered"* (Proverbs 17:27).

"Logan, if you think of anything, something you might recall later, call me any time, night or day." Cade passes me a card with his office and cell phone numbers on it, then touches me gently on the shoulder and walks away. He joins the young constable and three fishermen. Cade speaks to them for a moment, and the three men leave, heading for the weigh station office. They don't look happy about it.

I watch Cade open the driver's side door of his police cruiser while the constable opens the passenger side. While glancing at me, they speak to each other over the roof of the car.

Crocker lifts his middle finger at them. Cade and the constable only climb in the cruiser and shut the doors.

Crocker suddenly cuffs me lightly on the head. "Hey, wake up."

I take my eyes off the police cruiser and look at him. "What?"

"You look like you're in a daze or something."

I shake my head. I have Cade's card in my hand. I turn my body to the side and shove it into my coat pocket without Crocker seeing. "I'm heading home."

"No, come on, let's grab a burger."

"I can't. Mom and Gram are expecting me for supper."

"So, you can't eat a burger and supper too? I thought all young guys your age had hollow legs."

"I'm not hungry."

Surprisingly, his voice softens. "You're not still sick, are you?" Before I can reply, he puts an arm around my shoulder and hauls me toward his pickup truck. "Come on, some hot food will do you good. Settle your stomach."

"Crocker, no." I try to shake his arm loose.

He makes a fist and rubs his knuckles gently over the top of my head. At the same time, he shoves some bills into my coat pocket. "Come on, Logan, you know I have a thing about eating alone. Keep me company, just for a half-hour."

"No, and I don't want your money," I say, reaching into my pocket.

Crocker pushes my hand away from my coat pocket. He grasps each of my shoulders and looks into my eyes, smiling. "Keep it. You earned it. It's the money from our catch, not from Rupert's."

I give him a sceptical look.

"It is, I swear. Come on. Let's go grab a bite."

For some reason I cannot fathom, I agree. As I walk with Crocker to his truck, I see Cade and the young constable sitting in the cruiser. Their lips are moving. I'm conscious of both cops' eyes fixed on me, so I drop mine to the ground.

## Chapter 27

# LOGAN

I pick at my burger, pushing my fries around my plate. Crocker, on the other hand, is eating like a hog. He ordered the fisherman's platter, which has enough food on it for three people. He's stuffing it in, disturbingly emotionless.

Each time Crocker cuts into his deep-fried haddock, the whitefish reminds me of the bloodless white flesh on the boy's corpse and I can barely keep from puking onto the table.

The diner is busy and loud from clanking silverware, ice clicking in glasses, voices, and laughter.

"Crocker," says a male voice over the din.

I turn my head and see Andy Coldwell, Kurt Thomason, and Gage Kelly. They stand in front of our booth, all glaring at Crocker.

Crocker picks up his coffee mug, which he laced with whiskey from his flask, and drinks from it while eyeing the men over the rim of the cup. He casually sets it down. "What?"

"I hear you were poaching my lobsters," Gage says.

Crocker snorts. "Poaching your lobsters? Give me a break, Gage."

"I saw your boat stopped at Gage's territory," Andy says. "It was you, Crocker. You stole Gage's catch."

"It was too foggy out there to see anything clearly, Coldwell," says Crocker. "You're imagining things."

"I was using binoculars, Crocker. I know what I saw."

"Then you were stoned or you're losing it, Coldwell, because it didn't happen," says Crocker, mashed fries visible in his mouth as he speaks.

"You're a liar, Crocker. I saw you. Saw the boy too." Andy looks directly at me.

I feel my pulse ticking in my throat.

Gage leans over the table and points a stiff finger in Crocker's face. "You give me the money you got paid today for stealing my catch."

Crocker slaps Gage's finger away. "Get out of my face. I mean it."

Gage looks at me. "You're Logan Blanchard, Winnie's grandson?"

I set my burger down on my plate and push it away, untouched. "Yes."

"Logan, listen to me. You come from good stock. Your grandfather was a good man. Your grandmother's salt of the earth. And you're just a young lad. I don't care if you were stealing from my traps today. I know Crocker put you up to it. But I'm warning you, you need to stop working for Crocker now. My nephew, Jeremy Tanner, was Crocker's last helper. We all warned him against working for Crocker, but he wouldn't listen to us. Now he's missing. He fell overboard when he and Crocker were out setting traps, or so Crocker claims" Gage throws Crocker a furious look. "We never found his body. My sister's beside herself with grief. She won't eat, can't sleep. She paces the house all night long. For your mom's and grandmother's sakes, you need to stop working for this guy. He's a bad man. You don't want to end up like Jeremy."

The image of the corpse twirling in the air fills my mind again.

"He was only twenty-one, engaged to be married," adds Gage sadly.

I open my mouth to tell Gage about finding the body when suddenly Crocker kicks me in the shin under the table. He's wearing steel-toed rubber boots and the pain is excruciating.

I manage not to cry out, not even to grimace.

"Get lost, Gage. Leave the boy alone," Crocker says in a heated voice. "Jeremy went around in a daze most of the time. He's half-Kelly, lazy and careless just like his uncle. That's why he fell overboard."

Gage's face goes white with fury. "You sorry excuse for a human being," he says, his voice rising. "I should knock you right through that wall."

"Yeah, go ahead, try it!" Crocker jumps to his feet, fists clenched, his face darkening. "I'll put you through the wall right into next week."

The diner goes deathly silent. Everyone's watching us. Everyone's listening.

"Come on, Gage," Andy says, putting his hand around the man's arm and pulling him away. He eyes Crocker with revulsion. "He's not worth it."

"Yeah, he's just a lowlife piece of scum," Kurt adds.

Crocker just throws his head back and laughs at that.

"This isn't over, Crocker," Gage calls out over his shoulder as the three fishermen leave the diner. "I promise you."

Crocker lifts his hand and gives them the finger, then goes back to stuffing his face.

Two men on stools at the counter have watched the whole exchange. Their eyes meet, then look away. They shake their heads in disgust.

Their looks feel like a boot to the chest. In their eyes, I'm no better than Crocker.

Crocker lifts his eyes from his plate and looks at me. "Am I wrong, or were you going to tell them about the body?"

I take a breath, turn my head, and look over to the counter area.

I shrug. Crocker's eyes fill with a cold fury. His face goes utterly still, other than for a thick vein pulsing in his right temple. He swipes at his cheek once and then wads up the napkin, tossing it at my face. It hits me in the eye.

"Hey, look at me when I'm talking to you."

I ignore him.

He swiftly reaches across the table and grabs my chin with his thumb and index finger, twisting my head so that I'm looking at him.

*The eyes on him,* I think. *They make my blood turn to ice.*

"Remember your mom. You say nothing, got it?" Then he lets my chin go, sits back against the booth. He puts a finger across his lips and smiles chillingly.

## Chapter 28

## LOGAN

I find Cade's cruiser in the driveway when I get home. I'm not surprised.

I remove my running shoes on the step and enter the house as quietly as possible. Voices are coming from both the kitchen and the living room. I pad down the hallway, stop at the open door to the living room, and peek inside.

Audrey, Grace, Maxine, and Shaye are all watching a movie on television.

"There I am, ladies," I hear Audrey say with an affected English accent. "This is where I tell my handsome co-star Michael Caine to—"

I slip past the door and come up to the kitchen. I hear the soft murmur of voices coming from inside. I peek around the open doorway, heart thudding.

Gram's at the sink with her back to me. Mom and Cade stand at the counter talking quietly. It bugs me just how close they're standing, with their bodies practically touching. And they're talking with their heads bent way too close together. But there's nothing I can do about it right now. I'm in too much trouble.

*I might as well get this over with.*

I take a deep breath and step into the room.

Mom looks over at me. She wears a blue cotton sweater and blue jeans. Her dark hair is loose on her shoulders. She has shadows under her eyes and lines at the corners of her mouth, none of which were there before dad died.

Gram shuts off the tap and turns around from the sink. She smiles tenderly at me, but I see profound disappointment too.

Cade gives me a kind smile. I ignore him and look at Mom.

Her eyes smoulder. "So there you are."

I glance at Cade, wishing he would leave now. He's already done enough damage.

Mom folds her arms over her chest, livid. "So you've been fishing lobster? Skipping school? Lying to me?"

I feel my heartbeat in my chest, but I manage to keep my face neutral. "I guess."

"You guess?"

I shrug, but watch her face carefully. It's turning a worrisome grey colour.

Her anger gives way to despair. Tears fill her eyes. "Logan, how could you lie to me like that?"

Gram studies her carefully. "Sit down, Olivia."

"I'm fine," she tells Gram.

But she doesn't look fine to me. Her body is trembling. She sways a little.

"Mom, listen to Gram. Sit down."

She might be shaky, but she gathers enough anger to shoot me a glare.

"Why don't you sit down, Olivia." Cade gently cups her elbow and leads her across the room to the table. He pulls out a chair and Mom collapses into it, putting her head in her hands.

*Oh, so she'll listen to him?*

Mom lifts her head and looks at me. A tear runs down one cheek. "I can't believe you've been lying to me, that you've been fishing all week. I'm beyond shocked, Logan."

Gram's soft brown eyes moisten. She turns her back and walks over to the stove, pretending to be busy at something there. Her sorrow and disappointment nearly kill me.

Cade is back at the counter, concerned eyes on Mom. I can't believe he's still here. He looks a bit uncomfortable, but not enough for him to leave, which sends a hot flash of irritation through me.

"You can leave anytime," I snap angrily at him. "This isn't any of your business."

"Logan, watch your mouth. I mean it," Mom warns. "Cade's only doing his job."

"Cade," I echo sarcastically. "Nice, Mom."

Mom's face reddens, but she draws in a soft breath, composing herself.

"Constable Stone's only doing his job. You will speak to him with respect."

It infuriates me that she used his first name, and the way she said it. So familiar. After Dad died, I felt myself pulling away from Mom. Lately, especially after a day in Crocker's company, I find myself retreating even more, not so much pulling away as turning against her. My usual mild anger and resentment build up inside me.

Mom gets up from the table and faces me. "Show me your hands right now."

I lift my hands palm out. Thick yellow calluses cover my hands.

She takes three shallow breaths. Her father more than likely had identical calluses. "How long have you been working for Mack Crocker?"

I shrug. "A week or so."

Her eyes fill with fear. "It's bad enough you went fishing, and worse that you went fishing at the most dangerous time of the year, but to go out with Mack Crocker of all people? Logan, that man is evil."

I say nothing. I know she's right.

"You need to listen to your mom, sweetheart," says Gram. "Mack Crocker makes bad decisions. He's lost helpers in the past."

I shake my head impatiently. "I know that, Gram. He told me about those guys. They weren't careful. Besides, that's the risk of being a fisherman. Fishermen die every day at sea."

Gram gives me a pained look. "*I* am well aware of that, sweetheart. I still grieve your grandfather. He was the love of my life. The Coast Guard found debris from the *Olivia-Winifred*, but they never found his body. They never brought him home so we could bury him." She looks at Mom and gives her a small, sad smile. "Your mom and I feel like we've never really had closure after his death. Do you understand?"

I feel my cheeks burn. "Yes, I do, Gram. But I love fishing. It's in my blood."

"I'm sure it is. But you're too young to fish. You should be in school."

"I'll be careful, Gram," I say. "Besides, it's too late. I told Crocker I'd work for him. He has no one else. I have to go fishing with him in the morning."

"Over my dead body, Logan!" Mom shouts.

I turn back to her. "Oh, come on, Mom. I'm going to be fourteen in a couple of days. I'm a man. Crocker says I'm a born fisherman. I'm good at it and I'm careful. I don't make mistakes."

"Come on, Mom?" she repeats in a voice that says she wants to wrap her hands around my throat and strangle me. "I don't care if you love fishing or *think* it's in your blood. And you are not a man. Fourteen is still a boy. You're not old enough or mature enough to make that kind of decision. And I don't care what kind of compliments Mack Crocker pays you. He's a bully, a liar, and a thief. He'd say anything to keep you out there."

I make a face, snorting softly.

"That's true, Logan," Cade puts in. "Mack Crocker is ruthless, reckless, and irresponsible. He goes out when the seas are too rough and high. He ignores the Coast Guard warnings. Even when all the other captains have brought their boats in during storms, he stays out. And often it's because he knows he's the only out there and can steal other fishermen's catches without fear of being caught."

I exhale loudly, frustrated and embarrassed that Cade is even here to take part in this.

We all fall silent. The voices from a cooking show blast in from the living room.

Mom crosses the room and shuts the kitchen door. Instantly, the TV noise is silenced. She turns back to me. "Well, it doesn't matter whether you believe us or not. You are done fishing. And you're grounded. You will not leave this house other than for school. And you will come straight home after school. Do you understand me?"

My shoulders sink. I don't respond.

Silence falls on the room once again. Outside, there's the long, solemn peal of a foghorn. The sound of it fills my heart with longing for the sea, to be out there right now fishing.

"Logan? Do you understand me?" Mom repeats.

"Yes," I grumble.

"Give me your cell phone. You won't need that for a while. I don't want you or Crocker texting or calling each other."

"Mom, no," I protest. "I need it to text Keltie and Jared."

"Give it to me," she orders, holding her hand out.

I blow out an angry breath, then pull it out of my jeans pocket and hand it over sullenly.

"Thank you," she says. "You can have it back in one week. Now go up to your room and don't you come down until I say you can."

I look at Cade. His arms are folded over his chest, his eyes moving from Mom to me to Mom again, but mostly they linger on Mom.

"Why, so you two can be alone?" I say with deep disgust.

She narrows her eyes. "I said, go to your room. Now!"

That does it. I start out of the room.

"Sweetie, wait."

I turn around. Mom's right there, looking sad. She reaches out her arms, pulls me, and kisses me on the cheek. "I'm sorry if I seem harsh, but I have to discipline you."

My face burns red. "Mom, don't. I'm too old to kiss."

"You'll never be too old for a kiss," she says, then kisses me on the other cheek before I can dodge her.

Behind her, I see Cade smile.

"Okay, Mom, enough."

I go upstairs and into my bedroom, shaking my head. Since Dad died, Mom's had these weird mood swings. She's mad enough to choke me one minute, then hugging and kissing me the next. Bizarre! I don't get it. Seconds later, I hear footsteps and then the front door opening and closing. I know Cade's left.

*Good, and don't come back,* I think.

I lay on the floor and press my ear against the furnace vent. I hear Gram's voice in the kitchen and chair legs scraping across the floor.

"I called the school right after Cade arrived," I hear Mom say. "The principal, Mrs. Lahey, told me that Logan's been absent all week. Apparently a woman pretending to be me called and said Logan had the flu and would be out all week, maybe as long as two weeks. Who would do that?"

"My money would be on Crocker's wife," Gram says. "Monique."

Mom gasps. "What? Why would she do something like that?"

"Poor thing, he'd have made her do it. Try to understand, Olivia. She has a difficult life with that man."

"The principal also told me Logan's grades have been falling steadily since September. And that she finds Logan dangerously quiet."

I nearly groan aloud at that. I have to bite my lower lip to stop it from slipping out.

"Dangerously quiet?" says Gram. "Oh, what foolishness. He is not."

*Thank you Gram.*

"I've trusted him," Mom says, "but he's been lying to me all week."

"That doesn't make him dangerous, Olivia."

"I'm terrified of losing him."

"You're not losing him," says Gram. "He's a good boy. But Olivia, he's lost his father. He's had to move from Alberta, leave his school, all his friends. He's had to leave military life for civilian life, and military life is the only life he's known. To make matters worse, he's had to move into this house, a special-care home with six women. That would be hard for anyone, let alone a thirteen-year-old boy. He feels alone, he's angry, confused, and hurting. But who wouldn't be? He needs time to adjust, to heal. I think you need to be patient with him."

"I hope you're right."

"I am right. We'll make sure he never goes fishing again, even if we have to drive him right to the school doors and march him into his classroom. Don't worry, Olivia. Everything's going to be fine."

Mom's soft weeping and Gram's sad voice trigger a wave of regret and shame. In this moment, I hate my lying, callous self. I'm no better than Crocker. Proverbs 10:1 comes to mind: *"A wise son brings joy to his father, but a foolish son grief to his mother."*

"Way to go, Blanchard," I chastise myself, and flop down on my bed.

## Chapter 29

# LOGAN

I shift my backpack on my shoulder and head to school. There's a veil of fog this morning that clings to the blue cedar shingles of Gram's house. As I walk past the side wall, I run my fingertips across the wet shingles, then shake the water droplets off.

I look back at the house from the driveway. *Big, draughty old dump,* I think, in a bad mood for two reasons. The first is because I have to go to school. The second is that both Keltie and Jared didn't respond to my texts in the days before Mom took my cell phone. And now they aren't responding to my emails or Facebook messages. I don't understand it.

I hear someone knocking on the living room window. I turn around and see that it's Shaye. She's standing with her face pressed against the glass, giving me goodbye kisses like I'm her boyfriend off to the war. It's not even eight o'clock in the morning and she's wearing bright red lipstick, which is leaving red lip imprints all over the windowpane.

Grace and Maxine shuffle up to the window on either side of Shaye. Grace sees me and waves; her hand falls, her chin drops, and then she's asleep. Maxine's eating a cookie likely pilfered from the cupboard when Gram wasn't looking, and she's waving at me with her free hand. Then Audrey joins the group, one hand raised in the air holding an imaginary cigarette.

Instead of feeling my usual irritation and frustration, to my surprise I feel my heart softening toward them. It strikes me that I'm growing very fond and protective of them.

I lift my hand and wave back. Of course, that sets them all off waving and grinning like a pack of loons.

I reach the end of the driveway and start down the road toward town.

Halfway there, I hear the roar of an engine approaching but can't see it in the heavy fog. I step closer to the culvert, worried the driver won't be able to see me. Seconds later, dull white headlights shine through the haze and a pickup truck bursts into view.

My heart jumps a little. It's a blue Chevrolet, Crocker's truck. He's behind the wheel, driving too fast and straight toward me. He squeals to a stop beside me, leans over the seat, and rolls down the passenger-side window.

"Hey, Logan, what's going on? Where've you been?" he yells.

I look at him without replying.

"Logan, get in. It's time to fish!"

His eyes are bloodshot and the capillaries across his cheeks and nose are bright red. He's half-drunk and it's only early morning. I shake my head and start walking again.

He takes his foot off the brake and steers with one hand while the truck rolls along beside me. He leans over and pushes open the passenger door. The dome light comes on in the cab, illuminating his translucent icy blue eyes.

He softens his voice. "Come on, get in, will you? I need to pull my pots up. I told you what happens when you leave lobsters in the traps on the seabed too long. They cannibalize each other. And there's a big storm coming in a few days. If I lose them, I lose everything."

"That's your problem. You knew the storm was coming and you set them anyway."

He shakes his head back and forth, eyes dark, getting angry. "What else am I supposed to do? Quit fishing just because you don't show up for work or some bad weather's on the way? Now, come on, I have to get out there before I lose my whole catch."

"Not my problem."

"What do you mean, not your problem? We're a team. If I don't make money, you don't make money, either," he says, plumes of his breath vaporizing in the cold air.

"I don't care, Crocker. I'm done working for you."

He scowls. "Are you still ticked at me? Look, I told you, I have to make a living. I couldn't bring the dead guy in."

"Yeah, you could have. You didn't have to throw him back in the sea. The odds of anyone finding his body now are slim. His family may never have closure." I think of Gram and Mom and how sorrowful they looked when they told me about never finding my grandfather's body.

"You give me more grief than my wife. Fine, okay, I admit I made a bad decision. I should have brought the guy in. I was wrong. But stop acting like I'm some kind of monster. You know me better than that."

I stop, turn, and face the truck.

Crocker hits the brakes. He puts an arm on the back of the seat and gives me a fond smile. "Logan, give me a break. I went out alone yesterday and only got a quarter of my pots up. I need you bad. It's not the same without you. I miss you out there. We make a great fishing team."

I say nothing. Behind him, the sea roars in, smashing the wall of rocks, sending up a white spray that lands on the opposite lane. The spray mists my face.

His smile and compliments seem genuine. Even though I hide it, they have an effect on me. "Okay, maybe you're not a monster, but you are a liar and a thief. You cut other fishermen's lines and poach their lobsters. I hate that."

He shrugs a shoulder, unconcerned. "So I'm a lying thief. So what? Get down off your high horse. You're no better than me. You're quite the liar yourself, in case you've forgotten."

"Was, you mean. Mom knows everything, so that's all over. No more lying to her."

He smirks. "I'm not talking about that."

"What then?"

"You let me think your father's plane got shot down in Libya when the truth is that it crashed in Alberta, didn't it?"

I feel my neck and face burn.

Crocker snorts a laugh. "Yeah, thought so."

"That doesn't change anything. Cade Stone was at the house on Friday. He told my mom everything. I can't work for you anymore, even if I want to."

I start walking again, but the truck cruises along beside me.

He smiles knowingly. "And you want to, Logan. You can pretend the sea doesn't call you, but you don't fool me one bit. It's in your blood. You're a natural fisherman, a first-rate fisherman."

I stop and look at him. I like that he sees that in me, because Mom and Gram sure don't. They don't understand how much I love fishing. Only Crocker seems to get me. I feel my earlier resolve soften.

"Okay, maybe that's true," I say. "But I'm not going out with you again until you tell someone we found the body."

His facial features stiffen. "No, I can't do that, and you'd better not, either. Look, why can't you understand that? I can't tell anyone now. It's too late. I'll be ruined. I'll lose my boat, my living. I'll go bankrupt and my family will have nothing. I thought we already talked about this and came to an agreement."

I let out a breath. He's unbelievable. "If you call threatening me and threatening to hurt my mom talking, then yeah, I guess we talked about it."

He hits the brakes, puts the truck in park, and opens the door. He comes around the truck and faces me. He puts his hand on my arm. "Now come on, don't be like that. You make me mad sometimes and I say stupid things I don't mean." His face goes soft. "Logan, I wouldn't hurt a hair on your head, I mean that. You're like a son to me. Truth is, you're more of a son to me than my own boy. And I think the world of your mom. I wouldn't hurt either one of you." He reaches into the passenger side of the truck and pulls out a gift-wrapped box. "Here, this is for you. Happy birthday."

I'm taken aback. Crocker doesn't seem like the type to remember anyone's birthday, let alone buy a gift. I study his face, suspecting manipulation, but his goofy smile seems genuine.

"Don't look at me like that. It's yours, whether you come back and fish with me or not. So go on, open it."

His gift and words touch a part of my heart. I accept it. "Thanks, Crocker."

I tear off the wrapping and find a stainless steel one-litre thermos bottle. There's an engraved picture of a fishing boat on the front, and below that the engraved words:

THE SEA PREDATOR
LOGAN C. BLANCHARD

I love it. I grin at him. "Whoa, cool! It's great, Crocker. Thanks."

He ruffles the top of my head. "You're welcome. I almost got you a liquor flask like mine, but I figured your mom would kill me." He laughs. "Now come on, get in the truck. Let's get that thermos filled with hot coffee and go fishing. What do you say?"

I point to the road behind us. "I can't, I'm grounded. And Mom's following me in her car making sure I go to school."

His smile vanishes. "What? Your mom's following you?"

I nod as I slip my backpack off my shoulder and stow the thermos in a side pocket.

He drops his hand, looks back over his shoulder to the road, then back to me again, smiling in disbelief. "Your mom's back there, really?"

"Yes. I heard the car start up a few seconds after I left the house. She's been staying out of sight, but it's her. She wanted to drive me to school, but I refused, so she's been following me all week. Listen, you can hear the engine. It's a crappy little four-cylinder, sounds like a lawn mower."

Crocker goes silent, cocks his head to one side. Over the screams of gulls and the tide surging against the seawall, there's the clear sound of a four-cylinder engine in the not-too-far distance, and it's approaching.

He throws his head back in laughter. "Unbelievable. That Olivia always was a feisty little thing."

"I have to go, Crocker. It sounds like she's getting close."

Crocker slaps his thigh and roars in laughter, looking at the road behind him. Suddenly, Mom's green Focus emerges through the fog and rounds a bend in the road.

"Crap, there she is," I say.

I see Mom hunched over the wheel, eyes searching the road for me. Her mouth falls open when she sees us. She hits the gas, the engine roars, the tires shriek, and she speeds toward me. She steers around Crocker's truck and then pulls over in front of it, screeching to a stop alongside us. The window slides down.

"You leave my son alone, Crocker!" she shouts, leaning across the passenger seat. "He's not fishing with you anymore. Get away from him now, I mean it."

Crocker shakes his head. "Hello, Olivia. Still have that quick temper, I see."

Mom ignores him. She looks at me, lifts a hand, and points down the road. "*You* start walking! Get to school!" Then she glares murder at Crocker and jabs the same finger at him. "And *you* get in your truck and leave before I run you right down like a snake on the road."

"You know, I'm a little afraid of your mom. I believe she actually might just do that." Crocker leans in close and whispers, "Meet me at the wharf at 3:00 a.m."

"I can't tonight, Crocker."

"Thursday then. Come on, I need you. Don't let me down." He punches me lightly on the arm.

"Crocker, get away from him!" Mom shouts and guns the engine to make her point.

"All right, Olivia, calm down. I was just giving Logan his wages. I'm leaving now." Chuckling under his breath, he starts for his truck. He climbs in the cab and drives away, giving me a quick toot of his horn. Through the cab window, I see his shoulders shaking with laughter.

"Logan, go to school. *Now!*" Mom hollers.

"Okay, you don't have to scream at me like that," I say sullenly. "It's embarrassing. I bet half the town can hear you two kilometres away."

Seething, she raises her index finger again and points to the road. "Move it."

I let out a breath and set off down the road toward town with Mom in her hideous little station wagon following slowly behind. She stays far enough back that I can't see her, to spare me the humiliation of the other kids seeing her when I reach school. But I know she's there. I can hear the sound of her engine in the quiet morning air. I find it mortifying.

I want to tell her to go home, that I'm going to school, but I know I'd just be wasting my time. Crocker's right about Mom being feisty. But I know she's also stubborn, and right now she's furious with me. Nothing and no one could keep her from following me to school this morning.

## Chapter 30

# LOGAN

"Happy birthday, Logan," Audrey says as she sets a brightly wrapped gift down on the table in front of me.

Maxine steps up beside Audrey and gives her a shove out of the way with her ample hip. "Oh, excuse me, Audrey, I didn't see you there." Then she smiles at me and sets a long, thin, and shiny blue-wrapped gift box down on the table in front of me. "Happy birthday, Logan. Here, this is for you. Go ahead, open mine first."

"I have a birthday present for you too, handsome. It's in my bedroom," Shaye says in a seductive tone. "Come on up later tonight and we'll open it together."

"Shaye!" Gram yells, losing it. "Now you have gone too far! What are you trying to do, traumatize the poor boy?"

"Oh, Winnie, calm down, I was just kidding," says Shaye, grinning. "Go ahead, Logan, open mine first. It's on the table there in front of you, the small one with red wrapping."

Grace smiles and points at a medium-sized gift with silver wrapping. "Happy birthday, Brogan. That one's from me."

I look at the stack of gifts on the table. There are six gifts of all sizes. I don't know which one to open first. Mom and Gram are standing with their backs against the counter, tender smiles on their face. The four residents sit around the table, watching me with their rheumy old eyes, each one hoping I'll choose hers first.

Mom steps over to the table and picks up Shaye's, which is the smallest, and hands it to me, saving me from the choice. "Let's start from the smallest to the largest so we don't hurt anyone's feelings."

I tear off the red paper and open the small box. My face burns. Inside is a pair of silk men's boxers. They're black and patterned with bright red lips and the words *Hot Stuff* printed in white lettering across the front and backside.

Gram sees my face flame red. "Oh no, don't tell me," she murmurs, hurrying over. She looks in the box, closes her eyes, and releases a weary breath. "Shaye! I can't believe you bought this. What were you thinking? This isn't an appropriate gift for a fourteen-year-old-boy."

Shaye lifts a napkin to her mouth and pats her lips. "Sure it is. Fourteen? He's a man now. And a good-looking young man," she says, winking at me. "Aren't you, hot stuff?"

Gram points a rigid finger at her. "One more word like that out of you and you're going to go upstairs and stay in your bedroom for the rest of the night."

Shaye pushes her lips out in a pout. "Oh, Winnie, don't be such an old stick-in-the-mud."

"I mean it, Shaye, last warning." Gram scoops up the box and carries it out of the kitchen. She looks back over her shoulder as she leaves the room. "I'll just put this in your bedroom, Shaye, and you can return it and buy something more appropriate the next time we're in town. If you can't do that, you won't give him a gift at all."

"Party pooper," Shaye mutters under her breath.

Gram skids to a stop, turns around. "Pardon me, Shaye?"

Shaye smiles innocently. "I said I'll give it the old E for effort, Winnie, but I can't promise anything. I guess I'm just a good girl with bad habits."

Gram takes in a breath, turns, and is gone. We all go silent waiting for her to return.

Tree branches hover over the window in the kitchen, eerily scratching the glass whenever the wind blows hard. I look out the window just as a branch scrapes across the pane. I gaze out to the sea where whitecaps foam on the roiling swells all the way to the horizon. A pale blue lobster boat churns across the water of the bay as it heads back in. My heart feels leaden with despair and longing.

"Yoo-hoo, Logan," says Maxine, pulling me back. "Winnie and your mom are making your favourite food for your birthday dinner: chicken, French fries, corn on the cob, and coleslaw. That's one of my faves, too. I can hardly wait." She rubs her hands eagerly.

I smile at her. She's way more excited about it than me.

Gram walks into the room again. "Go ahead, Logan, open another gift."

I pick up the second smallest gift. It's from Audrey. I tear off the gold wrapping and find a DVD of the movie *Hitchcock*. I stifle a groan.

Audrey puffs away on her imaginary cigarette, smiling at me. "That's my latest movie, Logan. Sir Anthony Hopkins plays the male lead of Alfred

Hitchcock and I play the role of Hitchcock's wife, Alma Reville. I'm sure you'll enjoy it tremendously and agree with all my fans that so far it is, without a doubt, my best work."

"Um, thanks, Audrey," I say.

The tag on the next gift reads *To Brogan, Love Grace.* I open it and find three pairs of wool socks—one black, one grey, and one navy blue. They're so long they'll likely fit from my toes up to my knees. But I know Grace spent many hours knitting these for me, mostly because she can't help falling asleep every few minutes. Her gift touches my heart. I thank Grace, lean over, and give her a hug. She beams at me.

"The black socks will nicely match the boxers," notes Shaye with a lusty grin.

"Oh, Shaye, what am I going to do with you?" moans Gram, near tears by now.

"Make her go in her room," says Maxine, jealous over all the attention Shaye is getting. "You always threaten her, Winnie, but you never send her up. About time you started following through on your words, I think."

"I always threaten to move you to one of the upstairs bedrooms, Maxine," Gram replies.

Maxine laughs "Oh, don't be so foolish. I can't climb those stairs all day long. I'll have a coronary."

"I've decided to install a stair lift, Maxine," Gram tells her. "Someone from Monroe's Home Health Services will be here tomorrow morning to take a look and give me an estimate."

"But there's no extra bedroom up there!"

"You and Shaye will switch bedrooms," Gram tells her.

"No, Winnie!" Maxine says, horrified.

"Yes," Gram tells her sternly, then quickly looks at me and changes the subject. "Go ahead, open another one, sweetheart."

"Open mine next, Logan," Maxine says.

"No, Maxine. It's smallest to the biggest," Mom reminds her.

"Oh, who made up that stupid rule?"

"I did," says Mom patiently.

"Well, there are already too many rules in this house, if you ask me." Maxine gives Gram a hurt look. "On top of that, this place is nothing more than a glorified starvation camp. That's just one hungry woman's opinion."

"And there are too many females and not enough males in here, if you ask me," adds Shaye. "That's just one lonely woman's opinion."

"And is everyone in here completely mad?" puts in Audrey, shaking her head in frustration. "I mean, who is this Audrey Piper, and why do all of you insist on calling me by that name? It's dreadfully tiresome, I must say."

Gram briefly closes her eyes before reaching for the next gift, which is hers, and passes it to me. It's a Swiss Army multifunctional tool that has ten functions—three small jackknives, a bottle opener, scissors, two mini-pliers, two screwdrivers, and a compass. I love it. I give her a good long hug. Her eyes get all teary and she blows her nose when we're done. Mom is smiling but her eyes grow moist too.

Maxine's gift is next and it's awesome—a brand-new metallic blue fishing rod, and a fishing tackle box full of great lures and hooks. My heart speeds up just looking at it. Dad and I used to go trout-fishing in Alberta all the time.

"In case you miss fishing, which I think you do," Maxine tells me with a tender smile. "It's not like lobster fishing, Logan, I know. But it's fishing, right? And this is Nova Scotia, after all; there are plenty of brooks, rivers, and lakes to fish in."

I feel a lump in my throat. I nod and smile back at her, then get up give her a hug.

"Oh, stop that now," she says, but she hugs me back so hard that my ribs start to hurt.

Mom's gift is the best of all. It's a round-trip airplane ticket to Alberta for spring break in March. Mom tells me she already called Jared's mom, and they agreed I would stay there for the week.

I can't believe Mom did this for me. I can't believe that after all the lying I've been doing, she's allowing me to fly to Alberta alone, *and* trusting me to come back. I think of Jared and Keltie and can hardly wait. Lately, they haven't been keeping in contact as much. And Keltie's e-mails seem cooler somehow, like she's pulling away from me. I've been chalking it off to our long-distance relationship, but deep inside I have an uneasy feeling. I'm worried that I'm losing her. Now, though, I'll see her in person, and we'll feel close again, like we used to.

"Thanks, Mom. I love it." I give her a kiss on the cheek and the biggest hug of all.

"Just make sure you catch the return flight," she says, her eyes welling up.

"I will," I say, noticing Gram's eyes welling up too. Mom and Gram are both like that, one cries and instantly sets the other off. I've even seem them yawn like that. It's weird.

After supper, which was so good I ate more than anyone else, Mom lights the fourteen candles on my chocolate cake, which she and Gram made.

Maxine's eyes dart to the cake and then to me, pleading. "Would you be so kind as to cut me a slice of your cake, Logan?"

"No, Maxine!" Gram steps over to the fridge and reaches inside for a piece of chocolate cake she bought at the grocery store. She sets it down on the table in front of Maxine. "This is yours."

"What in blazes is that?" asks Maxine, horrified.

"It's low-fat, sugar-free chocolate cake."

Maxine's face collapses. "No, Winnie, come on. It's a special occasion. It's Logan's birthday. And just this once won't kill me."

"Your sugar levels have been running high all week. I'm sorry, Maxine, I can't chance it," Gram tells her.

"But I don't like that cake, Winnie. I've had it before and it has no flavour. It tastes like styrofoam. Besides, a little bit of sugar won't hurt me."

"A little bit of sugar will hurt you." Gram picks up her cup of coffee from the counter and sips from it, looking over the rim at Maxine and shaking her head.

Maxine turns her head away. She looks like she's going to cry.

My heart breaks. "Gram, come on," I say. "Can't we give Maxine just a tiny piece?" Maxine whips her head around, looking hopefully at Gram.

Gram watches me for a minute, then smiles. "All right. Just a sliver, though."

Maxine reaches out her hand and grabs mine, giving it a squeeze. "Thank you, Logan."

"Now, before we cut the cake, Logan has to make a wish and blow out the candles," Gram says. "While he does that, let's all sing Happy Birthday."

"Yes, let's," says Mom with a big, goofy smile on her face.

"No, let's don't," I say.

Mom and Gram ignore me.

Gram lifts her hands, waves them like a choirmaster, and leads them off. Five croaky old voices and Mom's sweet alto voice fill the kitchen and reverberate throughout the rooms of the old house.

I'm a little embarrassed, yet deep inside I like it. When they're finished, all six women laugh and clap their hands. Then, to my horror, they all get up from their chairs and surround me, each giving me a big hug. Shaye, the last, gives me a little pinch on the backside before Gram swats her hand away.

Later, as I climb the stairs to my room carrying my gifts, I have to admit that it wasn't a bad birthday party at all. In fact, I had a really nice time.

## Chapter 31

# LOGAN

On Thursday, I head straight home after school. When I step into the house, I hear subdued female voices coming from the kitchen, and one soft sob.

I hurry into the room and find Mom, Gram, Grace, Shaye, and Audrey all sitting at the kitchen table, holding hands, heads bowed in prayer.

"In Jesus' precious name, amen," says Gram as they all release hands and lift their heads.

Shaye and Audrey wipe at their eyes with a tissue.

"What's going on?" My eyes fall on the empty chair at the end of the table where Maxine always sits. "Where's Maxine?"

Mom lifts her head to look at me. "She's in the hospital, Logan."

"What happened?"

"Her blood sugar levels shot up so fast she had a stroke," Gram explains. "It happened shortly after you left for school this morning."

I think of the tiny piece of birthday cake I gave Maxine. I remember that she was eating a cookie this morning when she stood in the living room window waving goodbye. That's two mornings in a row I saw her do that. I feel a bit guilty. I shouldn't have given her any of my cake. I should have gone back in the house and taken the cookie from her this morning, or at least told Gram about it.

"Will she be all right?" I ask.

"Yes," Gram says. "I just got off the phone with her doctor. It was a mini-stroke, thankfully. They're going to keep her in the hospital for a few days until her sugar levels stabilize, to do more tests."

I feel like I might cry, so I drop my eyes to the floor fast. "Can we go see her?"

Mom notices and steps around the table. She softens her voice and puts her arm around my shoulders. "They're moving her out of the ICU and into her own private room later this afternoon. We can go up and visit after supper if you'd like."

"Oh, good," I say stupidly, and to my horror, tears fill my eyes. I don't know what's wrong with me. I'm usually a pro at holding my emotions in check. I drop into a chair, shoulders slumped, head down. "Yes, I would, of course." My voice cracks.

The five women all go silent. I can feel their eyes on me as they get up from their chairs and surround me. Five pairs of hands tenderly pat my shoulders, back, even the top of my head, while murmuring soft, soothing words. For once, Shaye leaves my backside alone.

At 6:30, Gram leads our small, forlorn group to the hospital. We follow her down the aisle toward the last room on the right-hand side. We stand just inside the room, staring at Maxine in the bed. She looks terrible. Her eyes are closed. Her face is bloated and white. Tubes protrude from every part of her body, including her nose. She's so still that she looks dead.

Gram is carrying a large bouquet of yellow roses. Yellow is Maxine's favourite colour, and yellow roses are her favourite flower. Shaye holds a pale yellow, vanilla-scented candle. The flowers and candle are from all of us. Audrey is wearing an ankle-length floral gown and silk scarf, both yellow, as if she's off to the Oscar's. Shaye's wearing blue jeans and a banana-yellow cotton top. Mom's wearing a butter silk blouse and black dress pants. Gram's wearing grey pants and a way too big, lemon cardigan that Grace knitted her. I'm wearing a white dress shirt with a yellow tie. Personally, I think we've gone overboard with the yellow thing.

A mournful sigh escapes Audrey's lips. A low moan comes from Grace, who's standing on my right. I hear a sniffle come from Shaye. I turn my head and see her pull a tissue from her purse and blow her nose. She passes the packet of tissues to Mom, who hands it down the row of women until it reaches me. I pass it back to Mom, shaking my head.

Hearing a noise behind me, I glance over my shoulder and see Cade standing in the open doorway, holding his own bouquet of yellow roses. He smiles at me, then enters the room and slips up beside Mom. He touches her arm gently, leans sideways, and whispers something in her ear. Mom smiles. Beams almost. I don't like how her face lights up when she sees him. I don't like how close he's standing to Mom, or how affectionate he is with her. But I do like that he thought to bring yellow roses for Maxine, so I let it go.

As we watch, Maxine's eyes flutter open and she coughs.

Gram steps over to the bed, sets the flowers on her nightstand, and takes Maxine's hand in hers. "How are you feeling, Maxine?"

"Not good," Maxine croaks. "Not good, not good at all, Winnie."

All the women rush over and stand around her bed.

Mom picks up a glass of water, puts a straw in it, and holds it to Maxine's mouth. "Here, have a drink of water."

Cade steps away to stand next to me. I shuffle from one foot to the other, not sure what to do. He shuffles from foot to foot too, then takes a step forward, lifting the flowers as if he's going to set them down on Maxine's nightstand. He then stops and steps back again. I don't know which of us is more uncomfortable.

"We brought you yellow roses and a scented candle," Shaye says, holding the candle under Maxine's nose. "Smell it. It's called vanilla ice."

Maxine sniffs the candle and her eyes go wide. "That smells good enough to eat."

Shaye quickly pulls it away and steps back, looking around for somewhere to hide the gift.

Gram motions to her and Shaye hands it over. Gram opens her big purse and slips it safely inside, murmuring, "What was I thinking?"

"Where's Logan?" Maxine rasps.

I step up to the bed between Mom and Audrey.

"Hi, Maxine," I say.

"Hi, Logan," Maxine says in a scratchy voice. "I'm glad you're here."

"I'm glad you're okay."

She takes my hand and hangs on tightly, smiling back at me. "That's a gorgeous tie you're wearing. I love yellow. It's my favourite colour, you know."

"I heard that," I say with a smile.

Cade sets the vase of flowers down on Maxine's nightstand.

Maxine smiles a bit weakly. "Thank you, Constable Stone."

"You're welcome, Maxine."

Shaye gives Cade a lusty wink. "For your information, *handsome,* my favourite flowers are pink carnations."

"Do you want to wait out in the hall for us?" Gram warns.

Shaye looks back at Cade. "I was wondering, do police officers have a photo calendar? You know, like the one firemen do every year to raise money for muscular dystrophy? Because if there is one, and your picture is in it, well, I would love to—"

"That's it!" Gram cuts her off, moving around the bed. "Let's go."

Maxine lifts a hand and waves it madly in the air. "Yoo-hoo, Winnie, I'm over here on the bed half-dead of hunger. Any chance I can something to eat before I fade away?"

Gram frowns. "I'm not sure, Maxine. I'll talk to the nurse." She gives my shoulder a warm squeeze on her way out of the room. "Shaye, come on."

"Atta girl," says Maxine with a happy grin.

Shaye follows Gram, then stops in the hallway, hands on her hips. "Where are all the hot doctors, anyway? Wow, this place sure isn't anything like *Grey's Anatomy*, I'll tell you that."

"Never mind," Gram says to her. "Go back in the room and wait for me."

"Well, make up your mind, woman." And then, a split second later: "Oh my, who is this?" With that, she takes off down the hall.

Grace walks around the bed and sits in a chair under the window. Her eyes close. Audrey turns on the flat-screen television on the wall, searching for one of her movies so we can all watch her in it.

Cade and Mom step back in one corner of the room, talking softly together, oblivious to the rest of us. I frown. Things seem to be changing between them; they're getting awfully affectionate with each other, and I'm not exactly sure when that happened.

It's all too much. I decide to flee, when Maxine, still clasping my hand, looks at me and nods to a chair. "Will you sit with me for a while, Logan? Please?"

I want to bolt so bad that I open my mouth to tell her I need to leave, but the look in her eyes moves my heart, and I change my mind.

"Sure, Maxine," I say gently, reaching back with my foot, hooking the chair, and dragging it up behind me.

## Chapter 32

# OLIVIA

We all file silently into the house. I go into the kitchen with Cade. Mom takes Shaye, Audrey, and Grace upstairs to get them ready for bed. Logan follows them up, pretending he's not really helping my mother with the women.

I pick up the kettle from the stove and fill it with water at the sink for tea. Cade leans back against the pantry door, loosening his tie.

"Logan seems to be growing closer to Maxine and the others," he notes.

I smile sadly. "He is, I know, and that's good. But he's still so remote, so quiet. Don't you find?"

Cade shrugs. "He is quiet, but I get the feeling he's a naturally quiet, serious boy. And he's mourning the loss of his father. Though I've noticed he wears his grief like body armour. Keeps people away."

"Yes, his dad's death has hit him so hard. The day they came to tell us Luc had died, when neighbours began arriving with food, Logan went down to the basement and stayed down there for hours. He didn't come back up until everyone had left. He changed after that, grew even quieter. He doesn't say much to me or even his grandmother now. And he always has this distant look in his eyes. He seems to have sunk deeper into himself."

Cade nods thoughtfully. "Well, that's understandable."

"Maybe, but it's hard. I feel like I've lost both my husband and son."

"That's understandable too."

When the water's boiled, I make the tea and pass Cade a cup.

"Thanks, Olivia," he says as we sit down at the table.

I sip my tea, studying him. He still has that quality of containment, that inner confidence I always found attractive. His deep blue eyes are serious, yet at the same time they reveal a kind, gentle heart. Once again, it strikes me that I've never stopped loving Cade. I remember the day I broke up with him and chose Luc instead. And I wonder how he can sit here with such love in his eyes for me.

"He'll be okay, Olivia," Cade says, drawing me back from my memories.

I turn my cup around and draw a quiet breath. "I don't know, Cade. He's so angry at God, it scares me. He refuses to go to youth group or church. In Cold Lake, he never missed church or his Friday night youth group."

"Well, he's young, and death is a tough thing for an adult to understand, let alone a boy. He'll come back to God, Olivia. I've been praying for both of you."

I allow a small smile. "Thank you, especially for praying for Logan. We pray for him every morning here. If he knew that, he'd probably run away."

Cade laughs softly.

"He may fool others, but I'm his mom. I can see through him, see that he's hurting so badly inside."

"Like so many of us are, Olivia," he says very gently.

I feel my cheeks flush. I see the sorrow in his eyes and remember that he too suffered a terrible loss. "I'm sorry about Bridget, Cade."

"Oh, but I didn't mean that. I meant you, with Luc."

I nod. "But you're suffered a terrible loss too."

"So you heard about it?"

I nod sympathetically. "Yes, I was in Alberta when it happened. Mom called and told me."

A wall of grief crosses Cade's face. "It was almost four years ago now, but I remember every mind-numbing detail as if it happened yesterday." He draws a breath. "We were out snowmobiling on the Cutter River one night in February. Bridget was driving her own machine and was leading. I was right behind her. We hit a pressure crack in the ice and our snowmobiles plunged into the water. I surfaced, and she did too, but only for a second or two." Cade's voice cracks badly and he pauses to take a breath. "I saw her go under and tried to grab her, but the undertow was too fast. It dragged her beneath the ice as soon as she hit the water and she was swept out into the bay."

"Oh, Cade, that's terrible. I'm so sorry." I reach out and touch his hand.

He nods and drops his head, staring at the floor. "It was my fault, Olivia."

I shake my head, dismissing that. "Cade, no. I know you did everything you could to save her."

He shakes his head. "It doesn't feel like I did enough. You know, being her big brother, I always looked out for her, always protected her."

I move my hand up to his arm and give it a tender squeeze. "That's just survivor's guilt talking. Mom told me you stayed in the water so long trying to find her that you suffered severe exposure and lost a toe."

Cade looks up, lifting a shoulder morosely.

"Mom also said you would have died if the rescuers hadn't forcefully dragged you out of the water. She said you fought them the whole time. You have nothing to feel guilty about."

"Yes, I do. It was the middle of winter, and usually the ice over the river is frozen solid by then. I thought it was safe to drive on. I should have known better than to trust the ice, the way the winters have been getting so mild," he says, letting out a soft breath. "The ice is so much less predictable now than when we were teenagers, Olivia."

My heart goes out to him. As grief-stricken as I am, at least I didn't see Luc's plane go down. I didn't see him die. I understand that it had to have been a horrendous thing for Cade to see his sister, his only sibling, die right in front of him and be helpless to save her.

Cade's eyes grow moist. "We didn't find Bridget's body until June. All those months to wait, no body, no funeral, watching my parents mourn her loss. It was the worst thing I've ever gone through."

We hold each other's gaze. I feel that familiar intense connection that has always both thrilled and calmed me. It pulls me to him. It's all I can do to stay seated in my chair; I want to reach out and embrace him. I always felt drawn to him, always felt that melding of our souls.

Cade clears his throat, lifting his cup to his mouth. He drains his tea and sets the empty cup down on the counter. "It's getting late. I should get going," he says, his voice slightly hoarse.

I nod, smile.

He smiles, doesn't move.

And then he leans toward me, I lean toward him, and we kiss softly.

He pulls his head back, running a finger down my cheek. "Good night, Olivia."

"Good night," I say, heart thumping in my chest.

After Cade leaves, I put our cups in the dishwasher, then start across the room to shut off the light and go up to bed.

Logan enters the kitchen, eyeing me angrily. "I saw you guys kissing, Mom," he blurts.

"You did? Oh, yes, ah…" I let my voice trail off, not sure what to say.

"I can't believe you kissed him."

I'm quiet for a moment. "I'm sorry, Logan," I say finally, gently.

His face is half-wounded, half-angry. "How could you? Didn't you love Dad?"

"Of course I loved your dad. It's just—"

He looks at me imploringly. "It's just what, Mom?"

I let out a small breath. "It's just that Cade was... is..."

"Yeah, whatever, Mom. I don't think I want to hear this." His face white with anger, disbelief.

"Logan, please try to understand."

"Dad hasn't even been dead a year, and you're kissing another man? And you want me to understand that?"

"I don't know what to tell you other than that I'm sorry."

He shakes his head hard, spins around, and storms out of the room.

"Logan," I call out again, but he's pounding up the stairway to his room.

His door slams so hard behind him that it sounds like a gunshot.

## Chapter 33

# LOGAN

I'm leaning against the side wall of the picnic shelter at Puffin Point. I'm there because last night, after getting home from the hospital, I went online to email Keltie, to tell her about Maxine. I found two emails in my inbox. One was from Keltie, another from Jared. Shockingly, Keltie wrote to tell me she's breaking up with me, that she and Jared are dating. It feels like someone has hit me in the chest with a sledgehammer. Keltie's words were so excruciatingly painful that I moaned aloud in my room.

I didn't bother reading Jared's email. I just deleted it and shut down my computer. A flaming rush of hurt and anger for the both of them went through me. I opened my desk drawer, pulled out the airline ticket Mom bought me, ripped it up into a hundred tiny pieces, and threw them up into the air. They're still there, scattered all over my bedroom floor.

My severely broken heart, my anger at Mom, and the call of the sea all prove too much for me. So here I am, at 3:00 a.m., waiting for Crocker. The chill fog carries the sharp tang of the sea. It's as thick as a grey blanket settling over the trees and road, shrouding all in eerie silence. It reminds me of winter days in Alberta when a heavy snowfall came down, smothering the prairie in solemnity.

The picnic table in the middle of the shelter is too covered with dew to sit on. Even standing in the relative dryness of the shelter's wall, my hair and clothing are damp and I shiver. I shuffle my feet, wrap my arms around my chest, and tuck my hands under my armpits in a losing attempt to stay warm.

I can't stop yawning as I watch the road for the headlights of Crocker's pickup truck to break through the fog. I tossed and turned all night. Keltie's and Jared's shocking betrayal and the image of Mom and Cade kissing whirled around and around in my mind.

I squint and try harder to see through the mist, but I know I'll hear Crocker's truck coming long before I ever see it. Earlier, a taxi burst out of the fog and took me by complete surprise. I had to duck fast behind the wall of the shelter, but I doubt the driver would have seen me through the thick fog.

I hear the roar of an engine and Crocker's pickup bursts out of the murkiness. I jump in and we take off with a squeal. Crocker's smoking a cigarette, so I roll down the window to let out the smoke. Ice cold air flows into the cab.

"Roll that window up. It's freezing," says Crocker, taking a last drag of the cigarette before cracking his window and flicking it out. But he's speeding and the strong wind blows the butt back into the cab. It lands on his lap.

He cries out, takes one hand off the wheel, and reaches down for it, but it rolls under him. He lifts his bottom and pats the seat under him for the burning cigarette. As he's looking down, the pickup crosses the yellow line into the other lane.

"Crocker," I warn him.

He looks up, yanks the wheel to the right, and puts us back in the correct lane. He still can't find the cigarette and the harsh smell of burning fabric fills the cab. He frantically sweeps the seat beneath him with his hand. "Where is that stupid thing?"

I lean sideways, looking for the burning ember.

Crocker screams and shakes his hand in the air. "Ow, I burned my thumb." The cigarette, the end glowing hot red, flies through the air and lands on the floor at his feet. He reaches for it and the truck swerves across the yellow line again. Suddenly, the headlights of an approaching car shine through the fog. We're moving fast, in the wrong lane, straight for it.

"Crocker, watch out!" I yell, pointing out the windshield.

Crocker, his eyes on the floor and hand carelessly on the wheel, lifts his head and looks out the windshield, "What the—"

The car bears down, its headlights filling the cab, blinding us.

Crocker wrenches the wheel to the right, but the other driver, trying to avoid a head-on collision, yanks his wheel to his left to go around us.

"No, you idiot!" Crocker screams and hauls the wheel even further left.

It's not enough. We sideswipe the vehicle—a small white car, some kind of foreign make. The impact sends the car careening wildly back and forth from one lane to the other.

Crocker slams on the brakes and the truck's rear-end fishtails. He grips the wheel tightly and the truck screeches to a halt, tires burning black stripes on the asphalt. We turn and watch in horror as the white car skids off the road and onto the gravel shoulder. The passenger side of the car makes contact with the steel guardrail and orange sparks leap into the air. I roll down my window and hear a hair-raising screech as metal grazes metal.

The car and guardrail scrape together for a good ten yards. The driver fights to keep his car on the road, but his efforts are futile. The car's right side lifts up, sails over the railing, and is suddenly, horribly, airborne. It soars through the air, tires spinning and engine still roaring. The car seems to stop, suspended in the air over the rocky seawall for a few seconds. Then it drops, smashing on its wheels onto the large boulders. The sound of the violent impact and the shattering of glass explodes in the early-morning air.

Through the fog, I can just make out the car sliding slowly down the slippery slope of rocks toward the water. I watch, horror-struck, as the headlights begin to slip into the sea.

I open my door a little. I hear, at first, the hiss and sputter of the hot engine as it enters the water. Over that, a terrified scream comes from the car, and then it fades to soft whimpers and then silence. I throw open the door and leap out.

"Logan!" Crocker shouts, grabbing my arm.

"Let go, Crocker!"

His hand locks around my forearm. "Get back in here!"

"No, let go!" I try wrenching my arm free of his grip. With brute force, he tries to pull me back into the cab. I drag my feet on the asphalt, still yanking, struggling to get free. "Let me go, Crocker," I say breathlessly.

He clamps down harder on my arm. I'm sure his nails are slicing right through my clothing to my skin. I hear him grunt as he leans across the seat and reaches for me with his left hand.

I lift my foot and kick his hand away. This startles him and his right hand loosens on my arm. I rip it free, sprint across the road, and clamber over the guardrail. My heart pumps erratically as I make my way down the rocky seawall to the car. I slip and fall twice on the slimy rocks.

The hissing sound of its engine and the smell of steam fill the air around the car. All its windows are shattered. The back bumper has been torn free and is lying on the rocks behind the car.

I reach the driver's side door and look in through the broken window. The driver, a tall blond man, is slumped forward over the steering wheel. He's wearing a white cotton shirt peppered with dark spots at the collar that must be blood. He looks dead.

I take a deep breath, reach in, and gently shake him. "Mister, are you okay?" He releases a low moan.

*Good. Unconscious, not dead,* I think. I shake him again, but there's no response at all this time.

I yank on the door handle, but the door's jammed shut. I brace one foot on the rocker panel and pull for all I'm worth as the car continues its descent into the cold black water. It won't open.

"Logan!" Crocker's voice carries down to the car.

I look back up to the road. Under a streetlight, I see Crocker standing on the gravel shoulder. I reach in my pocket for my cell phone, but then remember that Mom has it.

"Crocker, the driver's hurt. He's unconscious. Call 911!"

"No, leave him and get up here now," Crocker says coldly.

I freeze, utterly confused. "What?"

"I have to get out of here. I had a few sips from my flask on the drive. I'll blow over the limit. I'll lose my licence, go to jail. I can't have that happen."

"What? We can't just leave him here," I protest.

"Is he alive?"

"Yes."

"Then he'll be fine. Come on. Get your butt up here, now."

"Are you crazy? No way. I have to get him out. The car's falling into the water."

I lean inside the broken driver's side window and unbuckle the man's seatbelt. I slide my hands under his arms and try to lift him up and out through the window. But he's a big guy and limp, and I only lift him an inch or so off the seat before I drop him again. He moans, but doesn't regain consciousness.

The underside of the car screeches a bit over the rocks. The bumper is almost completely underwater now. Panic sends blood rushing to my head with such force that a vein throbs sharply in my forehead. I pull with all my strength, but he's deadweight. Too heavy for me.

"Crocker, hurry up, come down here. I need a hand!"

"Logan, listen to me," Crocker bellows back. "I can't go to jail. I have a wife and two kids to support. He's alive, and the car will get hung up on the rocks. I'll call the EMTs and the cops once we get down the road a ways. Leave him and get up here."

"No!" I yell at him, shocked. "Come down here and give me a hand."

"Logan, don't do this to me! Don't be responsible for me going to jail, for my family ending up on the street."

Despite Crocker's obvious attempt at manipulation, I look at the driver more closely. He's got a huge lump and a gash on his forehead, but his pulse is strong and he's breathing. Still, I don't know how bad his head injury is, and the car is inching further into the sea with every passing second. I can't leave him. I won't leave him.

Suddenly, I gasp as Crocker's wraps a hand around my neck, the other around my arm. He squeezes, cutting off my words and my wind, dragging me back up the embankment.

"Now why won't you ever listen to me? I said he'll be fine, okay? I'll call the EMTs as soon as we get down the road some."

"Let me go," I try to shout, but my words are choked off by his grip around my neck. I kick and fight, but the rocks are slippery and he's got me from behind, pulling me up and over the boulders. I struggle to free myself, but it's futile. He's just too strong.

"Calm down," he whispers in my ear.

I can't say another word. I'm trying to concentrate on breathing.

Then, in what seems like no time at all, we're at the top. My jacket and jeans are soaked from the slimy rocks and fog. An icy gust of wind kicks up and cuts through my wet clothing. I feel the cold, rigid stub of his pinkie against my throat and it gives me the creeps.

"Let go of me," I sputter.

"Quit fighting me." He maintains his hold on my neck, using his free hand to grab my arm. I drag my feet on the roadway, trying to free myself from his crushing grip.

We reach his pickup truck and the driver's side door is open.

"Man, you're shivering. Come on. Let's get you in the truck before you catch your death of cold." He grabs my belt and hoists me up, giving me a firm shove so that I tumble past the steering wheel over to the passenger side.

He quickly vaults in behind me, making sure I don't throw open the passenger door and bolt. He puts the stick shift in gear and stomps on the gas. We peel away from the accident scene, tires squealing, veering back and forth over the yellow line.

Crocker leans over as he steers and turns the heater up full-blast. Then, unbelievably, he starts whistling some tune I don't recognize.

I straighten up in the seat, trying to get my breath.

"Crocker?" I say in a raspy voice.

"What?"

I massage my throat. "Call the EMTs."

"Can't do it," he says without taking his eyes off the road. "I'm driving right now."

I hold out my hand. "Give me your cell phone and I'll call them."

"No use. The battery's dead. "We'll have to wait till we get to the boat and call them on the CB."

"We can't wait that long!" I shout in disbelief. "He may not have that much time."

"You said he was alive and breathing."

"I don't know how seriously he's hurt, but I do know that shock can kill someone pretty fast. Besides, the car is disappearing into the water. Turn around and go back."

"No."

"Crocker, he'll die if we don't go back!"

He glances at me with a cold half-smile on his lips. "That's how it goes sometimes, Logan. Life's tough. You should know that."

I lurch against the seat like he's just kicked me in the teeth. By now, his cold indifference shouldn't shock me. But it does. As cold as he is, I didn't expect this kind of callousness. I believed he would call for help. Too late, I realize I should have trusted my instincts.

"Crocker, you gave me your word."

He shifts his eyes from the road to me, his expression slightly amused. "Oh, come on, you didn't really believe me, did you?"

I stare at him, speechless. Things are escalating too fast— cutting lines, poaching lobster, throwing the body back in the sea, now a hit and run. I can't keep my lies straight anymore. I've lost my dad, Keltie, and Jared. I feel disconnected from God, Mom, and Gram, from everyone and everything. I doubt my life can get any worse.

I slump against the door, staring vacantly out the windshield. I feel dead inside.

## Chapter 34

# LOGAN

Crocker's at the helm. I stand stiffly beside him, watching the waves smash into the hull, sending a wall of white spray up over the bow. It's cold, below freezing. The skies are cloudy, the seas churning. A stiff wind blows from the northeast and large whitecaps glisten on the water under the boat's running lights.

I pick up my mug and take a gulp of hot, acidic coffee. It burns all the way down to my already churning stomach. Crocker and I haven't spoken since we came aboard, him dragging me out of his truck and onto the *Sea Predator*. The tension between us is electric, more responsible for my roiling stomach than the coffee. It's nearly a ninety-minute trip to the fishing grounds, but today, in the strained silence, it's going to seem a lot longer.

"Rough seas today," Crocker says, breaking the silence.

I ignore him. I keep my eyes straight ahead, my expression sullen.

"I hear poor old Maxine nearly ate herself to death."

Anger fills me. I turn my head and glare at him. "She did not."

He waggles his eyebrows, laughter in his eyes. "Well, she's in the hospital, isn't she?"

"Yes, but she had a stroke. She's a brittle diabetic and her sugar levels run too high."

"Sure she is," he laughs.

"Just shut up about it, Crocker," I shout, clenching one fist.

He stops laughing and stares at me. I return his stare with a cold one of my own, making it clear I don't want to talk to him.

He shifts his eyes back to the windshield and curses under his breath. He rams the throttle to full speed and we ride swiftly down a wave.

The engine roars and vibrates under my feet. The bow of the boat heaves up on the waves, then plunges fast. I reach out and grab the edge of the dashboard to stay on my feet. The waves ram the hull with more force than I've ever experienced. A high spray of white water explodes over the bow each time the boat drops. At other times, the boat cants sharply from one side to the other. When it tilts to the port side, it dips down so low that green foaming water splashes over the rail. This would normally make my heart pound, filling me with excitement, but he's really pushing the boat today. It's a bone-rattling, heart-stopping trip out to the grounds.

For the entire trip, Crocker stares fixedly out the windshield, ominously quiet. He's fuming because I told him to shut up. When we finally reach the grounds, he kills the engine and we bob on the surface.

"All right," he growls, not looking at me. "Let's get to work."

I watch him walk out of the wheelhouse, not wanting to follow. But it's not like I have much choice. I go out on deck, vowing that this is my last day working for Crocker. Before I pull on my rubber gloves, I finger Cade's card in my jeans pocket. I decide to go to his office as soon as we get back in today and tell him about the hit and run. Crocker may have dragged me away from the accident scene and forced me onto his boat, but once I'm on the wharf I'll do what's right. I won't let him have any more control over me.

The white plumes of our breath spiral from our mouths into the freezing air. I work in sullen silence, not saying a word. Crocker keeps trying to get me to talk, and when I don't say anything, he just whistles song after song.

I'm repulsed by his whistling, sickened that he can fish with no emotion after the hit and run. He doesn't know if the car sank with the driver trapped inside it. He has no idea if the driver is dead or alive, yet shows no more concern for the man than if he had run over an empty can on the road.

At noon, we're getting ready to take a lunch break when Crocker, coiling a line around his forearm, glances at me over his shoulder. He smiles, a mirthless smile. "Another thing I heard was that your mom's seeing Cade Stone."

I pay no attention to him. I don't care about that right now. I'm worried sick about the driver of the car. I'm still furious with Crocker for dragging me away, not calling the EMTs.

Crocker clears his throat loudly and spits over the side. "The talk in town is that they were in Lucky's sitting all cosy in a booth. Heard they even kissed."

My hands tremble as I too coil a thick rope and hang it on a hook on the back of the wheelhouse wall. I pretend it doesn't bother me. "He seems okay," I say casually, wanting to rankle Crocker, knowing my words will do just that.

Crocker gapes at me. "He seems okay? Are you nuts? It's a bad idea, if you ask me."

"No one asked you," I say, keeping my back to him.

"Look, I know you're ticked about the accident thing, but you need to listen to me about this. I'm only thinking of your mom. You don't want him around her."

"The accident thing? That's what you call it?" I say through gritted teeth.

"Look, I'm trying to warn you here, so listen to me. Keep Cade Stone away from your mom. That man is a stone-cold killer."

I turn around and face him. "What are you talking about?"

Crocker sits down on an empty milk crate and yanks his gloves off. "I'm talking about the night a few years ago when he and his sister were snowmobiling on the Cutter River and went through the ice. A friend of mine, Joe Bouvier, was out there on his snowmobile too. He heard them screaming for help. When he got there, he lit them up with his headlight. And guess what he saw?"

"What?"

"Cade Stone standing above the waterline from the waist up, waving his arms for help." Crocker narrows his eyes and points a thick finger at me. "Think about it."

I frown. "I don't get it."

"Stone was standing on his sister's head!"

"No," I say in disbelief.

"Yes, Joe swears it's true. Stone and his sister were treading freezing water for almost twenty minutes before he got there. Joe thinks Stone's sister was too exhausted to stay afloat, and when she sank under the water, Stone climbed on her head. That's the only possible way he'd be visible above the waterline from the waist up. Our big, brave constable stood on his own sister's head to save himself."

I feel my body stiffen. I can't believe it. "Maybe it was an accident. It was dark. Maybe he didn't see her go under. In his panic, he may not have even realized he was standing on her head. If he was…"

Crocker snorts. "That coward knew exactly what he was doing. He saw her go under and he stepped on her head to keep himself up long enough for Joe to pick him out with his headlight. Once Joe got to him, Cade sank back down until just his head was above the waterline. I'm not making it up. Joe swears that's what happened."

I don't know what to believe. I stay silent.

"The man's a rotten coward." Crocker stands and kicks the milk crate into a corner. "I've seen the way he acts around your mom, seen the way he looks at her. I didn't want to tell you this, but I saw him kissing her myself the other day on the sidewalk in front of the library. Out in public like that. It makes me sick, so I can just imagine how you feel."

What I feel is shocked, confused. I don't know Cade well, but he doesn't strike me as stupid or cowardly. He seems mild-mannered, but once you get to know him you realize that all that outer mildness belies an inner toughness and quick, sharp-edged mind. In fact, with his kind, steady way, he reminds me a lot of my dad. But I do hate how he and Mom act so intimately in front of everyone when they're together. Kissing in front of everyone on the sidewalk in town? The thought mortifies me.

"You don't want the likes of him around your mom, Logan. You should keep him away from her."

I don't respond. I'm pretty sure it's too late for that.

"By the way, I called my wife, and she called a friend of hers who's a nurse at the town hospital. The guy we hit is there now. Two guys pulled him out of the car before it went into the bay. He's banged up pretty good, but he's fine. He's going to be released tonight."

The guy *we* hit? "No thanks to us, Crocker."

"What? I told you he'd be fine, and he is."

I stare at him dubiously.

"I swear. The guy's fine. There's nothing to worry about." Crocker drapes his arm affectionately around my shoulder. "We're cool again, aren't we, Logan?"

I just shrug his arm off. The man is remorseless.

## Chapter 35

# CADE

"That poor driver," Austin says. "It's a miracle he wasn't killed."

I take my eyes off the crushed remains of the car and look at the young constable. He's shaking his head solemnly at the terrible scene in front of us.

"It is," I say quietly.

The car has been winched up out of the water and now rests on the right lane of the Lighthouse Road. The front door is horribly twisted. All the windows are shattered, the front tires are flat. Seawater drips from the sides of the car onto the road with a steady *plopping* sound that echoes into the night and raises the hair on the back of my neck. On the other side of the guardrail, glass litters the seawall. A crumpled bumper lies on top of a large grey boulder, half of it submerged in the bay. To my right, four members of Shipwreck Cove's Fire Department sombrely pack up their equipment.

The scene is chilling. Besides the fire engines, three town police cruisers are parked along both shoulders of the road, their emergency lights revolving, lighting up the trees and bushes along the two-lane highway. Flares burn on the road just before and after the accident scene. Thick black skid marks on the southbound side veer over to the broken railing.

Some time after the accident, a car with two fishermen pulled up. The men removed the unconscious driver from his car only moments before it was completely submerged. Considering the extent of the damage, he's lucky to be alive. Moments ago, I spoke with the emergency room doctor and he informed me that the driver briefly regained consciousness. He isn't able to remember much other than that a dark pickup truck, driving in the wrong line, sideswiped him. He has a concussion, two broken ribs, and a badly fractured left femur.

Using our halogen flashlights, Austin and I search the area meticulously. We find deep gouges in the dirt shoulder of the road, scrapes in the metal railing where the car grazed along it for a short distance, and then nothing more where it rocketed over the railing. From that, the victim's story, and the black paint on the driver's side fender, we know the driver of the pickup crossed into the opposite lane and sideswiped the Honda, sending the car off the road, over the railing, and nearly into the sea.

What I find so disturbing, what angers me, is that that after hitting the car, it appears the pickup driver stopped. Footprints lead down the seawall near where the car slammed into the ground, and they don't belong to the two fishermen who rescued the driver. Those footprints give clear evidence that the driver and another person clambered down the rocks to the Honda. Shockingly, they left the driver in his car as it slowly dipped beneath the waves, then jumped back into the truck and fled the scene.

Cold winter fog surrounds us, so damp and dense that I feel like I could grab a fistful of it. When I reach out to touch it, my hand slips right through it and water droplets cover my palm. I walk over to the car again and lean inside, probing the seats and floor with the beam of my flashlight. I clamber down the rocks of the seawall again to the spot where the car first hit the ground. I aim the beam between the large boulders, study the footprints more closely, then spot drag marks. Frowning, I follow them as they go back up the embankment. I even spot something reflecting on the sand between two big rocks. I reach down and pick it up, holding it in front of my flashlight beam. I let out a long, grim breath.

It's a stainless steel liquor flask, and engraved on the front are the initials *M.C.C.*

## Chapter 36

# LOGAN

I stop dead in my tracks. I can't believe what I've just heard. In the kitchen, a few seconds ago, Cade told Mom that there was a hit and run on the Lighthouse Road last night. He told her that a vehicle travelling eastbound collided with a small car driving in the opposite lane. The driver of the car that was hit was found unconscious and unresponsive. He was rushed to the hospital, had surgery, and is now recovering in the ICU.

I lean against the wall next to the open kitchen door. Crocker lied to me again. He made up that whole story about his wife and the nurse. I recall the words from Proverbs 17:4—*"A wicked man listens to evil lips; a liar pays attention to a malicious tongue."* I clench my jaw, shake my head. I can't believe I trusted him again. I should never have believed him.

"I was just about to have a cup of tea. Would you like one, Cade?" says Mom.

"No thanks, Olivia, I don't have time."

"All right," says Mom. I hear a trace of puzzlement in her voice. She's wondering why Cade stopped in to tell her this.

I lean forward and hear him tell her that the driver of the Honda was on his way home from his job as a night shift manager at the local McDonald's. He suffered a fractured skull, four broken ribs, and a fractured left femur. Cade adds that it could have been much worse. The driver could have died, but thankfully two fishermen came upon the scene, stopped, and pulled him out of the car only seconds before it sank.

"Who would do something like that?" Mom says, shocked. "Take off after hitting another car, especially when the car they hit is slipping into the sea?"

Cade clears his throat, but doesn't answer.

"The cold-heartedness of such an act, I find it incomprehensible," says Mom.

"I know. I feel the same way."

Mom pours a cup of tea and sits back. I hear the ping of her spoon hitting the side of her cup. "You didn't come here just to tell me about the accident. And you seem so troubled by it. What's going on?"

Their voices drop. As quietly as possible, I move nearer to the open door. I hold my breath, listening hard. I still can't make out what they're saying. I move my head a quarter-inch and peek into the room.

Cade lifts his hands and rubs his face hard before beginning to speak. My blood freezes as I hear Cade tell Mom that he found a stainless steel liquor flask at the scene with the initials *M. C. C.* engraved on it.

I pull my head back, paralyzed in the hall, a ball of ice in the pit of my stomach. Crocker's full name is Macklin Charles Crocker and he owns a silver liquor flask just like that. He showed it to me the first day we went out fishing, said it was a birthday gift from his wife. I know he keeps it in his jacket pocket. It must have fallen out when he was dragging me up the seawall to the road.

Cade goes on. "With the tides that night, we know it could only have fallen there around the time of the accident. Any earlier, any later, and it would have been washed out to sea. Also, we found black paint on the driver's side door and front fender of the car, a white Honda Civic. The paint was high up on the Honda, so we're sure it was a black pickup or SUV that struck it."

"So someone who drives a black pickup and owns a liquor flask with the initials *M.C.C.* was the driver who hit the car and fled," Mom says, going suddenly quiet. I hear her set her teacup down on the table.

"Yes," says Cade. "Mack Crocker's middle name is Charles, and he drives a black pickup truck, Olivia. I know he owns a silver liquor flask with his initials on it. I've arrested him many times over the years and have taken it from him every time I booked him."

I'm panic-stricken, torn. I want to bolt, I want to hear more. I take in a quiet breath to slow my heart, cock my head, and listen more intently.

I hear Mom draw a breath. "Cade, what aren't you telling me?"

"We also found two sets of footprints at the scene, right in front of the driver's door of the Honda. One print is a size eleven boot and the other's a size eight running shoe."

My throat goes bone dry. This is getting worse by the second. I slip my head around the door a little and look in the kitchen. Mom is shaking her head back and forth at Cade.

Cade covers her hand with his. "We think it belongs to a small man or a young person, more likely a teenage boy."

168

I'm numb with horror. Crocker wears a size eleven boot, and I wear a size eight running shoe. Those are our footprints on the wet sand between the boulders. I can't hear their voices anymore over the thundering of my own heartbeat. I lean forward and hold my breath to hear better over my pounding pulse.

Mom's staring at Cade. "I know what you're thinking, Cade, and you're wrong. It wasn't Logan. I know my son. He would never leave the scene of a hit and run. It was someone else with Crocker, it had to be."

Cade's face fills with love and compassion. "He's the only teenage boy who's been working for Crocker."

Mom pulls her hand free, shaking her head vehemently. "No, you're wrong. Crocker must have hired another boy. Logan went to school today."

"Was he home when you got up this morning?"

"No, but he told me he was leaving early to go over to Shane Orson's house first and they'd walk to school together from there."

"Olivia, I need to talk to Logan."

"Fine," Mom says, voice trembling. "He should be home any minute now. You can ask him yourself. I know Logan has lied, has skipped school to go fishing with Crocker, but that's over, in the past. He gave me his word he was going to school today."

Cade once again takes Mom's hand in his and tenderly caresses it with his thumb. "Olivia, I called the school and spoke to the principal. I'm sorry, but Logan didn't go to school today."

Mom emits a harsh noise, a half-gasp, half-cry. Her shoulders collapse and her face goes the colour of yellow wax.

"Oh Olivia," says Cade, his voice breaking.

Tears spill down Mom's cheeks. "No, don't tell me that, Cade, don't."

Cade puts his arm around her shoulder. "I'm so sorry, Olivia."

My stomach wrenches. It's clear they are deeply in love, always have been.

I lean against the wall and close my eyes. I hear them talking, softer now, and I can't make out their words. But it doesn't matter. Cade's going to arrest me. He only came here first as a kindness to Mom, to tell her what I've done as gently as he can, because he loves her.

"Olivia, there's more and it's—"

The furnace kicks on with a rumble and warm air pours out of the vent beneath my feet. I can't hear a thing Cade says.

I should have gone straight to the police department when I left the wharf a half-hour ago, but instead I got scared and came home. Now it's too late. Cade will never believe that Crocker dragged me away from the accident scene and onto his boat.

I hear a noise behind me and turn. Gram's standing there, arms folded over her chest. My face burns with shame. My lower back is slick with nervous sweat.

"Logan, what's going on?" she asks.

"Nothing, Gram."

"Are you in some kind of trouble?"

"No," I say in a low voice so Mom and Cade won't hear me.

She cups her chin in her hand, watching me silently for a moment. "It takes bravery to tell the truth, sweetheart," she says, gently but seriously. "Only a coward lies."

Her words slay me, but I keep my face blank. "I know that, Gram," I whisper.

"Sweetheart, I want you to think about something your grandfather used to say. The sea is unforgiving, but God is all-forgiving. Do you understand?"

I nod. "Yes, Gram."

She watches me for what seems like an eternity, her eyes tender. Then she exhales a slow, sorrowful sigh. She turns and goes back into the living room without another word.

I hear the biting December winds howl and beat against the walls of the house as though in accusation. *Liar, liar, liar. Coward, coward, coward.*

I slink up the stairs and into my bedroom. I sit on the edge of my bed for a moment, trying to think. What to do, what to do. I reach out and turn my dad's photo facedown. I can't bear to look at him. It doesn't help. I pick it up and open the top drawer of my nightstand, ready to set it in there out of sight.

Then I see my Bible in the drawer. I feel a sharp pang in my heart and let out a sob. I set dad's picture back on the top of the nightstand and pick up my Bible. It falls open to a passage from Luke I underlined last year during a devotional at youth group. It's about the slippery slope a Christian can find himself on when he turns his back against God. I don't feel like I'm sliding down a slope; I'm rocketing down one. First I was a liar, then a thief, and now a criminal. Cade's going to arrest me and put me in jail. Part of me wants so badly to fall to my knees beside my bed. I yearn to be alone, quiet, with God. But I can't seem to do it, for in my heart lies a cold, hard stone. I believe my dad cried and prayed out to God as his jet plummeted to the ground. And did God help him? No! I can't pray to this same God. I just can't!

This will be too much for Mom and Gram to bear. It's better if I'm gone and out of their lives. I toss my Bible back in the drawer and take in a shuddering breath. Steeling my shoulders, I go to my closet and grab my gym bag. I pull out clothing from my dresser and stuff it in the bag along with the cash I've made working for Crocker.

I quietly descend the stairs, stopping at the bottom. Cade is still in the kitchen with Mom. Gram's in the living room with the others. There's no way I can walk through the hallway without being seen, so I turn right and go past Maxine's bedroom. I slip out the back way and shut the door silently behind me.

## Chapter 37

# LOGAN

"Cade found your flask by the Honda. I heard him tell Mom it was on the sand between two boulders, right next to the driver's side door."

Crocker makes a fist and slams it down on his thigh. "No, no! I knew I lost it, but I figured it was in my truck or on the boat."

"And he found footprints too, Crocker. He knows it was us."

Crocker puts his hands on his hips and glares at the trees in his backyard. He takes in breaths through his nose, then lets them out again while he thinks this over.

"Another thing," I tell him, reluctantly. "He found black paint on the driver's side fender and door. Between that, your flask, and our footprints, he has enough evidence. We're done, Crocker. We're both going to jail."

Under the glare of the security light over the doors on Crocker's garage, I see his face go a bloodless white. "Nooooooo!" he roars, shattering the late day's quiet. He grabs an old wooden lobster pot from the pile stacked behind him. With a howl, he catapults it across his driveway. It slams into the side wall of his garage, leaving a mark and tearing away a chip of white paint.

I just stare at him, my pulse thudding in my temple.

Crocker faces the garage, clenching and unclenching his fists, his whole body a shaking rage. "You talked to him, didn't you? What did you tell him?"

I jerk my head back, my own anger rising. Where did that come from?

"No, I didn't talk to him. I was out in the hall listening to them. He didn't even know I was there. But it doesn't matter. I didn't have to tell him anything. Look at your truck," I say, pointing to the extensively damage. "It's obvious you were in an accident. He's probably on his way to the wharf now to arrest us."

"Yeah, well, he steps on my boat when I'm not there, and I'll make sure it's the last step he takes," he says chillingly.

"Don't touch him, Crocker. He's only doing his job."

Crocker swings around. "Whose side are you on, anyway?"

"There is no side, Crocker."

"There most definitely is, boy." He steps to within an inch of me. He raises a clenched fist in my face, trying to make me step back in fear. But I know him too well by now. I know the coward that lives inside him. This time I hold my ground, staring him down. After a few seconds, he steps back and drops his hand.

He gives a false laugh. "Relax, I was just joking. Can't you even take a joke anymore?"

I hold his gaze until he lowers his eyes, turns, and walks toward the back entrance of his house, feigning nonchalance.

"Get in the truck," he barks over his shoulder. "I'm going in the house to grab some clothes and then we're taking off."

"What do you mean? Where're we going?"

"I've got over half my pots sitting on the seabed. We're going to bring them up and sell the lobsters to a good buddy of mine in New Brunswick. He owns a seafood market and two restaurants there. He'll buy them from us under the table. Then we'll take the boat up the coast a ways and hide out until this blows over."

"Hide out where?"

He looks at me like I'm a moron. "Didn't I just say? We'll cross the bay to New Brunswick. My buddy owns a big summer home right on the water a few miles up the coast from St. Andrews. He's got a two-slip boathouse where he keeps his powerboat. We'll offload our catch into his truck and hide the *Sea Predator* in the vacant slip. We'll lay low at his place for a few months. You bring any money?"

"Yes, I've got over a thousand dollars."

"Good, we'll need it to buy food for the next couple of months."

From the corner of my eye, I see Crocker's wife push back the curtain on the lit kitchen window and peer worriedly at us. She has wheat blond hair and a thin anxious face. Next to her, I see the blond hair on the top of a child's head.

"What about your wife, your kids?" I ask. "How will they manage?"

He follows my eyes to the window, frowning at his wife. He gestures irritably for her to close the curtain, which she does, fast. "I have enough money to tide them over until this dies down and it's safe for us to come back."

I nod doubtfully, thinking the minute we step back in town, three months, six months, or a year from now, Cade will arrest us.

Dark storm clouds are rolling in, covering the sky like a thick black tarp. The temperature has plunged. It's freezing now and plumes of our breath spiral into the air around our heads.

"But Crocker, there's a storm coming. I heard Gram say the Coast Guard have already advised all fishermen to come in to port. Look at those clouds moving in."

He looks up at the sky and blows out a scoffing breath. "I've been out in a lot worse than this. We have time to pull up the pots and make for New Brunswick before it gets really bad. Coast Guard always jumps the gun. It's probably nothing more than a squall."

I shift from one foot to the other, sliding my backpack more comfortably on my shoulder. I'm terrified of going to jail, but I'm having second thoughts about running away. And it's not because of the storm.

Crocker scowls. "Look, you let me worry about the weather."

"It's not that."

"What then?"

"It's Mom and Gram. If I take off and they don't know where I am, I'm afraid of what the shock and worry will do to them. Mom's kind of fragile as it is, and Gram's sixty-five years old. This could kill her."

"Yeah, well, what do you think will happen to them when they see you locked up in jail? You think that shock won't be the end of your mom and grandmother just as easily?"

My mind's whirling. My heart's turbulent. "I don't know, Crocker. I don't know what to do."

"Look, you can stay here and wait for Stone to arrest you if you want. But I'm leaving, with or without you. If you're coming, get in the truck now because we don't have much time. There's no way I'm going to give that idiot the satisfaction of putting the cuffs on me and taking me to jail. I'd rather die, you understand?"

I'm plagued by the image of Mom's and Gram's faces, of how distraught they'll be if I run away, of how heartbroken they'll be if they see me sitting in a jail cell in the town police station. I feel like I'm being torn apart. I don't know which is worse.

Crocker suddenly snaps his thumb and index finger. "Wait a sec. I have an idea. We can buy one of those disposable cell phones once we're in New Brunswick. My buddy sells them at the gift shop in his restaurant. You can call your mom and let her know you're safe. As long as you give me your word you won't tell her where we are."

I consider it. That might just work. And I really don't think I have much choice. My life here in Shipwreck Cove is over.

I nod in agreement. "Okay."

"Good." He turns and heads for his house.

I walk over to the truck, the frozen gravel in the unpaved driveway crunching beneath my running shoes, shattering the night air like gunshots.

## Chapter 38

# CADE

An icy mixture of sleet and snow pellets rain down on Fisherman's Wharf. An easterly is on the way. Soon the sleet will turn to heavy flakes and cover everything. The winds will worsen and the temperature will fall to about minus twenty Celsius.

Beside me are Austin, Rupert Bowness, a local fisherman, and Rupert's son Brad. While Austin and I were driving to Crocker's house to arrest him, the dispatcher radioed me to say that Rupert and Brad had found a body at sea and were bringing it in. I immediately turned the cruiser around and headed for the wharf. When I arrived, I called in the town coroner. It's now five o'clock and the coroner's here.

I study the body lying before me on the wooden planks. In the bright light thrown down by the street lamp, I can see it's a man, but I can't tell if he's in his late teens or late forties. He's missing his eyelids, his lips, most of his nose, and both earlobes. His eyes are just two holes staring up at me.

Rupert steps up beside me. "That looks like Jeremy Tanner."

"Might be," I say.

"It is, Cade. Look at that rat tail. Jeremy's the only young fellow in town who wore one. And we all know he was working for Crocker on the *Sea Predator* when he supposedly fell overboard. Mack Crocker should be charged with murder."

"We don't know anything yet, Rupert."

"Where is Crocker anyway?" Rupert says, rubbing his bristly chin with the heel of his hand as he looks around the wharf. "His boat's moored in its slip."

I look over at Crocker's berth. The *Sea Predator* is tied up, bobbing and swaying in the strong wind, but it's dark and its engine isn't running. Crocker's likely at home.

Rupert leans in, whispers in my ear. "Look at the gash on the top of Jeremy's skull. There's something not right about that. You know Crocker's hard to work for. A violent man."

"Yeah, this stinks," Brad says. "Crocker has a bad temper and Jeremy wasn't the type to back down. I bet they got into a fight and something bad happened. I warned Jeremy not to work for him."

I hold my hand up and caution the men. "Now, we don't know anything for certain. Listen, would you please go back to your boat until the coroner's finished here?"

The father and son nod and move away silently. They don't look happy.

Austin steps up beside me. "They're right about one thing. I knew Jeremy. With that rat tail, and the build, it looks like him."

I nod grimly and look down at the body. It's a chilling scene. The body is on its back, lidless holes staring sightlessly at the black sky. The boy was slim but well-built, about five-eight and one-fifty. Other than for a pair of blue jeans, he's nude and his exposed flesh reminds me of cottage cheese, bloodless white and mushy looking. The build fits Jeremy and not the other missing boy, Cullum, who was about six feet and two hundred pounds. I think it's Jeremy and I don't like the gash on his skull either, but I keep my thoughts to myself.

Dr. Cameron Bryson, both the coroner and one of the town's physicians, squats down next to the body. He leans in close to the face. "Darn eels," he mutters. "They do most of the damage."

Cam is chewing gum. Every other minute, he lets out a long burp. He turns his head and glances up at me, looking a little embarrassed. "I quit smoking. Chewing gum is supposed to help curb the craving. I don't know, though. About all its doing is giving me gas."

I give him a small smile.

"Will you guys give me a hand?" Cam says. "I want to turn him on his side."

Austin and I get down and put on clear surgical gloves. I place my hands under the corpse's hips. Austin places his hands under the corpse's legs. Cam slides his hands under the man's left shoulder and then regards us for a moment before giving the signal to lift.

Not pretty, hey?"

"No," I murmur.

Austin gives a silent shake of his head.

"A human body is like a floating buffet for marine life. They make an awful mess of a person," Cam explains. "When a person drowns, they sink to the bottom. Once the process of decomposition begins, once the gas gets built up inside the body, the belly swells, and up it floats to the surface. The skin wrinkles and turns to mush, the body bangs into rocks and logs, and with the marine life feeding on it, it's not long before the floater hardly looks human anymore. With the amount of decomposition on this body, it's hard to guess its age exactly, but I think he's between twenty and thirty years old."

"Uh-huh," is all I say. I feel the corpse's spongy skin under my gloved hands and it's making me sick.

"Look at his face," Cam continues. "See how the eyelids, eyeballs, nose, lips, and ears are all gone? That's where scavengers like crabs, seals, and fish like to start, where the skin is as smooth as a baby's bottom. It takes them a little less than a month to fully devour a decaying corpse."

From the corner of my eye, I see Austin turn his head and look out across the harbour. He puffs his cheeks and blows out a soft breath.

Cam studies Austin briefly. He smiles apologetically. "Well, I guess that's enough details. You two ready?"

On Cam's count of three, we lift the body onto its side. Cam reaches out and slides a hand inside the back jeans pocket. He pulls out a sodden brown leather wallet. We lay the body back down on the wooden planks and then Austin and I step back.

A few seconds later, Cam heaves himself to his feet and holds the wallet out to me. "There's a nasty gash on his head, Cade. And there's some major trauma to his face, but that can happen from bumping into logs and debris. I'll do further tests, and also test for traces of alcohol and drugs." He lifts his eyes, looks at me, and speculates. "I'd estimate he's been in the water anywhere from eight to fourteen days. His skin's mushy and is starting to detach from the bone. The medical examiner in Halifax will be able to pin down the age, time, and cause of death for you."

"All right, Cam."

Cam whips out a hanky and blows his nose while looking down at the body. "Well, we've got a couple of young fishermen missing, don't we?"

"Yes, we do. Cullum. And then the most recent, Jeremy Tanner." I open the wallet and pull a driver's license from one of the slots.

Cam burps loudly, watching me. He sighs, takes the wad of gum from his mouth, and tosses it in the water. "Likely Jeremy then. The decomposition fits the timeframe."

I study the card and release a sad sigh. The photo's ruined, but some of the ink is still readable. The driver's licence belongs to Jeremy Tanner. "It's him."

Cam turns and clamps a hand on my arm. "I feel bad for the boy's family. Terrible thing to hear so close to Christmas."

I nod. "It is. But maybe they'll find some peace now that they have his body to bury."

"True enough. Well, I'm done here. I'll take the body now and do a preliminary autopsy, and let you know what I find before I send it on to Halifax for a full autopsy."

I close the wallet and drop it into a plastic bag. "All right, Cam."

Austin and I watch as two men put the body into a white body bag, lift it up, and lay it gently on a stretcher. They fasten the red straps at the head, chest, and legs, and then roll the stretcher over to a plain white van and slide it into the back.

Once they've closed the back doors, I tilt my head towards the group of bystanders gathered under a streetlight at the entrance to the wharf. We'd closed the wharf off, but the crowd has grown larger as word spreads. The way news rockets through this town; it's only a matter of time before this reaches the Tanner family.

"Let's head over to the Tanners' place, Austin. I don't want them to hear about this before we get there. We'll pick up Crocker as soon as we're done."

As Austin and I walk to my cruiser, my heart is heavy for Alicia and Liam Tanner,. I mentally prepare myself for what I know from experience is the most unpleasant, heartbreaking duty of a police officer.

My sadness is tempered by the thought of arresting Mack Crocker. At the same time, I'm glad I won't be arresting Logan Blanchard. The footprints at the accident scene reveal he was trying to pull the driver out of the Honda when he was pulled away. Another town fisherman, Pierre St. Onge, also reported seeing Crocker pull Logan out of his pickup truck and onto the *Sea Predator*. From the evidence, it's clear Crocker forcefully dragged Logan away from the accident scene, and then later onto his boat. It was a huge relief to tell Olivia earlier, but I need to find Logan and talk to him. He is, after all, an eyewitness.

## Chapter 39

## LOGAN

The *Sea Predator* is docked at Fisherman's Wharf. Thick, purple-black storm clouds scud across the sky and a brutal, icy wind gusts off the harbour. I'm about to unmoor us when I hear angry voices. I glance over my shoulder and see three fishermen heading straight for Crocker's berth. I lift the line around the bollock, but my pulse is ticking in my throat.

"Hold on there!" a voice shouts. I freeze with the line in my hand. "Where's Crocker? I want to talk to him."

I loop the line back around the bollock and slowly turn around. The three fishermen stand right behind me, facing the *Sea Predator*. I'm not surprised. I knew something bad happened the minute Crocker and I drove past the weigh station and saw them gathered in front of the building, saw the way their faces changed when we drove past.

The engine's rumbling and diesel fumes pour from the pipe in the wheelhouse roof. The wind carries it into my face and I choke. My stomach churns and bile lurches up into my throat. Crocker's in there and can't hear us; he has no idea what's going on. But I know. Seconds ago, as the three men strode down the wharf, I heard one of them say something about Jeremy Tanner's body being brought in earlier. A shiver of fear goes through me.

"Hey, boy, look at me," Gage Kelly says, his eyes blazing. All three fishermen's eyes are on me. "I'm talking to you. Is Crocker in the wheelhouse?"

I shove my hands in my coat pockets to hide their trembling, then nod.

"Then go in and tell him to get out here. I want to talk to him."

I don't move. Can't move.

Gage grabs me by the shoulders and shakes me. "Did you hear me? Go tell Crocker I want to talk to him!"

Andy Coldwell pulls Gage away. "Easy now, Gage, he's just a boy. He had nothing to do with Jeremy's death. He wasn't working for Crocker then."

"Let me go, Andy." Gage shrugs his shoulder free from Andy's grasp.

At that moment, Crocker emerges from the wheelhouse, his stride fast and angry. He's irritated because I'm taking so long to unmoor us. He sees the fishermen surrounding me and skids to a stop. Rage fills his face. He tears across the deck, leaps over the railing, and stomps toward us, his boots cracking explosively on the cold wooden planks of the wharf road.

"Get away from him!" Crocker comes up behind Gage and gives him a furious shove. Gage stumbles sideways, crashing into Kurt Thomason. He quickly regains his balance and goes after Crocker.

Andy and Kurt step between the men. Andy pulls Gage away, and this time holds him in a tight bear hug. Kurt hangs on to Crocker.

"Rupert found Jeremy snagged in his trap lines today, Crocker. He brought him in a couple of hours ago," Gage yells, struggling to break free of Andy's grip. "You want to try explaining to me how he got that big gash on his head?"

Crocker, strong as an ox, easily slips free of Kurt's arms. "He probably smacked his head on the railing when the line yanked him over the side, you idiot."

"Or you hit him over the head with a pipe and threw him overboard," Gage accuses.

Crocker snorts a laugh. "Don't be so stupid, Gage. I was working the winch. I didn't even see him go over."

"Yeah, sure, Crocker."

"If you had half a brain in your head, you'd know that's ridiculous," Crocker says with a sneer. "Why would I do something like that? I needed Jeremy to help me set my traps. If I threw him overboard, I'd be cutting my own throat."

"You lose that smile right now before I wipe it off your face," Gage seethes.

Crocker's smile broadens. "What smile? This one?"

Gage steps forward, fists clenched. "I should knock you right into the harbour."

Crocker's smile vanishes. He stiffens. "Try it, go ahead."

Andy pulls Gage away. "Come on now, Gage, let's go. Let the law deal with him." He gives Crocker a knowing look and nods his chin over to where Crocker's damaged pickup is parked under a streetlight. "Strange, isn't it, how there was a hit and run last night on the Lighthouse Road and your truck has a dent on the driver's side. What happened, Crocker? You want to try explaining that too?"

"I hit a deer, Coldwell. Not that it's any of your business."

"Sure you did, Crocker," Andy says with an edge to his voice. "You're not going to get away with Jeremy's death, or anything else. You're going to jail, and you know it. I can see the fear in your eyes, you rotten coward."

"You're crazy. Jeremy fell overboard and I don't know jack about any hit and run," Crocker tells Andy, but even I hear a tremble in his voice. He's scared stiff.

Andy just shakes his head. He looks at me with a concerned expression and his voice changes to a softer tone. "Go home, Logan. Think of your mom and grandmother. They'll be worried about you now. Be safe, be smart. Go home now."

Kurt nods. "Yes, listen to us, boy. You go home."

Gage only stares at me, but he doesn't speak. In his eyes, I'm no better than Crocker. His anger toward me is palpable; his disgust for me is gut-wrenching. I can barely hold his gaze.

"You need a drive home, Logan?" Andy offers. "Come with us now. I'll drop you off at your grandmother's."

"He's staying here with me until we're done cleaning up the boat," Crocker says. "I'll drop him off at home."

Andy looks at me again, waiting for me to respond. I'm scared and I want to go with him, but know I can't.

"I'm okay, but thanks for the offer," I tell him, trying to keep my voice cool.

He nods a bit sadly, then turns and walks away. Kurt and Gage leave with him, and I can hear all three men murmuring amongst themselves.

Crocker watches them leave, his eyes seething. "Idiots," he sneers at their backs. "Unmoor us, now!"

I lift the dock lines from the bollards and toss them onto the boat. I jump aboard, instinctively lifting my arms and planting my feet. Crocker guns the engine and pulls out of his berth. On the wharf, I see the three fishermen spin around in surprise. Soon, the three men and the lights of town disappear behind us.

Beyond the harbour, I spot Gram's house high on the hill facing the bay. Through the sleeting rain, I see colourful Christmas lights twinkling in the living room window. I realize they must have put up the tree and decorated the house this afternoon before they drove to the hospital to pick up Maxine.

It hits me like a boot to the gut that I won't be home for Christmas. The gifts I bought for Mom, Gram, Maxine, Shaye, Grace, and Audrey are all wrapped and hidden in my closet. I think of the love and laughter in Gram's house and my heart literally aches in my chest. The pain is so intense, it's almost unbearable. I want to be home so bad that it takes everything in me not to lay down on the deck and cry. I slump against the rail, head down, and feel tears spring to my eyes.

I can never go home again.

# Chapter 40

## LOGAN

The seas are heavy and the waves slam into the hull with a steady, bone-jarring thump. It's dangerous out on deck with the wind, heaving waves, and sleet coming down, but I stay out until I can no longer see Gram's house.

Then I go in the wheelhouse and stand next to Crocker at the helm. He grips the wheel tightly, fighting to keep the boat from being sent off-course.

I stare out the windshield, stomach queasy with fear. Thick black clouds roll in ominously. The sea is all heavy foam, the water patterns changing constantly. The waves swell and then break ferociously, hammering the hull with a deafening thud.

"Crocker, look at the sky. Maybe we shouldn't bother with the pots. Maybe we should just head for New Brunswick now."

Crocker's green eyes glitter unnaturally, like the perilous winter sea ice that covers the shoreline, that breaks away and floats in the treacherous waters of the harbour, often unseen until too late.

"No, we can't do that," Crocker says. "We need the money if we're going to hide out for a few months. I told you already."

"Yeah, but—"

The boat rises on the crest of a huge wave and dives hard. I have to grip the edge of the dash to stay on my feet.

"Yeah, but," Crocker mimics, laughing. "Relax, so far it's just a squall. If it gets worse, we can ride out the storm."

I look at him and understand by the look in his eyes that he takes strange delight in risking our lives, in terrifying me.

*Just a squall?* I think silently, sure he doesn't really believe that.

It's pitch-black when we finally reach the grounds. The moon's completely hidden by heavy, dark clouds. It's really storming now, a frigid, numbing sleet and snow mix that coats everything on the boat with a layer of ice. Large waves rise and slam down on the icy deck. The seawater washes across the deck boards and pours over the opposite side and back into the sea, taking anything loose on the deck along with it. A heavy wooden crate surges across the deck, smacking me painfully in the calf before sailing over the side.

I grit my teeth to hold back a scream, then grab the pot line and run it around the wheel of the winch. Head down, I grip the railing with both hands, bracing myself as I wait for the rising pot. I stare at the churning swells, struck with terror at the very real threat of being washed overboard into the freezing water. The wind howls in my ears, blasting through my foul-weather gear, wool sweater, and long underwear. Ice pellets mercilessly stab the exposed flesh on my face like a thousand knives. I'm drenched, I'm frozen. I shiver unceasingly.

The winch whines in my ear as a pot breaks the surface. I wipe my nose on my sleeve, then step forward and reach for the pot as it rises above the rail. My fingers are so frozen, my hands so numb that it takes me twice as long as normal. My feet are two chunks of ice in my boots.

With each passing minute, the storm intensifies. The winds worsen to near gale force. The temperature plummets. The waves get bigger and stronger and pound the boat so forcefully I think they must be pulverizing the hull. The thought fills me with such alarm that I feel my heart flutter wildly in my chest.

Crocker's a madman though, and we keep working. As I empty pots of lobster and stack them in the stern, I'm so frightened. I silently call for my mom. Not for the first time, I fight back tears, deeply regretting my decision to run away.

## Chapter 41

## LOGAN

We've hauled up our traps and stacked and secured them in the stern. The wind is against us as we desperately try to cross the bay to New Brunswick. It blows from all sides, increasing in power by the minute. It seems to almost hold us in place.

Crocker's hands are clasped around the wheel in a death grip, his posture rigid. I follow his eyes to the raging sea. Suddenly, the surface of the water shifts. The swells boil and heave with a terrifying new violence. I feel sick as they mercilessly batter the *Sea Predator*.

The boat tops a crest and plunges down into the trough. As we rise again, another wave slams us in the stern, swinging us broadside. Seawater pours across the deck. The noise is unlike anything I've ever heard before. It's like someone is using a giant sledgehammer to pound the sides of the ship while shaking it back and forth like a toy.

The boat gives a sudden, powerful shudder under my feet, then dips hard, water rushing over the bow. Crocker increases the throttle to try to lift the bow, but seawater is filling the bilge, pulling us down. When the bow finally lifts again, I see that the boat is sitting perilously low in the water.

Crocker sees too and shakes his head. "The water's coming in faster than the bilge pumps can remove it. It's the pots. We're too heavy. We're going to have to throw some of them off or we'll never make it."

I move to the starboard side window and look out. The boat's leaning dangerously to starboard. Water is washing over the railing, swirling on the deck. I watch a buoy marker roll over the side with the next wave.

The sea is in a rage; even its colour is a seething shade of greenish-black. The noise is so loud that I'm terrified the *Sea Predator* is breaking apart. Despite the overheated wheelhouse, the blood in my veins turns to ice.

Crocker sets the engine on idle while zipping up his foul-weather coat. He yanks on his wool hat and pulls his hood up over it. He's breathing heavily.

He heads out of the wheelhouse, yelling over his shoulder. "Come on, move it, let's get those pots off."

I can't move. My body is frozen with fear.

Crocker comes back, gripping my arm and squeezing. "Logan, come on, let's go!"

I stare blankly at him. Panic wipes out all logic and understanding. All I want to do is stay in the warm, dry wheelhouse.

"Logan, move it!" Crocker screams in my ear, giving me a brisk shake.

That snaps me out of my state of paralysis. "Okay," I mumble, pulling my hood up and tying it snugly under my chin. I yank on my gloves and stumble after him out of the wheelhouse.

The icy wind blasts me in the face and body. I slip and fall, banging my head against the deck. I stand again and lurch toward the railing, then grab it. Dizzy, black spots appear behind my eyes. I shake my head to clear them. Thick, foamy seawater pours over the low side of the boat and washes across the deck. The awful sloshing sound fills my ears, petrifying me. The wind slams into me and knocks me right off my feet. I stagger to my feet again, but the cold is paralyzing.

"Logan, come on!" Crocker screams over the wind as he reaches the stacks of pots.

I force myself to move, to follow him on shaky legs. I pull my filleting knife from the sheaf on my belt. I slip again and my knife flies out of my hand, sliding across the deck to the port side. A massive, rolling wave slams into the boat. It gives a groaning shudder and tilts, the port side nearly touching the water. I slide across the sloping deck on my behind and hit the side. Finally, the boat heaves and straightens.

I want my mom. I want my gram. I've never been this scared in my life.

Crocker turns and irritably gestures to me to get up. He's screaming too, but the wind whips his words away. I stand and slip and slide over to the port railing, grabbing my knife along the way. The dark storm clouds are so heavy and low that they seem to envelop the boat like a black cloak. The wind pummels my clothing flat against my body, nearly holding me in place.

Finally, I come up alongside Crocker, who's already sawing at the cord around the traps.

I lean over and lend a hand. When I get one cord free, I grasp both sides of the pot, draw in a breath, lift it, and stumble over to the railing to drop it overboard. At that moment, a powerful gust smashes into the boat, lifting it. I reel sideways, but somehow remain on my feet. The traps strain against their ropes, but they stay in place.

"Go, go, throw more over or we'll sink!" Crocker screams.

I reach out with my knife, slicing at the rope on another trap. I lift it and stagger over to the railing again. With a grunt, I heave it over the side.

I keep working. The icy sleet is coming down sideways, like knives to the face. My arm and leg muscles throb with pain, my body quivering from the cold and fatigue. After I throw my tenth pot over the rail, I look down at the turbulent waves. The boat is sitting lower than ever. We're taking on too much water, and faster than we can get rid of the pots. This isn't going to work.

I look at Crocker, who's just heaved a pot over the side and is staring down at the water. He turns his head and meets my gaze. He shakes his head grimly, motioning to the wheelhouse.

The *Sea Predator* is sinking. We are going to die.

## Chapter 42

## LOGAN

The boat dives into a huge trough, burying the nose beneath the water. The bow disappears, and then sluggishly rises again. Seconds later, another wave slams the boat, shattering a window on the starboard side. The wind howls into the wheelhouse, followed by a wall of spray. I stagger back, nearly falling down. I reach out and grab the dash, hanging on with one hand and wiping the icy water from my face with the other.

We dropped about thirty pots before we gave up and came back into the wheelhouse. It didn't make a bit of difference. The boat is sinking lower in the sea with each passing minute.

The boat groans and quakes as it climbs and plunges down the face of mammoth swells, over and over. I look out the broken window to the black, raging seas, my heart fluttering. Why didn't Crocker listen to me? If we hadn't stopped to collect his pots from the seabed, most of which we threw back overboard, we'd be safe in New Brunswick by now.

Crocker grunts and wrestles the steering wheel so fiercely that his knuckles are a bloodless white. When he guns the engine, the boat shudders and vibrates under our feet. He screams at me, but his words are swept away by the wind that howls through the broken window. It's viciously cold, burning my ears and the damp flesh on my face.

"What?" I shout back.

His face is a pasty colour, lined with sweat; his breath smells rancid, like an outhouse. "We're not going to make it."

Before I can move, another gigantic wave crashes into the boat, picking us up and spinning us sideways. The punishing swells pummel us, crushing the boat, one after the other. The boat pitches and shudders so fiercely that I feel it right up through my feet and into my lower spine.

Cursing, Crocker fights with the wheel, trying to straighten the boat, but as each new wave hits us, the bow dips further under the water, the portside leaning even more frighteningly. Each time we rise up atop a swell, we seem to stop for a second before hurtling down the face of it. I'm terrified we're going to dive down and never rise again.

I hang on to the dash with all my strength, shivering uncontrollably from the icy wind and spray blowing in through the broken window, pelting my face, freezing my flesh.

The biggest wave yet pounds the boat, shattering two more window panes, including the windshield. I'm thrown off my feet, slamming into a wall. The wind screams in. The boat lurches hard and feels more sluggish and heavy in the treacherous seas.

"Damn it!" Crocker's face goes concrete grey. "The rudder's broke, the rudder's broke."

The engine coughs and then dies. Crocker turns the key. It catches, runs ragged, coughs twice, and dies again. When he turns the key again, there's nothing. The lights go out. The wheelhouse goes dark and silent. The boat wallows helplessly.

I struggle to my feet and grab the dash. A swell rises up and hammers the boat. We roll to port about forty degrees. Waves sweep over the deck, filling the bilge. The bow sinks even further under the waves, and this time it doesn't rise.

Crocker reaches up and grabs the radio mic. "Mayday, mayday, mayday," he shouts into it. "This is the fishing vessel *Sea Predator* requesting immediate assistance. We're about twenty miles southwest of Skull Island. Our rudder's gone. We're floundering, taking on water in heavy seas. We need immediate assistance!"

The crackle of the radio suddenly fills the wheelhouse. There's a man's voice, but his words are unintelligible.

Crocker presses the button on the mic, tries again. "Mayday, mayday, this is the fishing vessel *Sea Predator* requesting immediate assistance. We are sinking."

He releases the button and we have to strain to hear over the howling wind. This time there's nothing—no crackle, no trace of the usual static. The radio's dead. At the same time, the wind inexplicably dies down. There is only silence. Deathly, sickening silence.

My heart lurches so badly that I feel dizzy. A terrible, stomach-turning jolt of fear twists my stomach into a painful knot.

The radio's destroyed. The rudder's broken. The engine's gone. The boat is crippled. Without any control now, the *Sea Predator* pitches and rolls helplessly on the waves. Seawater sweeps over the deck, most of it filling the hull, the rest taking buoys, ropes, anything loose.

Crocker's face goes slack. His arms fall limply to his sides. "No, no," he mumbles. "She's lost, I've lost her."

"Crocker?" I say. "Do you think they heard you?"

He stands with his shoulders slumped, staring emptily through the broken windshield. "I don't know. Doesn't matter," he says hoarsely. "They'll never get to us in time. I've only got an inflatable life raft aboard, too light for this kind of wind. It'll flip us over in two seconds."

"What?" I gasp. "You told me you had a hard-shell survival raft aboard."

"I lied."

"Did you lie about the survival suits too?"

"Suit, not suits," he replies grimly. "I have only the one. I meant to buy another one, but never got around to it."

The boat rises sharply on a wave, giving a horrendous creak. I grasp the edge of the dash as hard as I can to keep from falling backward.

"Well, what are we going to do?" I say, once I'm steady.

He gazes at me for a long time, looking scared, desperate, conflicted. Finally, he draws in a breath, places both hands on my shoulders, and squeezes hard. "You put the survival suit on and I'll wear a life jacket. We'll have to try the life raft. We don't have any other choice."

I look out into the deep, frigid Atlantic. The waves are huge, wild, slamming into each other as well as the boat. I can't imagine surviving in that icy water, clinging to a small rubber life raft.

I look at Crocker. How could he have been so negligent? "But you'll never survive in those seas without a suit."

"Sure I will," he says with a forced smile, pretending he believes it.

I shake my head, my heart full of fear and sorrow. Without a survival suit, he'll die. I can't put on the suit when he doesn't have one. It's beyond me.

Crocker squeezes my shoulders, looks right into my eyes. The sheen of sweat on his face and the terror in his eyes send my heart into my throat. "Think of your mom and grandmother. Do it for them. And listen to me. If the raft flips, you'll float in the suit, but try to swim as far from the *Sea Predator* as you can, or it could suck you down with it."

I don't reply. What's there to say?

He gives me a vigorous shake. "Are you listening to me?"

I try to remember how long a person can last in freezing water while wearing a survival suit. I read it in a book once, but in my panicked state I can't recall the details. Only six to eight hours, I think. I pray I'm wrong, that it's much longer. I do remember reading that a person will only last a few minutes without a suit before falling unconscious and succumbing to hyperthermia. Or drowning. But if no one knows we're in the water, it won't matter anyway.

"Logan, do it."

I stagger over to the cabinet on the side wall, trying to stay on my feet. I pull out the bright red neoprene suit.

"Crocker, I can't," I say in despair.

"Put it on, now, Logan!" he bellows over the howling wind.

He comes over. The suit is surprisingly heavy and awkward to put on, but Crocker gives me a hand. I slide into it, closing the bootstraps. I pull the hood over my head and zip it up. I yank the hood up. The face seal around the chin doesn't seem to fit right.

Crocker shrugs apologetically. "It's old. It might leak a little. But even a flooded suit will keep you alive for a couple of hours. There's a strobe light attached to the upper right shoulder. Turn it on and put a life jacket over it."

I find the strobe light and flip it to the on position, then grab two life jackets. I toss one to Crocker and put the other one on over my survival suit. Crocker puts his on and turns on the strobe light on the shoulder. He doesn't even bother to zip up the life jacket.

An enormous wave two stories high rises up on the starboard side and smashes down on us. The force of the water is unbelievable, like a black mountain crashing down on us, taking out the rest of the windows in the wheelhouse. Icy seawater surges through the destroyed windshield, drenching us. There's at least six inches on the floor now.

"Let's go, Logan. The boat isn't going to last much longer." Crocker heads for the wheelhouse door.

I will my feet to move, but it's hopeless. Fear keeps them frozen to the spot. Even though I know the boat's sinking fast, I don't want to leave the false security of the wheelhouse.

Crocker turns around and sees me. He grips my right arm, hauling me out of the wheelhouse to the deck. "Move your feet! Go!"

## Chapter 43

# CADE

Austin and I have just left the Tanner home when my cell phone rings. "Cade," Olivia says, voice breaking.

"What is it, Olivia?"

"Logan's run away. He took some of his clothes and he's gone." She begins to weep quietly.

"I know."

She's so distraught that what I've just said doesn't hit her.

"Mother told me he was in the hall outside the kitchen listening to us talk earlier. He knows you're looking for Crocker for the hit and run. He must think you're going to arrest him too. And there's more, Cade. When I went into his bedroom, I found the ticket I gave him for his birthday torn up and thrown all over the room. He must be scared he's going to jail." Her voice dissolves into sobs. "Oh, Cade, you have to find him. I don't know where he is and the storm's getting worse. Have you found Crocker yet? Maybe Logan's there."

My heart sinks. "Olivia, I was just about to call you. Only moments ago, I learned that Crocker showed up at the wharf sometime after six o'clock and had an altercation with some fishermen. Shortly after that, he left the harbour on the *Sea Predator* and headed out to sea." I pause, then continue as gently as possible. "Olivia, the men saw Logan aboard with Crocker."

"What! Oh my word, no," she cries. "In this storm… oh, Cade, no."

In the background I hear frantic female voices. Olivia is whispering to her mom and the other women in the house about what's happening. The voices grow more terrified.

"Olivia," I cut in. "Does Logan have his cell phone on him?"

"What?"

"His cell phone. Does he have it on him?"

"No, he doesn't," she sobs softly. "I have it. It's upstairs in my dresser drawer. I took it away from him a few days ago."

"That's right."

"Oh, Cade, look at the sky. It's turned completely black."

"Listen, Olivia, I'm on my way to the wharf now," I say in a comforting voice. "I've already spoken to Lieutenant Ramsey Keller at the Joint Rescue Coordination Centre. They've launched a helicopter and a Coast Guard vessel. If there's any break in the storm, and the Coast Guard permits it, I'll go out in our department's search and rescue boat. Some of the town fishermen have offered to help too, once the weather improves."

"But Cade, the storm's getting worse by the minute. It looks like a blizzard out there. The wind is so strong… how can a helicopter or plane go out looking for them?"

"They still have some time before the winds get too forceful. With an immersion suit and hard-shell life raft, Logan can—*will*—survive until they find him."

Olivia sobs quietly. "You're talking about Mack Crocker. You mean *if* he has a survival suit for Logan and a hard-shell raft."

She's right, and I thought the exact same thing. I hide my own fear from my voice. "I'm sure he does, Olivia. Try not to worry. The Coast Guard will find Logan in time."

"I feel so helpless."

"I know, Olivia. All you can is pray. Call Pastor Harris and get the prayer chain going."

"Yes, I will," Olivia says, her voice growing stronger. "I'll do that right now."

## Chapter 44

# LOGAN

Outside, gale-force winds smash into me, snatching my breath away and slamming me into the deck. Ice pellets hit my face, stinging like razors. The freezing spray coats the boat. The deck is as slick as an ice-covered pond. I try to stand, but can't.

Crocker pulls me back to my feet. "Keep moving!"

We slide over to the port railing close to the wheelhouse. I'm shaking so severely, I can hardly stay on my feet. The boat jerks hard sideways and emits a dying moan. I look over the side to the heaving, black seas. The entire bow is underwater now, pointing into the depths like a dart. I stop again, frozen in fear.

"Logan, come on, I need your help to get the lift raft's casing open!" Crocker yells over the shrieking wind.

Crocker's words jolt me. I haul in a big breath of icy air, feeling my senses sharpen. Alert now, we work our way along the deck to the starboard wall of the wheelhouse where the life raft is tied down. I help Crocker with the latches and the casing snaps open. We both lean over and grab it.

Then disaster strikes. A massive wall of black water rises up, sweeping us off our feet and over the side, into the howling, stormy darkness.

I fly through the air, arms and legs flailing uselessly, then plunge into the turbulent sea. But the suit does its job and the next thing I know I pop up to the surface and float on my back, looking up at the black sky. The swells lift me up, up, up and then I career down the face of the troughs so fast it's terrifying, disorienting.

The waves are at least seven to eight feet high now. The powerful wind shears the crest off the waves and crashes over me. It's like a punch, slamming my head backwards. It hurts so much; it feels like my nose and cheekbones are being shattered.

Lobster pots, ropes, and other fishing gear float on the water all around me. To my horror, I can feel icy seawater leaking into the chin area of my suit. I try to grab onto something that might help lift me higher on the water, in case the suit fails, but the suit's mitten-like hand coverings make it hard to grab anything. I scream in fear, but the wind whips my cry away.

My teeth clack uncontrollably. The ice pellets nearly freeze my eyelids shut. My breath is shallow and quick and I know I'm going to die. A sob escapes my lips at the thought of Mom and Gram and how heartbroken they're going to be. I think of my grandfather and it hits me that I'm going to die at sea just like he did thirty-seven years ago. I look up at the black sky, thinking of my dad. Is this how he felt as his fighter jet plummeted to the earth? Were my grandfather's last thoughts of my mom and grandmother? Were my dad's last thoughts of me and mom? I'm sure of it.

Thinking of my father has a calming effect. I feel my heartbeat slow down, my breathing grow more even. My dad always kept a cool, level head, no matter how dire the situation. He'd want me to be brave, to stay calm. He'd want me to pray and fight to live. I can't be the third man to die in my family. I have to live for Mom and Gram.

I let the buoyancy of the suit and life jacket do their work and just float, conserving energy. I close my eyes and pray to my heavenly Father for the first time since my dad died. I ask for His forgiveness, for His strength and help. I pray for Crocker too. As I pray, I sense God's loving presence calming me.

I turn my head from left to right, searching for Crocker. I see a bright red balloon from the *Sea Predator* sweep by. I reach out and miss it. I try again, and succeed in holding on. Holding it under my chest lifts me a half-foot out of the water. I cling to it and search for Crocker again. I spot him to my left, flailing desperately in the water. His life jacket has slipped completely off one shoulder. Then a big wave hits him and he disappears.

Seconds later, I see him again, but he's turned around, the back of his head visible. He lifts his arms up and down weakly, struggling to stay afloat.

"Crocker!" I shout, inhaling a big mouthful of water and choking on it.

Crocker turns in the water and faces me. His eyes are wild, bulging with terror. His mouth is open, like he's panting hard, so he's swallowing and choking on seawater.

"Logan, help me!" he screams. Through the wind, I just barely hear him.

"I'm coming!"

I hold the balloon out in front of me and kick my feet as hard as I can.

Another rolling wave washes over his head and I lose sight of him. I stop, straining to see him in the roiling seas. But when I rise up on a wave, he disappears in a trough. And when he rises in the swells, I go down.

Finally, we both rise at the same time and I spot his head bobbing at the crest of a large wave. I see his life jacket floating away, the flicker of the tiny strobe light growing fainter and fainter. He's lost it; he's going to drown. I kick my feet harder to close the distance between us, but the waves actually push me away from him. Gasping, I try to catch my breath and gather more strength.

His head rises above the water and he sees me. His eyes are wide with terror. His mouth opens as he screams for help, but the wind snatches his words away.

I push on, kicking as hard as I can, my eyelids freezing nearly shut. I draw close enough to hear Crocker cry out weakly once to God, who he doesn't even believe in, for his life. Then he slips beneath the waves and doesn't come up again.

Behind me, I hear a horrendous creak. I get myself turned around to look back at the boat. The *Sea Predator* is sinking. I swim away desperately so the boat doesn't pull me down with it. When I think it's safe, I turn and watch the boat go down.

The sea is like a giant serpent consuming its prey. The *Sea Predator* flounders helplessly in the water as wave after frenzied wave crashes over its bow and deck. Finally, the stern of the boat is swallowed by the icy Atlantic. With a final shuddering groan, the *Sea Predator* slips into the depths.

My suit is flooding faster with icy seawater, pooling in the boot area. Numbness is already creeping into my feet. My clothes were wet before I put the suit on, so I'm freezing and shivering. I can feel my heartbeat slowing down. I cling to the balloon and kick my legs hard, Mom's and Gram's faces in my mind.

*Fight!*

I hear an odd thump-thumping noise above. I look up and see a beam of light shining down from a black object. A helicopter!

Even with the flickering strobe light on my suit, its light misses me. Then a big wave hits and rips the balloon from my hands. A second later, a huge wave crashes over my head and buries me underwater. I claw my way up, the suit pulling me up at the same time. When I surface, the light is gone. All I hear is the screaming wind. I almost cry, sure I was hallucinating.

In what was likely only minutes, though it felt like an eternity, a brilliant strobe of light hits me. My jaw is frozen and my teeth no longer click together. My eyelids are covered with ice and I can barely see the light, can barely see anything.

More minutes pass. I can't move a muscle anymore. Surprisingly, I'm not even cold. I actually feel warm. I'm so sleepy too. I float helplessly and feel myself start to fade, to slip away.

Then I'm vaguely aware that someone's there next to me.

I can't see the man who shouts into my ear, but I can hear him. "Wake up! There you go. I've got you! Take it easy, son, take it easy."

I barely feel his hands wrap tightly around me, a harness slipping over my shoulders. A yell, a jerk, and I'm plucked from the sea. The wind whips around me as I'm hoisted through the air, seemingly straight up into those black storm clouds. Arms reach out and pull me safely onto a helicopter, barely conscious.

"You're all right now," a man says. His voice sounds like it's coming from way down in a deep, deep well.

## Chapter 45

# LOGAN

Mom hands me two copies of the *Halifax Chronicle*. One is yesterday's, the other today's. I read yesterday's first. The article is on the front page.

### ONE SAVED, ONE LOST AS BOAT SINKS

The lobster fishing boat *Sea Predator*, fishing from its home port of Shipwreck Cove, Nova Scotia, sank in the frigid Bay of Fundy around seven-thirty last evening. The boat went down about twenty kilometres off the coast of western Nova Scotia after going out in stormy winds and violent seven-metre seas.

A distress call was broadcast on Friday evening from the vessel's captain and a Canadian Forces helicopter and Coast Guard ship were immediately dispatched. The *Sea Predator*'s surviving crewmember, fourteen-year-old Logan Blanchard, was plucked from the raging sea and flown to hospital in Halifax. He was wearing a survival suit. He is reportedly doing well and will be released from hospital soon.

The search for the boat's owner and captain, Macklin Crocker, was suspended last evening due to zero visibility, volatile seas, and high winds, though it resumed at dawn today. A Hercules aircraft also joined in the effort. With the strong winds and icy conditions last evening, and because the captain was not wearing an immersion suit, there is little hope of his survival.

Officials have also said the volatile seas and fierce winds are expected to continue all day, making the conditions difficult. With every passing hour, the chances of finding Crocker diminish.

I set that paper down and pick up the second one. The article reads:

### SEARCH ENDS FOR MISSING FISHERMAN

RCMP in Nova Scotia say the search for a missing lobster boat captain, Macklin Crocker, has come to an end. Crocker, owner and captain of the lobster fishing boat *Sea Predator* was swept overboard when his boat sank on Friday evening during a storm at sea.

A second fisherman, Logan Blanchard, 14, was rescued from seven-metre seas after being spotted by the crew of a Canadian Forces helicopter.

Members of the Joint Rescue Coordination Centre in Halifax told police they made the decision at 11:00 a.m. Saturday morning to end the search.

I fold the paper and set it down on the nightstand next to my bed. A mixture of emotions slice through me—sorrow that Crocker is dead, sympathy for his wife and kids, and a sense of guilt that I'm alive. Strangely, I also feel a sense of relief that I'm finally free of him.

## Chapter 46

# LOGAN

I awake to an utterly gorgeous December day. The sky is a clear sapphire blue, the sun high and bright. The wind whips in off the bay, sending the waves crashing against the rocky seawall below Gram's house. Farther out, thick white foam caps cover the dark, wild sea. It looks cold out, but when I open my bedroom window, a surprisingly warm sea breeze caresses my face.

I shower and dress before descending the stairs and stepping into the kitchen. All four residents are sitting at the table. Four pairs of watery old eyes stare at me.

"Morning," I say with a smile.

"Morning, Logan," they all say in unison. I'm used to it by now. I don't even mind.

"We were so worried about you, Logan. We were praying for you," Audrey tells me when I sit between her and Maxine. For the first time since moving into the house, I hear her real voice, with no phony British accent. "I promised God that if you lived, I would give up both the stage and cigarettes."

"You did?" I say, astonished.

"And I promised I wouldn't cheat on my diet anymore," says Maxine, eyeing the bacon on my plate, looking and sounding clinically depressed.

"And I vowed never again to pinch, slap, or pat men's bottoms," says Shaye cheerlessly. "I only did once so far, at the grocery store yesterday. That hot bakery clerk I told you about. I couldn't resist. Well, wait now. Twice. When the cable man was here yesterday afternoon. Shoot, hang on, okay, three times then. I forgot about the newspaper boy this morning."

Gram turns from the stove, moaning. "Oh, Shaye, the newspaper boy?"

Grace looks at me and smiles proudly. "I have my hearing aids turned on, Logan. I promised God I'd turn them on if He would bring you home safe to us." At that, her chin quivers. "And He did. Praise the Lord, He did."

"Praise the Lord," Gram, Mom, Maxine, Audrey, and Shaye say in unison.

"Thank you, Grace." I look around the table. "Thanks so much everyone. That means a lot to me, that you were all willing to stop… ah…" I pause. "Um, well, anyway, it means a lot to me. But really, you guys didn't have to do that."

Maxine's face lights right up. "No? Well, then can I have your bacon?"

"No, Maxine," says Gram. "You're doing so well. Let's not ruin it."

"I don't call *starving to death* doing well, Winnie," counters Maxine.

"You're fine."

"Logan, dear heart, it's marvellous that you're alive and well," says Audrey with a sudden, thick English accent. "But I heartily agree with Maxine. Since you said we really shouldn't give up anything, and please accept my deepest, sincerest apologies if I have misconstrued your words, I cannot possibly last another second without a cigarette." She pulls an imaginary cigarette out of the pocket of her house robe and puts it to her lips. She pretends to light it, then inhales a deep shuddering drag.

"Just in the nick of time," says Shaye, her eyes shining with an unsettling excitement. "I do believe a certain hot police officer is on his way over here to see Olivia, and I didn't know how I was going to behave with that big hunk loose in the house."

"And these darn things whistle so bad I'm going to go right out of my mind if I have to wear them one more second," says Grace, ripping the hearing aids out of her ears and flinging them onto the table.

I hear Gram let out a long, despairing sigh.

Audrey pushes her chair back with a scrape. "I believe I hear Oliver Stone calling for me." She glides across the room, the fake cigarette in one hand and a blank sheet of paper in the other. Her lips are moving as she reads her lines to herself on the way out of the kitchen.

"What's on the menu for my mid-morning snack, Winnie? I'm so hungry I could eat my own leg." Maxine laughs hard at her own, often repeated joke, her mood improved now that her self-imposed diet is over.

Gram, Mom, and I all exchange looks.

"I guess it was too good to be true," says Mom.

"Yes, I think we may have had our hopes set just a tad too high," Gram agrees. We all laugh together.

## Chapter 47

# LOGAN

I stand in front of the stone monument at the entrance to Fisherman's Harbour, running my fingers along a new name engraved in the stone.

Macklin C. Crocker
*The Sea Predator*
December 21, 2012

I draw in a heavy breath and proceed down the paved wharf road. Because it's December 24, all the lobster boats are moored in their berths. Traps are piled in stacks on the boats or on the wharf. Sea gulls swarm the vessels, lured by the still-lingering scent of blood and guts on the bait bins.

I stop at the empty berth where the *Sea Predator* would normally be tied up.

Mom, Gram, and Cade all exchanged glances when I told them Crocker wasn't as bad as they all thought—glances that said they disagreed with me. But I know I'm right. In the end, by giving me the sole survival suit, Crocker showed bravery. He knew by doing that he would die. That took pure courage and selflessness. Despite all the bad things he did in his life, in the end, that's what he chose. So despite what anyone else in this town may think, that's how I choose to always remember him.

"Hey, Logan," a voice calls from behind me.

I turn around and find Sophie Thibideau, the girl from school who invited me to youth group back in September, standing behind me. Her dad is Rene Thibideau, a fisherman whose lines Crocker cut a few days before the *Sea Predator* sank.

"How are you?" she asks with a warm smile.

I look down at the road. "I'm good," I say, though I don't really feel all that good.

"It's awful what happened, Logan. I'm glad you're okay, but I'm sorry about Mr. Crocker. I feel bad for his wife and kids."

I look up, surprised. "Thanks." She's the only person so far to express grief over Crocker, and I like her even more for that. No matter what people think of him, he still died, and he left a young family behind.

"Once, when I was six and helping Dad on his boat," Sophie says, "he gave me money to buy an ice cream from the stand by the weigh station. I was probably more of hindrance than a help, so he was likely just getting rid of me for a few minutes." She laughs at the memory. "Anyway, I was on my way back to the boat, eating the cone, when I dropped it. I was so upset that I started crying. Mr. Crocker, who was on his boat and saw what happened, came over and told me not to cry, that he'd buy me another one. After he bought it, he walked me back to Dad's boat." She smiles sadly. "He wasn't all bad like everyone around here thinks."

I nod, swallowing hard against the lump in my throat. I don't trust myself to speak.

She lifts a hand and tucks her short dark hair behind her ears. She's a couple of inches shorter than me, slender, but strong and athletic. Her eyes are the colour of the Atlantic in the summer, a sparkling azure blue. She has freckles over her nose and dimples in both cheeks when she smiles. Her dark brown hair is cut short and always slips out from behind her ears; she constantly tucks it back in place. She's wearing blue jeans, purple knee-high rubber boots, and a purple jacket unzipped over a light blue Hoodie.

"Anyway, I need to get home," she says. "I was just helping my dad clean up his boat."

"Oh," I say, glancing back at the boat. "Do you fish with him?"

She snorts softly at that. "I wish. No, he won't let me. He says it's too dangerous. I can't go out until I'm sixteen. I think he's hoping I'll change my mind by then. But I won't ever change my mind. As soon as I turn sixteen, I'm going out with him and I'm going to save every penny I make so one day I can buy my own fishing boat."

I jerk my head back in surprise. "Really?"

She tucks her hair back behind her ears again and grins at me. "Hey, don't look so surprised! There are a couple of women in town who are captains of their own lobster boats. I have a goal that by the time I'm nineteen I'll have enough money and experience to be a captain."

I can only nod like an idiot. I'm amazed, awestruck, and impressed by her gumption.

"Are you doing anything right now?" she asks. "Want to come over to my place and see my boat?"

I frown slightly. My mind's whirling. She's incredible. I can't think straight. "Huh, what boat?"

"I bought a twelve-foot wooden rowboat off a town fisherman. It's in our garage. I was actually heading home to paint it before we head to church for Christmas Eve service. I'm going to use it this spring to fish lobster."

I nod, my mind still a blank.

"Dad said I can take the rowboat out in the harbour and drop in a couple of pots. Lot of kids around here do that. Dad says he'll let me as long as I promise to wear a life jacket and stay in the harbour."

My heartbeat triples in pace. She wants to be a lobster boat captain? She bought a rowboat to go lobster fishing? How cool is that? I've never met a girl like her before and I'm absolutely mesmerized by her charm, her blue-blue ocean eyes, dimples, and smile.

She catches me staring. I look away quick, face burning.

"What's wrong?" she says. "Your face is as red as a boiled lobster."

"I'm fine," I stammer. "That sounds great, really."

The wind picks up so I try to zip up my jacket, but my hands are a little shaky and I fumble with it, end up getting the zipper caught in the fabric. To add to my embarrassment, my ears feel like they're on fire, and my jacket's hanging crookedly now.

"You know Joel Cote and Tyson Kessler from school? They have rowboats and fish in the harbour too. They sell their lobsters to some of the restaurants in town. Hey, your zipper's stuck," she says, pointing at my jacket. "Anyway, it's a good way to make a few bucks. I was wondering, do you think it might be something you'd like to try?"

I free my zipper and zip it back up correctly. The idea of buying my own rowboat and fishing in the harbour isn't as exciting as the true lobster fishing I did with Crocker. Yet it does appeal to me. *Seriously* appeals to me.

"Yeah, sure, I'd like that."

Sophie smiles. "I thought you might. The reason I asked is that I know a guy who has a rowboat for sale. It's old, but it's good and solid. If you're interested, we could go over to his place and see it later this week."

"That'd be awesome." But then I think of Mom and my excitement fades. I shake my head. "Nah, forget it. My mom would freak out at the idea."

"Why? It's safe if we stay in the harbour and wear life jackets."

"You don't know my mom."

Sophie thumbs back over her shoulder to her dad's lobster boat, the *Sophie-Belle*, moored two slips down from Crocker's. "My dad does, though. He went to school with your mom. I could get him to talk to her, tell her how safe it is. Maybe she'll change her mind if she knows he's letting me go out."

Hope blooms in my chest, and then just as quickly vanishes. Her dad knows I was with Crocker when he cut his lines. He probably hates me. "I don't think your dad will do that for me, but thanks."

"Hey, he doesn't blame you for anything. My dad's not like that. He told me he respects you because Crocker was always bragging you up, saying how good a worker you were, and how you're a born fisherman. He's a Christian too. He believes in forgiveness and he lives it. He'd never hold that against you. He'll talk to your mom if I ask him."

I feel a twinge of hope again. "That'd be great, because I'm pretty sure I'll need him to."

We fall silent. A fat sea gull dives down and snatches a candy wrapper from the wharf road next to me. With a shriek, it soars away. A buoy clangs at the harbour entrance. The relentless wind whistles off the water, flattening my jeans against my legs.

I try not to stare, but my eyes are drawn to Sophie's face. With her sparkling eyes and cute button nose, I can't seem to look away. My eyes travel up from her nose, and when I reach her eyes I see that she's watching me.

She smiles. "You're staring again."

"Sorry."

We hold each other's gaze. I feel a little catch in my throat, a warm tug in my heart. I've never felt this way with any other girl. It's like our two souls have just touched, and then fused together.

"So, you want to come over to my place and see my boat? Maybe help me paint it?"

I consider it for all of a split second. "Sure."

She turns around and calls out to her father. He walks over to the rail of his boat and waves at her. He eyes me for a few seconds, then calls out, "Hello, Logan."

"Hi, Mr. Thibideau," I call back, my heart lightening. His face is unreadable, but his voice doesn't carry any anger or resentment.

"I'm heading home now, Dad," Sophie tells him. "I'm bringing Logan over to show him my boat. Is that okay?"

To my immense relief, he smiles and nods. "Tell your mom I'll be home shortly."

We turn and start walking down the wharf road toward town.

"I'm going to name my boat the *Sophie-Galene*," Sophie says, stopping to look at me. "Galene was my grandmother's name. She died last year. We were super close. She understood me better than anyone else. She loved fishing too, but never got to do it. She always supported me in my dream to one day own my own boat."

"That's cool, to honour her that way."

"Galene is a Greek word. Do you know what it means?"

I shake my head. "No."

"It means 'calm seas.' My grandmother's father was a fisherman," she says, laughing softly.

I laugh quietly along with her. She has a calm, serious side like me, but smiles and laughs easily. I like that about her.

We start walking again, closer this time so that our fingers brush against each other with each step.

After a few steps, she takes a breath to gather her courage. "I know I asked you this back in September and you weren't interested, and I don't want to push you, but my youth group is going bowling on Saturday night, if you'd like to come."

I turn my head and look out over the glistening blue water of the town harbour.

"What time?" I ask.

"Seven, but we're meeting at the church at six-thirty. If you like, you could meet me at my place first and we could walk over to the church together."

I nod. "All right, sure."

She looks right into my eyes. My heart tugs and turns to liquid.

I smile back and we start walking again.

Our fingers brush once more. Gathering my own courage, I reach out and take her hand gently in mine. She lets me, giving my hand a soft squeeze back.

And I feel the cold hard stone in my heart completely dissolve.

## About the Author

Karen V. Robichaud was born in Portage La Prairie, Manitoba and grew up on Canadian Air Force bases across Canada and in Europe. She is the author of four novels, including *Leigh Falls*, *Where the River Flows*, *Beyond Winter's Shadow*, and *An Evening Sky in Autumn*. *The Unforgiving Sea* was shortlisted in the Word Alive 2014 publishing contest. She divides her time between Halifax, Nova Scotia and Fredericton, New Brunswick. At present, she is at work on her sixth novel.